WHEN THE VILLAGE SLEEPS

A NOVEL

Sindiwe Magona

PICADOR AFRICA

The writing of this novel has been made possible by a bursary from the National Institute for the Humanities and Social Sciences (NIHSS) to do a PhD in Creative Writing at the University of the Western Cape.

First published in 2021 by Picador Africa
an imprint of Pan Macmillan South Africa
Private Bag X19, Northlands
Johannesburg, 2116

www.panmacmillan.co.za

ISBN 978-1-77010-629-1
EBOOK ISBN 978-1-77010-630-7

© 2021 Sindiwe Magona

All rights reserved. No part of this publication may be reproduced, stored in or introduced into a retrieval system, or transmitted, in any form, or by any means (electronic, mechanical, photocopying, recording or otherwise), without the prior written permission of the publisher. Any person who does any unauthorised act in relation to this publication may be liable to criminal prosecution and civil claims for damages.

This is a work of fiction. It is based on a wide range of personal experiences and observations. Names, characters, businesses, places, events and incidents are either the products of the author's imagination or used in a fictitious manner. Any resemblance to actual persons, living or dead, or actual events is purely coincidental.

Editing by Helen Moffett
Proofreading by Kelly Norwood-Young
Design and typesetting by Triple M Design and Setting
Cover design by publicide
Author photograph by Bjorn Rudner

Printed by novus print, a division of Novus Holdings

'Timely and truthful, this novel is vintage Sindiwe Magona, one of our wisest voices. Few capture the contemporary black South African female experience with such power and resonance. The voices of her protagonists linger in one's mind long after the reading of this book.'
— ELINOR SISULU

'This book is a wake-up call to the sleeping village that is our country. It's a multi-layered, beautifully woven narrative that takes the reader on a journey with unexpected twists and turns that challenge us to look beyond common assumptions to see the complexity of the human condition. Sindiwe Magona has outdone herself in using the power of language – her unique isiXhosinglish – to explore the healing that is made possible by embracing our culture and heritage as spiritual anchors in a country that is yet to find peace for its soul. Ubuntu is brilliantly presented here as the healing balm dispensed by an unlikely combination of a makhulu and a differently abled great-granddaughter. This is a must-read to feed our souls.'
— MAMPHELA RAMPHELE

'*When the Village Sleeps* could only come from South Africa's bravest, most enduring female voice. In this high point of Sindiwe Magona's literary oeuvre, the ancestors and a foetus find groundbreaking voices within a contemporary English narrative. Poetry mixes with tradition, anger with criticism, and guts with beauty in a deep-seated urge to resurrect values and build resilience.'
— ANTJIE KROG

'*When the Village Sleeps* is a compelling novel of sorrow, hope and possibility. In a thought-provoking narrative of relationships – human, societal and environmental – Sindiwe Magona leads us from destruction, despair and tragedy to the possibility of renewal, healing and wholeness through ancient wisdom and the generosity of the human spirit.'
— DUNCAN BROWN

WHEN THE VILLAGE SLEEPS

*To the community of Woodside Special Care Centre,
who show what is possible when every person is cared for,
and supported to allow them to realise their potential.*

PART ONE

CHAPTER ONE
◇◇◇◇◇◇◇◇◇◇◇◇◇◇◇

A-aah! Blessed day—

Saturday!

Busisiwe wiggled her toes. With all her heart, she hated her life. Not all of it – people like that committed suicide, her mother once told her – not that anyone took what Phyllis said seriously. Yes, Busi hated her life, but one of the few blessings, one thing she really appreciated, was the sixth day of the week. Not only was there no school, there was no one else in the house. Phyllis, her mother, gone; Aunt Lily, in whose house they lived, gone; Lily's husband, Uncle Luvo, gone. The whole lovely morning, she was alone.

OMG, she had all the space to herself. Just herself, by herself, no one else but herself!

Saturday! The grown-ups were away at work. They all worked over the weekend, including half-day Sundays for the two women, Mama and Aunt Lily. The two older boys, her cousins, were out, attending funerals.

Funerals were opportunities for feasting. On Mondays already, Themba and Sazi started prowling for houses with tents in their yards. Tents meant death, and death meant a funeral, and a funeral meant food galore. Food for all, and not per invitation either. Nobody would turn people away from a funeral. Funerals were much better than weddings. The ancestors (*and God and His angels?* wondered Busisiwe) were present. Now, what host would dare appear graceless before the ancestors and God, and demand an invitation card? The bereaved family welcomed all who came to honour the dead with proper respect.

Therefore, on weekends, the boys went funeralling. They were veritable funerongers. Busisiwe smiled as she shook out a blanket. The boys often chattered about how they helped the men slaughter a beast, how fantastic innards roasted on an open fire tasted, what was served during the Friday night vigil, how the really good meat was cooked and distributed. Lately, even her little brothers Owam and Esam had started tagging along, following the older boys, who didn't seem to mind the tails.

A week after the burial, the following Saturday, the family would be cleansed with the Washing of Spades ceremony, observed by all. Not as lavish as the funeral, it was nonetheless a feast for amahonkco – all aboard the gravy train.

Because she was a girl, Busisiwe was not allowed the same privileges. Women could go to funerals, of course. It would fall on them to clean, scrape and cook the veggies – a job tedious and back-breaking, with absolutely no reward. The older women saw to it that the job was done properly, for such a weighty affair as death; but they imposed their authority on younger women, who did the work while they supervised.

I don't need such supervision, Busi thought to herself. She had had the best teacher on cooking samp and beans, steamed bread, vegetable preparation and making ginger beer – her grandmother. *Khulu had me watch her since before I was even six or seven years old. Then, one day, she turned the tables on me – watched while I prepared. Said the way she saw things, my mother was not teaching me anything. Said that behind Phyllis's back, of course.* But it was the truth.

Her uncle Luvo, like the boys, was hardly ever indoors on weekends, because Sunday was the day the bereaved, having buried their loved one the day before, were drinking herb-infused and bitter water as though to say: accept the bitter taste of death and know that you will live, must live. These were the two inescapable sides of the coin. Accept death as you accept the skin in which you live, the skin that gathers all you are – protects you from harm that lives in the air.

Not that Busi gave such matters much thought. At first, she had resented being unable to benefit from the funeral bonanzas. But she would be dead in the water if she went mooching for food; yes, she would be ridiculed by both her kasi neighbours as well as her classmates at her posh Model C school, where she did not dare wear poverty too brazenly. Sometimes she even resented that her grandmother's former employer, Mrs Bird, paid her school fees so that she could have what the grown-ups called a 'decent education'. Nobody spoke about the pressure Busi felt, how she was always out of step at that school.

Now, brows scrunched, she surveyed the fruits of her labour: bed made, just so, as Lily liked; furniture dusted; floor swept ... She put away the duster and looked around – all she still had to do was to scoop up the little mound of inkunkuma and go put it in the cardboard box under the kitchen sink. That would spell HOUSE DONE!

In the comings and goings of the family members, she had no power or influence; hers was to do what she was told, and, according to her mama, be not only cheerful about it, but grateful; very grateful, in fact. Well, grateful was choking her, killing her – except on Saturdays. Then she *was* tremendously grateful.

She could breathe.

She could hear herself think.

She could sing out loud.

There was no one in the whole house to tell her, 'Stop it!' or 'Heyi, wena! You are not here all by yourself!'

Oh, yes! For one day of the week, she was truly happy.

Saturday meant a lot of chores, and of course, nobody regarded *her* work as their skutete, a blessing. No, they expected her to welcome it, enjoy it, and never forget she had to pull her weight, contributing to the wellbeing of the family, 'as we all are contributing to yours'.

Stepping outside, she picked a small piece of the peppery fennel bush along the hedge, took it back into the house and put it in a little fishpaste bottle on Aunt Lily's dressing table. She always left this room for last. With a long, deep breath, she braced her shoulders and lifted her tired arms, waved them about two-three times, stretched. She smiled as she reached for the remote and sunk herself onto the little sofa at the bottom of the bed. Now was the time to steal a look at the TV; sometimes *Utatakho* was on. It entertained her, but also made her sad when it reminded her of her own plight – tata-less. But now the smile stayed on

Busi's face, an idle smile, but a smile all the same.

My heart is light, she thought. See how I am watching television in Aunt Lily's bedroom; the only room in the house that has such a luxury. Who else has money not only to buy a set, but keep it running – pay for the electricity and DStv – to say nothing of paying for the licence – *every year*?

Busisiwe clicked, and up on the screen came: 'Heroines of Our Time!'

The only hero who came to her mind was, of course, Tata Mandela, whose picture was on every coin and note of South Africa's money. Perhaps he had a mine? Busi left the thought hanging as she turned back to the programme, where an advertisement for funeral cover for everyone in the family (including beloved pets) was playing. Aargh! What a waste of time.

She still had to wash the laundry soaking in the huge red plastic tub. Well, let it soak, she wasn't going to hang it out before she'd gone to fetch water for the house. She knew better than to take an eye off it; one wrong move and the clothes, the whole tub would be gone. Drug thieves had no qualms about stealing even wet clothes. Things simply vanished without a trace, and people became sightless to avoid being implicated, which could have nasty consequences.

She glanced at the bottom of the screen. Yhoo! Ten o'clock! A girl who did her chores late was considered lazy – that was why the smart ones always started with the laundry – visible industriousness. What's the point of doing anything if no one knows about it? Brag is the name of the game ... even about the most insignificant matters, such as who puts out the garbage bin first, or whose white laundry is whitest. Which reminded her: she had better get going.

As she got up, remote in hand to switch off the TV, an insert at the top right corner of the screen came alive: a group of young men performing the gumboot dance.

A young woman, all smiles, with a clear café-au-lait complexion, glowed on the screen. Her long black dreadlocks were swept up in a knot, crowning the top of her head. She wore a brown shweshwe dress that left her arms and one shoulder bare. Her well-toned arms rippled as she gestured. Brightly beaded bangles rose half-way up both her arms, and a necklace of the same colour draped across her chest. Two big silver rings flashed on each middle finger, big silver hoops dangled from her earlobes.

'Maybe this is what Aunt Lily calls African Elegance ...' said Busi to herself.

Introduced as a social worker, this elegant woman, her voice sweet and carrying, explained how she got involved with this group of gumboot dancers as part of a programme to address the perennial problem of youth unemployment in the townships. She encouraged these young men to do gumboot dancing instead of milling around in frustration, their self-esteem draining away like water in a leaky bucket.

'Anything is better than doing nothing!' she said, adding, 'And the boys took to it immediately.'

The camera zoomed onto this group of fit young men in overalls of different colours – red, yellow, blue, orange – some with one sleeve off the arm, and a few with both sleeves off and tied around the waist. Their bodies ... yhoo! The muscles! Busi's eyes bulged. All wore black gumboots, and their makarabhas finished the mgodi look. Right now, the group was shuffling around, warming up, gearing for performance.

The social worker said she had even found sponsors for the group. 'There is a lot of help available for programmes of social upliftment,' she said. 'People must help themselves if they want to get anywhere in life!'

On cue, the young men sprang into performance mode. The leader blew a whistle and like a well-oiled machine:

Tshisa Bo!

Paqa-paqa!

Tshisa Bo!

Paqa-paqa!

Tshisa Booooo!!!

Paqa-paqa-paqa-paqa-paqa-paqa!

Their smiles and the fierceness with which they exuded confidence were beamed straight at the TV camera. Aware of her blessedly untrammelled morning, Busi got up and paqaza'd right along with them, no matter that her paqaza came sans the rhythmic boom of the gumboots.

What a performance! The thunder of their heavy boots, accompanied by the insistent 'PREE-PREE-PREEEE!' of the leaping and gyrating leader's whistle, was in turn accompanied by rhythmic hand smacks. These hand sounds didn't quite alternate, didn't quite follow, but rather shadowed the stamping feet, coming just after them, so the two blended in a kind of thud-and-echo, thud-and-echo ... it was a perfect – NO, brilliant – orchestra.

'They have improved,' said the social worker. 'They are miles better than before!'

'Walala, wasala! You snooze, you lose!' said the host as he gave out the social worker's contact details in case anyone out there wanted to start something similar. 'There is a lot of help available. Don't just sit on your behind and expect things to fall into your lap. M-O-V-E! Move yourself. When you do, you'll find other things begin to move. Your life moves! Daxa phantsi; daxa your life too!'

Busi wished they had someone or something like that in her neighbourhood – a group right here in Kwanele that she could join. Scores of people around her were jobless, young people especially. Maybe if she joined a project like that, she could at last make a little bit of money.

And daxa phantsi is what she was doing right now. 'The laundry won't up and wash itself,' she muttered. Snatching the remote, she got up and made for the door. There, just at that teeny moment between pressing the remote button and the TV actually turning off, her eye caught something, and no sooner was the TV off than she switched it right back on again.

The social worker and the TV host had moved to the audience for a Q & A session. Now questions flew.

'Did you enjoy that?'

'What did you think of the dancing?'

'Would you like to do something like that too?'

'What do you want to be when you grow up?'

Busi squirmed. Ridiculous! Grown-ups asked such dumb questions. Children want to be grown-ups, of course; at least, she did. Grown-ups could boss everyone, every single child. It was the worst thing in the world to be a child – especially a child in miserable Kwanele.

Most of the spectators were young people; some simply responded with smiles, shy in the sudden limelight. Then a hand shot up, like a kid seeking the teacher's attention in a crowded classroom when they knew the answer to the question, and another kid had just said something they knew, absolutely knew, to be incorrect. The host stretched his microphone towards her. This little girl, younger than Busisiwe, but bold as brass, said something Busi couldn't catch. The host gulped visibly and urged, 'Again? Please repeat what you just said? What do you want to do when you grow up?'

'I want to marry a deformed man!'

'Yii-yhoo!' Busi gasped and took a second look at the scrawny little girl with her tired hair, the unnatural rust colour telling of long-faded chemical treatment. She could hardly believe her ears. Where had the child come upon such a mind-boggling idea?

The host, clearly also staggered, asked, 'Do you mean a man with a disability? Why?'

'So I can get a lot of money!' the girl replied without hesitation.

'Where will you get that money?'

'The grant! Everyone knows deformed people get more money!'

How much more? Busi screamed silently at the girl on the screen in the shapeless gym dress, her shoes badly in need of more than just polish – even the laces were frayed. *How much?* Why was the host not asking that question? Ask! Ask!

But the stupid man just thanked the girl and turned to the viewers: 'There you are!' he announced, 'You heard it on Mzansi 1017!' And, flashing his all-teeth-bared smile, he exhorted: 'Remember, your future is in your hands!'

Busi stood a long time. Then she made sure she left no trace she had been relaxing in Aunt Lily's room – put everything as she'd found it, the two remote controls just so, crossed, with the smaller one on top, at the corner of the bedside table.

Long after the programme ended, the girl's words rang in Busi's mind. That child knew what she wanted, all right!

She would not judge her. She'd heard the words, and they echoed what she'd heard before, but never so blatantly, so boldly; and never before from the lips of someone that young. How could such a child already know how to solve the ever-present crisis of money?

Maybe a disabled husband could get one money for airtime, for that swanky cell phone, new sneakers, a dress to wear to her best friend Thandi's party in a few weeks, the school's choir tour …

Take Thandi, for instance. Three years older and twice as glamorous as Busi, her father gave her his card to shop at Splendour, and her sugar daddy gave her a fat envelope every time they met. But how much did Mama get for her, Owam and Esam? Was it three hundred a month for each child? Less? More? No, surely not. Phyllis was always, but always, short of money.

And then Busi had a new idea: for a disabled child, the grant must be huge: a thousand … *at least!*

CHAPTER TWO

Khulu loved Sidwadweni, her home village not far from Mthatha and near Tsolo in the Eastern Cape. The name Mthatha spoke of grandeur, glamour, splendid living. Tsolo also had much of which to be proud, including great chiefs, but Sidwadweni was the village Khulu chose to retire to after working for the same family in the manicured white suburb of Bishopscourt for decades.

At the time that her knees began to ache after years of polishing floors, Khulu tore herself away from the clinging vines of family – and her employer, Mrs Bird, who over the years had also become friend and benefactress, fondly called MaNtaka (a take on her surname) by Khulu and her family.

'Now that I am retiring, I want to go back to the place my beloved Hlombe and I planned for our old age,' Khulu told everyone.

She and her husband Hlombe were newly married when she first got that job; Mr and Mrs Bird also a newly married couple. Both women thought it a good omen that they shared the date of their weddings. Both were blessed with two, and two children only. Girls for both; no boys – much to the secret lamentation of the husbands. As much as both men professed to love their daughters, each harboured a sorrow in his heart; for each, the girls were not true heirs. Perhaps this private sorrow accounted for their early demises.

While the two women both lost their husbands much too early, they did not lose each other. When Khulu lost Hlombe, Mrs Bird was a huge support to her; and Khulu returned the favour hardly a year and a half later.

The two remained together until Khulu's bones refused to go on co-operating with housework. 'Not my fault you don't want to move with the times,' said Mrs Bird. 'I bought the Hoover for you, you know?' She patted Khulu on the shoulder as she always did. 'Make yourself a cuppa Milo!'

The separation was far from unkind. Khulu received a golden handshake, plus so many extras even she was surprised. Even more surprising, Mrs Bird suggested that the famously unreliable Phyllis, take over housekeeping duties from Khulu: 'I've known Phyllis since she was born! Let her come here to char for me.'

She went on, 'Your room here with me will always be available. Leave your stuff here and take the key with you. I have a spare, but doubt I will ever need to use it. There's nothing of mine in there.'

And so Khulu was free to return to the house she and Hlombe had built eSidwadweni. They had planned to retire there; the place of their growing years. Now she would go to that place where his bones rested. That was her home now. She said only very soft words to her God. She said very soft words to her ancestors, the Old, the long line without end of which she was just a tiny dot, insignificant. Yet her God and her Old saw to all her needs, protected her from harm, forefended evil from her path so that her foot never on ungodly thorn did tread.

In serene Sidwadweni, placid land of rolling hills and soft valleys, here and there a silent stream gleamed past, only to return and do the same over and over and over. All around, broad-leafed lazy cabbage trees dotted the veld; aloes stabbed the hill flanks with their bloody spears; here and there, cattle dozed in the midday sun among sweet thorn and kei apple.

Human habitation appeared scant, sightings of hut, house or rondavel cluster were rare. And those visible appeared uninhabited or deserted, except for a few trading stations where white shopkeepers had called the shots until the political tide had turned, and one and all had fled to the cities. A few rare souls – ministers or doctors – stayed behind, as did the farmers. Not an easy thing to do, pack up a farm and cart it off to the city; so a lot of the farmers stayed on.

Here Khulu lived alone in Ekuphumleni, the homestead of Hlombe's and her dreams. Their little castle on the plain, where, if one stood quite still amidst the warbles of finches and starlings, one could hear whispers of the rushing waters of ages long gone. And here Khulu could live out her dream of gardening. She grew all her own vegetables – onions, carrots, tomatoes, potatoes, cabbages, beans and maize. She even had a few fruit trees: apricot, peach and pear. 'I only grow what I like!' she would say.

Her eyes softened and a smile parted her lips to show the gap between the front upper teeth, big enough to pass a mealie-pip through, as she thought back to planting those trees in her youth. Way back when Sidwadweni boasted lush bushes, pinned by impressive trees – thick forests alongside the streams and wide fields of maize on the plains, heavy-laden stalks swaying in the breeze as autumn winds breathed to ripen them. Some planted swathes of broad bean, squash on the vine, plump carrots in deep dark fertile soil. Buffalo grass, red grass boosted the rich milk of ewes, and the thickets rustled with the midday cooing of doves, the melodious boubou and raw crackling sounds of ravens – and starlings so black that the black hurt the eye, the black so black it was blue-tinged. So black it called out for praise in poem and song:

> Pitch black is the starling;
> Songbird of the thickets.
> Isomi limnyama thsu;
> Ngumlonji, imyoli ingoma yalo—
> Melodious is the song of starling.

Khulu also kept chickens. So when the shadows grew long, the chickens stopped scratching and sauntered toward the coop. Khulu would get up from where she was shelling beans or stamping maize on a stool in the sun, and head for the end rondavel. Here, from under the table against the far wall, she would haul out the chickenfeed. The hens flapped about her feet, clucking like there was no tomorrow. Khulu smiled and shook her head at their reflex anticipation.

And that set her thinking about the morning's call from Phyllis, one that always came at this time of the month. It was more than two weeks since the child grant had been in her pocket. She found it easier to ask for money when her mother was in the Eastern Cape. Phyllis would rather not see her mother's face screwed up, eyes slit like a cat's, mouth agape at the spectre of a daughter begging for money from a pensioner.

That SASSA pension! It added lines of care to her face. And lines of sorrow to her prayer: 'Uyaziwa umntu onemali yaye ehlala yedwa; ukukutya okuvuthiweyo.' There was no rest or freedom in her old age. Cooked food was she. After battling long unruly lines and the ever-present risk of on-site robbery for her pension, next she faced the ever-outstretching beggarly hands of her elder daughter. And the two add-ons, the babies born after Busi, whose fathers Phyllis did not even know, were red coals in Khulu's heart. They were sure signs her daughter was lost.

It will kill me, the way my daughter lives, thought Khulu, as she watched the satisfied chickens jostle and trip over one another as they hustled towards their coop. *It will send me to my grave. Long before the ancestors would have wished to see me, they surely will. I have fled here to avoid that early grave, but the phone, that most astute detective, bites into the innermost ear of my heart, lacerating my very spirit.*

Her daughter's pitiful voice as she said the same words Khulu heard each month: 'Apologies for waking you at so early an hour, Mama.'

Like she wasn't aware of this before she went to bed the night before.

'Siyashota, Mama – we are running short!'

The grant money did not seem to help Phyllis one bit. It never did. It made no difference at all, at least not as far as her children were concerned.

Khulu shook her head as she heard Phyllis wheedle and beg yet again. 'I know, Mama, it is not I who, in utter inconvenience and danger, have to travel solo kilometres to town. It is not I who have to wait the whole day in long, long queues! It is not I who have to cross wide fields to the tarred road, walking all alone while being observed by young men and boys who would like to help one travel lighter … I know, I know. Why are these tellers always so resentful? Really! The reluctance of people in jobs supposed to offer service is a national scandal. Prisoners hired out to farmers show more enthusiasm digging and tilling and heaving and shoving heaps of rock-hard turf.'

The phone conversation stayed with Khulu well into the night. *My elder daughter brays. Will she ever grow up? Will she ever sober up? Will she ever take responsibility? God help us if she foals again! Lily will kick her out. Lamb-like husband might also baulk.*

Fat chance of ever escaping her children! Phyllis was a heavy load on her shoulders; Khulu had thought that if she left Cape Town, maybe that would help. That her older daughter would learn to stand on her two feet at last. *Yhoo, ndikhe ndizibhanxe kanene! Golly, I do sometimes fool myself. Must talk to Phyllis one more time. Must do that. Next time I'm in Cape Town …*

And it wasn't just her. When she was still living at Mrs Bird's, at least once a month the phone would ring, and: 'That will be Marvin! Wonder what he wants,' her employer would say as she shuffled off to answer. Marvin was her most spoiled nephew and godchild. Khulu knew what Marvin wanted. What Marvin always wanted towards the end of the month – money!

Khulu shook her head. She and this woman she worked for were old, getting older, but the younger people seemed to believe they did not need the money they had: 'But where *mine* think I get the money they want from me beats me!'

◇◇◇

We, the Old, heard the cry of our daughter;
Looked at the long years of her living ... Awu!
What shall we say about earthly matters?
The blue cranes stacked in heaps lying dead at Hoho;
The black vulture and its dogs ate, at Hoho;
Our hearts are grieved
For we see no relief for her from her drainage;
Only growing sorrow; growing hardship;
All sprung from the death of ubuntu;
Even that grant to the poor:
What did it really grant the poor
Except more poor; more poverty?

CHAPTER THREE

Every time Busi travelled to and from Cape Town, she knew Cape Town had no idea of Kwanele at all. No idea it lay there, waiting, seething, ready, at minimal spark, to erupt. But the informal settlement was there *because* of Cape Town. It saw itself as part of Cape Town. No! Kwanele *believed* it *was* Cape Town. Knew its very existence, its evolution was inescapably tied to Cape Town: 'Here we are, Kwanele, rooted in, sprouted from and irrigated by Cape Town for Cape Town.'

Busi's thoughts guided her automatically: *Just let me get to my seat!* If she'd forgotten today was Friday, the noise in this overcrowded kombi told the story: over-excited children, relieved to be on their way from the centre of town to the townships for the weekend. *If those two girls get in, we'll be nearly thirty kids in here.* The rowdiness was always greatest on Fridays, and it seemed Tatomkhulu, driver, conductor and manager, wanted to join the celebration with his loud music.

Here come the traffic cops, slowly overtaking us. Hey, you two, don't you hear this rhythm belting out? Don't you see this potential slaughterhouse? But nobody cares. Let me look at the wide sweep of the sea as we hurtle along Baden Powell Drive.

Like my heart, the houses are getting smaller and smaller as the taxi gets closer and closer to home. Home? I have to call it that. But in my heart of hearts, it will never really be. Home is elsewhere; it is where, once upon a time, I lived with Mama and Tata. I was happy there. Very happy! Aunt Lily's house is a pretend home.

Here is the dreaded left turn towards Dunes Road, past the make-do soccer playgrounds on the left, opposite the white sand hill. Now speeding on to Lookout Hill, to be struck by another but totally different kind of sea: as endless as the ocean and as hurtful to the eye as that other sea is pleasing, uplifting to the soul. Khayelitsha. Within Khayelitsha lies Kwanele, which means 'Enough!' Funny that! Call a place 'enough' when it never has enough of anything, except more than enough squalor, crime and disease. I wonder whether anybody knows how many divisions and subdivisions Khayelitsha has? I can't even direct my school friends to my home! No matter how detailed the directions, they would get hopelessly lost. Thank God for that, actually! Nobody from my school must ever ever come here.

From the Main Road, Tatomkhulu turned left, and immediately the tyres of the kombi made a sound like soft ice being crushed under a stone. No tar on this road. On the left was the community centre with its bright-blue painted walls, on which leaders of a past era stared out at the passing world. *Tata Nelson Mandela is the only one I know, the others ... who cares! But why are no women there? What about Mama Albertina Sisulu, Winnie Mandela, and the other women Khulu always talks about? Her heroines.*

Let me get my things ready, I am the first to be dropped off.

Aunt Lily's house is the first house in this row. The taxi doesn't have to turn into Second Avenue, our street.

Jump out. Quickly slide the kombi's rusty white door shut. Don't look back. Scoot for the house. Through the gate and two, three, four strides; hand on the doorknob and inside!

The stares of always-lying-in-wait neighbours and the ever-ready sneers of passers-by are daily hurdles I must ignore, moving as swiftly as possible, eyes and ears closed. Not my fault I go to a Model C school. Not my fault I live in a Wendy house in a crowded yard. How I hate it here! But at least, unlike most RDP houses, Aunty Lily's has a back door so I can go in and out the back to change into street clothes.

Only one more dreaded task still to do: walk all the way back up the street to pick up little bhuti from the crèche. I will never go and fetch him in my city school uniform – no ways.

Thank God for kasi soccer practice; the boys, my cousins and Owam, are almost never home when I get here, but look at the dirty mugs and saucers left behind from their snacking. Boys! Anyway, today being Friday, they won't be around much.

Past the crèche, down the small hill, I can see the line of scholars waiting their turn at the communal tap, or as Thandi calls it: the Gossipmongers' Communal Tap.

Little brother settled. Washing soaking. What else can I do to shut up my mother? Shut out her loud, husky voice, followed with that long quick click of tongue. Head turned half-way to the shoulder, eyes slanted, glaring at where I am sitting, mouth corners turned down when she talks to me. And those sad traces of red on her lips and cheeks. But, hey! One: I don't care, and two:

the reasons for her fury are unpredictable. I have zero feelings for that woman.

>ntyilo-ntyilo uyalila
>uyalila umntan'akho
>take a good look at this girl
>her name is Busisiwe
>but everybody calls her Busi
>Busisiwe – She-who-is-graced
>Busi – honey-graced.
>Busi is nearly thirteen years old
>Graced-honey is soon to be my mother
>she will try
>she will want me
>want to be my mother
>she will
>eventually
>be
>my mother
>though herself still a child
>but I know she will be my mother
>I also know
>I will fight
>to the best of what power is mine
>not to be born to a thirteen-year-old child
>not yet done being a child

> *she will become my mother in the end, though*
> *that I also know*
> *I will be accepted*
> *if reluctantly*
> *if with much regret*
> *it has to be.*

◇◇◇

On that Friday in Kwanele, that ramshackle sprawl of a place, an hour by death-defying taxi away from Cape Town city centre, Busi was doing the ironing, Lily was reading the Bible in her bedroom, while Phyllis sat with her eyes glued to the TV. 'Can you believe this?' Phyllis yelled at nobody in particular. 'Thugs made off with all the grant money! At gun-point. Shame!' Busi looked up from her pile of ironing at the screen, as the reporter described how the recipients just waited and waited and waited. Some folded themselves down onto the drought-scorched grass, stretched their legs before them, and dozed off. Others slept where they had stood all day long, trusting that the next day the cash vans would come.

'A new vocabulary we have,' said Phyllis, counting on her fingers: 'Siyalamba/we starve; asinazindlu/no houses; imali yesikolo/school money; amayeza noogqirha/medications and doctors; ziyasityabula/chafe us ...'

She pointed at her daughter: 'This is what you can escape, if you put your mind to it!' Phyllis laughed, but with menace, before turning back to the TV, hanging on every word coming out of the mouth of the Minister of Women, Children, and People Living with Disability.

The gentleman was now speaking in Parliament, but every word was an exact repeat of what he had said so many times, at different venues, several per province, he could say them in his sleep.

'Do you still remember that you didn't get any grants from government during apartheid? Yes, my friends, if you were classified Bantu you were not allowed to even apply for grants. Grants were only given to Whites, Coloureds, Indians and Asiatics! But this is *your* government, and it is doing all in its power to support the poorest of the poor. Look at how much money your party, the party in government, spends. Hear how much grant money you get *every month*!'

At that, Phyllis sat up straight, hammering her fists on her thighs, and opened her ears wider.

'Yes, I am increasing the amounts. You are going to get more money in three months' time.'

Phyllis screamed, 'Liii-ly! Did you hear that? They're increasing the grant money!'

'Oh?' Lily could have guessed that one. Besides drink, the only thing that ever made Phyllis sit up and pay attention was money ... or rather, free money.

The Minister continued: 'Listen, all! This is how much we have raised the new grants.'

Phyllis stood and went even closer to the TV in case a car hooted or something else roared or boomed. She didn't want to miss a word.

'The Child Support Grant goes from R380.00 to R400.00; the Care Dependency Grant from R1 600.00 to R1 780.00. We can do this now because—'

But Phyllis didn't care what he was about to say, her excitement bubbled over. 'Yes!' she screamed, then burst into song: 'More money! More money!' she shrilled. 'Guess how much …' She paused, oblivious to Lily's marked disinterest in the news she was busy broadcasting. Receiving no answer to her question, she completed it: '… I will be getting now?' Thought better of what she'd just said, and clarified, 'Well, not immediately, unfortunately, but in three months' time.' She certainly didn't want her sister thinking she was loaded.

'So sorry for you.' Lily went back to her reading.

But Phyllis interrupted again: 'Uyaphoxisa? Are you being sarcastic? But it doesn't matter,' she sang. 'I'm going to get more money! I'm going to get more money!'

With a sigh, her sister asked, 'What difference will that make?' But Phyllis's song turned into a war cry: 'More money is more money! More money is more money!'

'More, to do what more?' retorted Lily, setting her Bible neatly down on the table next to her bed.

Busi, who had been silent until now, thumped the iron down on the board: 'Maybe I will get a new phone!' she cried. 'Nobody I know still uses these stupid things,' and she flung her old tilili onto the couch.

Unbeknown to her, via this action, Busisiwe had answered a call from the ancestors, from the Old. CAMAGU! They moved their bones. They rattled.

Awu! What can we say about earthly matters!
The blue cranes stacked in heaps lying dead at Hoho;
Steel ate blood, at Hoho;
The trees clashed, at Hoho;
The skin of the cow spoke, at Hoho;
Beating and beating, at Hoho;
The black vulture and its dogs ate, at Hoho;
A large flock ate and left some
For the white-necked raven, at Hoho;
The hyena ate and gave some
To the Cape hunting dog, at Hoho;
The green bottle-fly ate and left some
For the worms, at Hoho;
Ho-yi-i-i-i-i-i-na!

The Old had seen enough:
Do all the children need phones?
That one thinks she does.
And not any fanakalo phone either.
What's wrong with the one she has?
The children get it from their parents:
Give me! Give me! Give, give, give!
Terrible to say, they teach their children;
By example train them in feebleness.
Hands forever outstretched,
Begging begging begging!

Who can speak to them? We have found the one:

CAMAGU!
Livumile! Our wish granted, the call answered.

◇◇◇

... nty ... ntyilo ... ntyilo-ntyilo
ntyilo-ntyilo
someone is crying uyalila
someone is crying uyalila
someone is crying
uyalila umntan'akho
your baby is crying
that little girl throwing her phone
is twelve years old
uyalila, my mother, she will soon be—
this is my story
it is also my mother's story.
what we will go through, my mother and I?
a long and winding road shall we travel.
here and there, straight as the bridge on your nose—
at other places, hilly like a mountain range,
curved as a harvesting sickle.
expert in the art of gathering Earth's rich green grass
take a good look at me
look!
see?
I will be born perfect!
designed so

WHEN THE VILLAGE SLEEPS

by my mother
Busisiwe Mkhonto
Busi
take a look
a very good look
this is your story too
witness the crazy path to my birth
witness that
but know this
remember this
the meaning, the essence
far outweighs what the eye beholds
for the fruit is always in the seed
oh me! oh mama! uyalila uyalila
what act fruits me?
oh, the profligacy of men of power; men in the moment
men who forget the oneness, timelessness, the total
inter-relatedness
of all.

CHAPTER FOUR

The next morning, walking to the communal taps, Busi hoped to bump into her bestie. She had sent Thandi a 'Please Call Me', their sign to go fetch water together, but no response had come yet. Maybe her friend was already waiting for her.

Thandi had asked Busi to help design her 'SWEET SIXTEEN' invitation card, because she could use her time at the school computer to do it.

Can't wait to show her my design! Can't wait to see her face when she opens it! The party was strictly invitation-only. Thandi's dad was a cop, and the uninvited would know better than to even try to ambush his favourite daughter's Sweet Sixteen party.

The card had come out brilliantly. Busi had chosen an old-fashioned font, and now she admired its purple flourishes on her phone.

Obviously, as Thandi's best friend, she would be there. She just had to figure out how to attend without the rigmarole of asking for permission, which might either be refused, or be given with iron chains instead of strings attached! She could hear it all now: 'Go for an hour and a half ... no, okay then, three hours. You are a student; can't party all night. Wait, there's bound to be liquor there, with that older Thandi.'

Better if she just found a way to get there without anyone the wiser. *One good thing about my own mama being the way she is – she can't keep tabs on me. She doesn't even try or, as some mothers do, pretend to.* The only real hurdle would be if Khulu was around, paying one of her visits from the Eastern Cape. But even then, she always went to bed early, and once she fell asleep, she might as well be dead. Most parties didn't really start getting down till around midnight anyway.

At the tap, Busi spotted Thandi a mile away. Tall, dark as night, you couldn't miss her if you tried; not with those thick, gleaming braids cascading down her back to well below the waist, cutting her butt in half in a shimmering swirl that swayed this way and that as she gestured, hands up in the air, head and shoulders moving from side to side. In her ears, as always, she wore hoops you could shoot a ball through.

The two girls joined each other in the usual long, slow-moving line. Busi watched with dismay as water overflowed cans, pails or whatever containers were under the tap, the owners busy yapping and not watching them fill. Didn't they know South Africa was a dry country, prone to drought and water shortages? She caught herself: most of the people here had no idea. How could they? People believed what they wanted to believe. Truth stared them in the face, but they preferred to ignore it, letting the tap run on.

But now Thandi demanded her attention, and the two girls were soon sharing tingly secrets, keeping their voices low, although anyone with ears could hear them if they wanted.

'Ah, my blesser, Ganja Guru, is my bestest! I have no ring on my finger, so I owe him NOTHING! Yet he's my creamiest milk cow!'

Busi looked down sadly at her bare feet in the mud around the tap. She had also tried to get money. Had called Tata: 'Tata, what about me?'

'What about you?' her father sneered.

'Don't you love me anymore?' *Why ask him that?* His voice already held the answer.

Silence.

'What have I done?'

That had brought a loud and heavy sigh from him before he barked: 'What do you need?'

'A father ...' The thought had run out of her mouth, a loud whisper, before she could stop it.

'I mean, something I can get you!' he said, shouting as if she were deaf. Busi heard only denial. Tata denying her. There was pain in her throat: *money couldn't buy what she wanted* ...

'Sneakers,' she whispered again.

'All right!' He sounded relieved.

When Busi got back home, it was as if she heard Khulu dispensing wisdoms: 'A girl hanging laundry around lunchtime is lazy! No man will offer lobola for a young woman who sleeps until the sun has not only risen, but stretched and yawned its way up the sky, making shadows shrink before she gets up.'

Busi found herself chuckling. As much as she was glad that

Khulu was not interrupting her precious Saturday, she missed her terribly. In the days when Khulu still worked for Mrs Bird in Bishopscourt, it took just one phone call to arrange a visit after school or on Saturdays.

Of course, the ache was deeper when she was in the Eastern Cape. That was far. Busi was happy Khulu was coming to them for the holidays, due to arrive any day now.

When Khulu had worked and lived in Bishopscourt, she always spent Thursday nights with them all in Kwanele – the day she attended her church group, the Women's Manyano. Busi cherished these visits. Those Thursday nights were the only nights that were semi-normal; times when Busi felt she had a warm, loving family. For one, her mom would do her best to act normally; she would try to be a mother in front of her own mother; she'd have dinner and spend the night at home. However, even then, sometimes Phyllis would wait for Khulu to fall asleep and then sneak out, pretending the next morning that she had slept in the old children's room inside the main house.

Busi truly loved Khulu. She was grateful for her – the glue that held them all together. It was thanks to Khulu they all lived in Aunt Lily's house; or rather, the Wendy house attached to Lily's home. They had lived there since Busi was five.

Phyllis looked ten years older than her baptismal certificate said. Alcohol and stress, Busi heard Khulu muttering. Her mother had never recovered from what her best friend, who had been maid of honour at her wedding, had done. Phyllis had caught her and Busi's father, Mzi, red-handed so to speak … in bed together! Even though she was only five at the time, Busi's memory of that day remained fresh. After Phyllis kicked Mzi out, his uncle in turn kicked her and Busi out the shack they were renting.

'My shack, my nephew – no nephew, no shack,' he reasoned.

Phyllis had nowhere else to go except her sister Lily's home. At first, Aunt Lily was kindness itself: would she let her mother's daughter sleep under the railway bridge? But only one year into their Kwanele stay, Mama had given birth to another baby. Thank God Khulu had intervened – that was when she had put up the back room for Phyllis, Busi and the new baby, Owam.

Soon the words 'Ingxaki nguPhyllis: The problem is Phyllis!' spouted from Lily's lips. Even at the age of six, Busi knew this meant that her mama was unacceptable, ugly and unwelcome before the eyes of God. Worse, she heard even her sweet-tempered uncle refer to Phyllis as a slut. It was too much to bear: Tata gone; Mama, ingxaki; a new baby, one she had to mind, too. No one to love her. And there was no help from above, either. Prayer was nothing but fooling your sweet, sorry self. Prayer only worked for that minute you did it. Knees on the floor, heart and mind in some cloud, trying to pass the burden to the unseeable, untouchable, unresponsive One.

As Lily's resentment grew, Phyllis had her own resentments to nurse: Lily, her younger sister, at least had a house. Yes, an RDP house, but a house all the same. Phyllis had never had a house of her own. And that was cancer to her very soul. She would tell any with ears to hear that she had been on the waiting list for housing since the dawn of democracy – she'd put her name down even before Busi was born. Yet she had as much hope of getting that house as landing on the planet Venus.

And Busi heard. She absorbed all the venom spewed by and about her mother, and the older she got, the more she had to accept it as the truth. She had to listen to the gossips saying that Phyllis got so hot, many a night she didn't find her way home at all. Missing at night became Mama's second name.

The first time this happened, alarmed, the family had notified the police. Where was she? Statements were taken, but a day later, Phyllis turned up back at Lily's. The third time it happened, no one called the police – not after that unforgettable second time, when the phantom had reappeared.

That time, it was the police who came to them. The van screeched to a halt outside the house very early in the morning, before people crawled out of their beds. Two burly police officers, male and female, marched up and banged fists against the door.

'Yes, she lives here,' said Uncle Luvo who'd answered the summons.

The police, alerted by a concerned citizen, had found Phyllis mindlessly wandering along Baden Powell Drive.

'When?'

'Oh,' replied the woman police officer. 'Three-o-three! That is when the call came in.'

Aunt Lily had joined her husband, and wanted to know who was with Phyllis when they found her.

'Alone,' answered both police officers. After a brief discussion, voices dropped low-low, Lily exclaimed, 'But she might have been—' She caught herself, dropped her voice again. She and Luvo followed the police to the van and dragged out a pap-dronk and stinking Phyllis. They shooed away the children, Busi's eyes borrowed from a bull frog, and took Phyllis to the garden hose at the back of the house.

Afterwards, the three adults never referred to the incident. They hid it from Khulu, too. But now and then a look, a word recalled it. Much worse, less than a year later, there was another baby in the Wendy house, another little brother, Esam, for Busi to mind.

'If I had known that Phyllis would make a habit of making children without a husband, I would have thought twice about letting her come stay with us,' Aunt Lily grumbled. 'Yes, she's my sister, after all. But the add-ons – aba songezile bakhe – are red coals in my heart, I tell you!'

Of course, all this happened years and years ago – a lifetime for Busi. Back when she was Mama's only child. With Tata gone, it couldn't have been easy for Mama. Busi understood that now, at least more than when she was only five, and blamed her mother for making her fatherless. But what she still did not understand was how Phyllis could not only go on letting herself down, but Busi down as well.

CHAPTER FIVE

I have to wait to be sure-sure they're all asleep, said Busi to herself. She was nearly dying from the tension of lying awake in bed, pretending to sleep. In her mind's ear, she could already hear the noise of kwaito, see everybody vibing. Wait wait wait and die, bit by bit. Now! All was quiet; out the window she flew. She was soooo late for Thandi's Sweet Sixteen party!

But here she was at last, and the two friends jumped up and down upon seeing each other, squealing with excitement. Then Thandi pointed towards this pretty boy. Busi held her breath, walked away nonchantly. *First check him out*, she told herself. *What's he like? Cute, not tall, but hefty as hell. Could lift a whole horse. Eyes like a chief when he lifts them. Ah there, he is eyeing me when he thinks I'm not looking his way. I make sure he sees I AM NOT ... HA-HA-HA-HAA!*

Thandi intervened, pulling him towards her friend: 'Dance, you two!' she shouted above the roar of the music. She had drunk a bit more than Coca-Cola. 'He's from Section B ... hotter than hell! I saved him especially for you!' she said in Busi's ear.

She raised her voice again: 'Brian, this is Busi. Make sure you're happy; neither of you's allowed outta here before noon tomorrow!'

And off she sashayed, shouting to another friend, waving her arms as she disappeared into the gyrating crowd of cuddling, bobbing, bubbling bodies.

Busi and Brian got down, dancing without wasting words. Rhythm was king that night. But then she heard his voice: 'Girl, you look hot!'

That was all she got from the boy: that, and his name. And oh, let's not forget: his number! Got that when he buzzed her right back after she gave him her number.

Wait, there was more: he fished out a small bottle from his pocket, twisted off the cap, and held it out to her. Thirsty, she took a gulp, then had to hide her coughing as the liquor burned its way down her gullet. After that, whenever he offered her the bottle, she was careful to sip, the warmth soon spreading to her outstretched fingers, her gyrating hips.

Although Busi sneaked back home early the next morning, before six, that whole Sunday, she was more nervous than a brooding hen. She kept to herself, pleading a headache (that was true) and loads and loads of homework. Not quite a lie that either ... just an overstatement of fact. Had anyone detected her absence? Did anyone know?

Busi knew if one knew in that house, all knew. She hoped that no one had noticed her empty bed during the night. She'd been very careful, but everyone knew about Thandi's party – also that she, Busi, was too young to attend.

But soon she picked up Khulu's eyes following her, one brow raised, one corner of mouth drawn down – a piercing look of disapproval. Sadness was there, too.

Khulu saw the alarm and brooding on her granddaughter's face and troubling thoughts, most unwelcome, inveigled her mind. No good could come from Busi's meetings with that ougat Thandi ... no good at all. Khulu felt this in her old bones. But how to stop Busi from taking what she had been fed? Khulu thought about it. She picked at it like a dog with a bone.

Then she called Phyllis.

'Busi will see her moon time soon!'

'Hayi, suka, Mama! Ngumntwana lo. This is a child.'

'A child who has sprouted! You don't see the peaches on her chest?'

'No! You imagine things!'

'And the oily face?'

'Oily face?'

'Uyafikisa. Coming into womanhood, she is.'

'Hehake! Goodness!'

'Uza kumthombisa nini? When will you give her the rites-of-passage ceremony?'

Phyllis jumped to her feet. 'No, I am not doing that! Not me.'

'And why not?'

'That is backward, Mama.'

'Backward? No, that is tradition!'

Lily heard their heated discussion and joined in. 'The child will be laughed off the face of the earth. Even here in Kwanele – and I don't want to think about that posh school of hers! Times have changed, Mama. Please leave the poor girl alone.'

The 'poor girl' eavesdropping on this adult discussion, soundlessly punched her right fist into her left palm, said to herself: 'Good!' She couldn't remember when last she'd been in full agreement with her fussy aunty.

'If you say so,' Khulu retorted. 'Kodwa, nakundikhumbula ngenye imini. But one day you will remember what I said today!'

The older woman looked at her daughters, shook her head and murmured, 'Mark my words. Yes, you mark my words. I must take Busi to the village. She will learn a lot eSidwadweni. But also just to get the poor child away from this place ... if only for a while.'

Busisiwe, in Grade Seven, had no such concerns. She felt quite grown-up now that she was almost in high school. Just a few more months and the year would be dead. The principal talked about nothing else: 'You all have one foot already in high school. You had better behave yourselves. You're not quite there yet, remember that and act your age!' What she meant by that, Busisiwe had no idea.

What she did know was that she was hopelessly moneyless. Had always been, but now, for some reason, it was just more pronounced, more terrifying. The only thing she seemed to see was how other kids at her school flaunted their wealth ... well, those from the suburbs, the blessed ones, not those travelling in the minibus back to the township. She definitely saw and felt that divide more keenly. One couldn't help be embarrassed by one's nakedness when everyone else was wearing clothes. But never mind! There were many tricks a girl could come up with to tart up her school uniform, and Busi had learned them all. Had had to learn them, or she'd have been dead in the water.

She was lucky that way, Busi told herself. Her sister-friend Thandi in the township was not only older; that girl was a fashion-maker. She could take an insignificant piece of nothing, wrap it around her lower body, and BOOM! Thandi had an elegant designer skirt. It was from her that Busi learned the trick of shortening her tunic with an extra set of buttons hidden in the shoulder seam.

Thandi's horror stories about the school she attended in the township made Busi aware that perhaps she should be grateful for her opportunities. No, *definitely* grateful, she corrected herself. Kasi schools, it was a well-known fact, suffered chronic shortages of textbooks; had no computer or science labs; many had taverns right around the corner from the school premises, and it was not uncommon for learners and sometimes even teachers to sneak off there – they did that during school hours, or, for the few still with some sense of shame, right after school.

In an effort to save her sneakers, Busi went to fetch water in an old pair of Mrs Bird's shoes, which were too small to be useful until they were cut open at the back. As she stood there, waiting her turn at the ever weaker-running tap, hopelessness sifted into her. Somewhere deep inside her, desperation grew. Every second she was consumed by burning thoughts about the gross unfairness of her life. Imagining how Thandi spent the past weekend with her Ganja Guru choked her. Yhoo, Thandi didn't spend it in a hokey-pokey shack, or even an RDP leg-out or apartheid four-room. The girl had stayed in a HOTELE. For a whole long weekend – Thursday through to Tuesday morning. And then she was driven to school! Although she didn't disclose the exact amount her sugar daddy slipped her, Busi suspected, KNEW in fact, that Thandi had at least five grand in her pocket.

Imagine that! To have that!

And that's a girl attending a rickety-rackety nothing school while she, the blessed one, a learner from a posh Model C school with a saint's name, stood here with her cut-down, throwaway shoes in the mud.

Busi felt caught between a rock and a hard place. When she wanted, needed something, her mother stubbornly refused to pay for it. For Phyllis, the education Busi was getting courtesy of Khulu's old employer was already more than she could expect. She should concentrate on doing well at school, an opportunity many in her position – fatherless and mother a domestic worker – could not even begin to dream of. She was very, very lucky, Phyllis kept on saying. Hers was an opportunity many would give anything, everything to receive.

But she couldn't begin to tell her mother how difficult, how anxiety-making it felt straddling Kwanele and Cape Town every single day. Moving from the one to the other was like climbing in and out of two different TV shows: one full of colour and strangeness, the other drab but familiar.

'We had no such chances during our time!' Phyllis would snap.

This irritated Busi to no end. Why should she be punished because she was getting a better education? Mama and Khulu's suffering under apartheid was not her fault. Besides, it was not Mama herself who had suffered, nor had she personally defeated the apartheid government. That had been the job of Tata Mandela and the ANC.

Sitting next to a white kid at school! That was Mama's idea of freedom. But Busi did not feel the freedom. If her Mama could only see the 'to-die-for' three-grand sneakers her desk-mate Shona wore when she went out with her parents. Mama did not know how hard she had to pretend not to show envy while chatting to happy, kind-hearted Shona with her long straight hair, who was always nice to her. Why couldn't she be an awful snob so that Busi would have a good reason to hate her?

To crown it all, with frowns and jeers, Mama forbade Busi to ask her absentee father for anything. 'Why do you think he stays away ... because he loves you and wants what's best for you?'

This crushed her spirit, deterred her from calling her father. Well, sometimes.

◇◇◇

'Are you sure?' asked Ms Priscilla, the school secretary. Busi had not yet paid the fare money for the trip, although her name was down as a definite. Mortified, Busi told the secretary she'd been given the money, but had forgotten to bring it.

'Well then,' said Ms Priscilla, 'bring it tomorrow.'

Busi wished the ground would just open up and swallow her. The school was planning a trip to a clothing factory. The learners would not only see how evening gowns were made, but some would be allowed to dress up like mannequins and parade on a real ramp, modelling dresses for teenage girls!

Back home, she pleaded and scolded and wept until her uncle couldn't bear it any longer. He gave her the money. Gave it to her, and then suffered through the hours of fighting with Aunt Lily behind the closed door of their bedroom that followed. As if that were not bad enough, Phyllis bitched: 'Do you want them to throw us out?'

Busi felt as if she stood on a crumbling piece of clay, while all around her roads led to wonderful new and exciting possibilities. The only thing needed to step off that lump was money.

And then nosy Shona asked Busi where she was going during the holidays. Busi shrugged and said, 'Family's keeping it secret so far.'

'Oh, my dad is taking us to Mauritius.'

Busi's head swirled with names and words like this, thrown around during school time. Names of places, foods, brands of clothing, hobbies, gym equipment, cars, names names names ...

'That's nice,' she said and painted a big, lips-only smile: 'Enjoy!' But Shona was already racing off and away to another group, no doubt to discuss their holiday plans before all the Grade Sevens trooped into the assembly hall for a lecture.

The speaker was there to talk to them about respect for self. Busi's mind started burning. Did she respect herself? Did her Mama respect herself? She didn't love herself, that's for sure. Is respect possible without love – or the other way round? Love without respect?

That evening, Busi asked Mama about respect and love.

'The Bible says: Beka uyihlo nonyoko,' Phyllis replied.

'Awu, Mama, the Bible assumes one has a yihlo – father!'

'Miss Know-all!' Mama slapped the table, got up, pushing the chair she was sitting on so hard, it tottered backwards like a drunken wooden robot. Uncle Luvo stopped it from toppling over, shook his head and put it back in its place. 'Respect your furniture,' he said.

Busi looked at the figure of her mother disappearing out the door, and her usual thoughts started up: *There she goes again! She'll most certainly get herself soused. Any wonder Tata left? Or am I blaming the victim again? Didn't the teacher in Life Orientation the other day say we must be loyal to members of our families? Trouble is, which one must I be loyal to? Tata, who said he loved me, but left me, or Mama who stayed, but is always out and about, leaving me to babysit the fruits of her actions?*

Busi knew that the enraged Phyllis would disappear for the whole night, and with her charring for Mrs Bird finished for the week, she might stay away even longer. The two little boys would sleep with Busi. That meant getting up and settling a crying child several times in the course of the night: 'Been there, done that, more times than I care to remember!'

She sighed. The teachers told them, 'When you get home, rest for half an hour after a snack, and then hit your books.' She arrived long after even the possibility of a snack; then she had so many chores to do. If only they could all sit down like the families she saw in advertisements, be together like a real family.

Busi had another anxiety. She hoped Tata would remember her birthday this year. He forgot it last year, after promising, nogal, he'd come especially to be with her. The man hadn't even called, and had his phone off all day long. So much for fatherly love!

Her mind was buzzing. She simply had to come up with a plan for new sneakers for the outing. Although the principal was strict, very strict about uniform – brown lace-up shoes only – uniform rules always relaxed when they went on an outing. She couldn't have the class see her in her regular tatty mud-splashed sneakers. No way!

Although all the blood in her veins screamed against it, she texted Tata and appealed for money.

'Sure, baby!' came the prompt response. No explanation about not sending the money he'd promised her last time round – and forget any apology. But surprise, surprise! This time the man actually honoured his word. Within an hour, Busi got a notification of cash received. Wow! Papa had sent her a lousy R200 via Checkers.

'How big-hearted of him,' Busi fumed. What kind of pathetic sneakers could one buy for that miserable pittance? But when she complained, Aunt Lily snapped: 'Be grateful for small mercies.'

Phyllis's response was to scream: 'I could kill the swine!'

'If he's a swine, are you a sow?' Lily countered. The sisters glared at each other with scorn-filled eyes.

Then Lily turned back to Busi: 'You're at that place to learn, not to be a fashion modeller!'

Phyllis chimed in: 'Perhaps Mrs Bird can help. Why don't you go ask her for money?'

Busi made a face. She didn't like asking Mrs Bird for anything. 'Khulu doesn't want me to bother Mrs Bird.'

'Don't tell me you expect *me* to go on my knees for you! I have news for you: nothing doing!'

'You're the one who sees Mrs Bird, Phyllis,' said Lily. 'Don't be selfish. The child needs to go on school trips ... you work for the woman.'

Phyllis turned to her daughter and spat: 'Go ask Mrs Bird yourself!'

Busi felt as if she was splintering into nothingness. In the back room, she went straight to her bed, lay face down. Buried in the rough corduroy overcover, she stifled groans. She couldn't go on the trip. It was as simple as that. She couldn't make a friend because she had nothing. She was a nothing.

The next day, Phyllis came home in the evening, her face longer than a pole.

'What's the matter?' Lily asked.

'MaNtaka is something else!'

'You two had a fight?'

'Well,' answered Phyllis, 'I did what you said I should do, and you have should heard the mouthful I got!'

'From Mrs Bird?'

'No, from Jesus Christ!'

Lily burst out laughing: 'That bad?'

Phyllis went into a rant about the lecture she had received on the difference between needing and wanting things. She couldn't remember which of the two Mrs Bird said was right, and which was wrong. Cutting coat according to cloth, lying on the bed one had made, there are many poorer families, and so on and so on ...

Lily sighed and turned to Busi: 'Know what our father used to say to us – your mother and I – when we were your age?'

Phyllis shouted, 'Choose which you want: education or swank!'

The sisters laughed out loud, looked at each other, and there was an amazed spark of recognition, of admission, remembering who they once were ... who they still were: Hlombe's beloved daughters. Remembering their father, wordlessly, they reached for each other, embraced.

So surprised was she by this rare show of kinship between the two sisters, Busi found herself tearing up at the same time that a slow-spreading smile split her face. That minute, something was born in her heart: recognition of kinship. Love of family. She'd always understood the concept, but it had not been a living thing, real and tangible.

Despite all the ups and downs of her family, love was also present. She must not forget that. Their living in Kwanele, living under Aunt Lily's roof – well, in her backyard – was proof positive thereof.

CHAPTER SIX

All day long Busi could hardly pay attention to what the teacher was saying. The number so loud in her mind she could hear her heart beat it loud and clear. THIR-teen – two-beat strokes; loud-gap-soft.

THIR-teen THIR-teen THIR-teen! Hello? She was grown. Finally, she was grown. At the stroke of midnight tonight she would be a teenager, no less!

Sleep was scarcer than a hen's tooth that night. Now life could begin to happen. Now she would be able to live out the things she felt churning inside her. Her mind had a million zillion crazy things to think about. She could hardly wait for the coming morning.

Her phone alarm buzzed, but she was already up. Up and waiting. Surely ... now? Now he would call, for he knew perfectly well she'd be awake. Knew what time she woke for school.

But everything was stubbornly quiet.

Busi's thoughts went round and round in her head. *This can't be happening. It can't be happening to me. I went to bed expecting a midnight call. It didn't come. So I told myself: he considerately thinks I should rather sleep and will call first thing tomorrow. Even as I drifted off to sleep, I imagined his deep bass voice singing: 'Happy birthday to you! Happy birthday to you! Happy birthday, dear Daddy's girl! Happy birthday to you!' Yes, and he would drag that last note, making it dip and rise, dip and rise, his voice deeper on the dip and shooting up like a wave on the rise.*

Why hasn't he called yet? He can't possibly forget the day, as we share a birthday. If I'd arranged the year's calendar myself, I could not have organised it better: a double birthday with my father.

Busi realised she'd forgotten how old her father was, even as she remembered how handsome he was, and how much he had loved her as a five-year-old. Long ago he'd promised to spend this important day with her. Surely he wouldn't break his promise this time? Of course not! This birthday was special. Maybe he hadn't called because he wanted his visit to come as a surprise.

As Busi emptied the wash basin onto the garden, the rest of the house suddenly descended on her, singing at full throttle, no stopping them, the chorus loud and out of tune. Now the whole neighbourhood knew it was her birthday.

> Happy birthday to you!
> Happy birthday to you!
> Happy birthday, Busi-Busi!
> Happy birthday to you!

And then they sang again, translating the whole distinctly inharmonious song into isiXhosa. OMG, her family was something else. Embarrassment meant nothing to them.

Surprise, surprise! Even Mama made it. Not only was Phyllis

present; she looked good, quite pleased with herself. Just because, for a change, she had slept in the house and was sober in the morning for her daughter's birthday, was no reason to look as though she deserved a prize.

Although it was her birthday, it was also still a school day, so the family made short shrift of the cream biscuits and Oros.

'There will be chocolate cake when you come back from school,' said Phyllis.

Really? But aloud Busi said, 'Of course!' even though she didn't believe one word.

'Nyhan-nyhan!' said her mama.

Lily shrugged, eyeballs going north until only the whites showed.

'Believe it when I see it,' Busi shouted back as she ran out the door to catch the school taxi. Although she wasn't looking at Phyllis, the girl felt her mother wince – a cat caught stretching for milk not in her saucer. Busi told herself: *She so desperately wants me to think she loves me, and maybe she does. But I know she loves her liquor more. I'm done with her lies. Yes, I know we shouldn't say a grown-up lies. That's rude. Grown-ups make mistakes – bayaphosisa.*

Busi kicked her mother out of her thoughts as she got into the transi, switching back to Tata. He was more important – more reliable. Well, she hoped so.

All the way to school, and all day long, the same thought kept turning and turning in her mind. *He will not forget my birthday. It is also his. No way could he forget his own birthday. Surely he remembers he shares it with me, his beloved daughter. We* spoke about it during our weekly 'visits', as he calls our scheduled Sunday afternoon telephone talks. And today is not any old ordinary birthday, either. THIRTEEN! I am a teenager at last. Certified, verified, glorified.

Should I call him? No, it is a special day for me: he must call first!

Thina sobabini? We two?

We jive!

Except, that whole long day, no call came from her father.

At her school, a learner got detention if a teacher had to warn her to be quiet more than once during the day. Busi had got detention during her very first week there. Was it her fault she had a loud voice and was not so good at whispering? But the teacher also said she was cheeky. Cheeky? Cat's whiskers.

So today, although distracted, in fact more like subtracted from what the teacher said, Busi trod carefully — today of all days she didn't want detention.

But what a tedious day as it stretched out and no call came. That day the benevolence of her big-hearted class teacher stuck in Busi's throat. And then busybody, know-it-all Shona had to broadcast to the entire school that it was 'Boosie's' birthday. Boosie — why the belungus exploded the soft 'b' was beyond her. After so many years, it had stopped jarring her ear. Once Shona had alerted all the silly girls in her class, break was a nightmare of thanking people for cupcakes, juice and gaudy birthday cards quickly handmade by classmates.

On her way home, Busi still nursed some hope her father would call. At home, no surprise, Phyllis had not only forgotten her promise of the morning; she forgot to come home at all. No card, no cake. As they sat around the table joylessly drinking tea, poor Aunt Lily scuttled to her room and miraculously returned with a box with a cake and some soft drinks in it. 'I know my sister,' her eyes said.

The boys were delighted, but something vile lodged in Busi's new teen throat. *Broken promises from both of those who bred me! A washout day!*

Busi felt she no longer even had a heart – it had been hammered and trampled, torn and crushed into a clot. That was the gift she had to mark this supposedly special day, this milestone passage. A bleeding clot where her heart had been.

As she lay sleepless in the dark that night, she agonised over how long it had taken her to wake up to the truth, to see her parents – especially her Tata – clearly. She had only herself to blame. All these years, she had been fooling herself.

She had wasted half her life chasing a father who did not love her, maybe never had. The staggering fact was that for eight of her thirteen years, she had lived a dead life without knowing it, waiting and praying for the miracle of being loved for herself.

Later that night, the back-room door blew open. It was Mama stumbling in, making such a lawaai …

'Why does your father call me when it is your birthday? Why doesn't the swine call you, his dropping?'

Busi could hear the neighbours complaining about the noise.

'He called *you*? I waited for his call all day long …'

'No, he wanted to call me so that I could listen to his pitiful excuses! He has his other children and his wife … do you hear that? His *wife*, my dear – the man has no shame telling me, the woman he abandoned and left holding his baby with nowhere to live – tells me about his wife who is not working. I told the dog what I thought of him and cut him off. Flipping wasting *my* airtime!'

'But how did he waste your airtime? You said he called you.'

But even as she spoke, Busi knew it was the absolute last straw. Why hadn't he called her, even if he couldn't make the visit he'd promised? Even a 'Happy Birthday!' message would have been something!

Stupid! Stupid! Stupid Busi!

Phyllis wasn't done yet. In the mood to punish, perhaps to make up for her own failure to materialise a cake, she went on: 'Your father has moved on, Busisiwe. You'd better move on too! He has forgotten all about you. He has his other children to love. Yes, that's it. He loves his other children and does not love you. That is, if he ever did.'

CHAPTER SEVEN

Fully thirteen-year-old Busisiwe told herself: 'Enough is enough. I must come up with a plan … a plan that works. Forget the father! Forget the mother! I cannot live like this any more. I'm on my own.'

A plan was percolating in her mind. A plan that could generate breathing space. Trouble was, how was she going to get Brian to agree to this? They hadn't been dating long, but he was the only reliable human being she knew.

Her plan was simple. Lots of girls were doing it; why shouldn't she? She'd just make him. Convince him. She had to.

Busi read the signs. Busi calculated the dates. Meticulously, she went over all the facts. Brian had kissed her on the lips. He had begun frequenting her neighbourhood. She would tell him: it was love at first sight at Thandi's Sweet Sixteen party! He would believe her.

She had to brush up her act, and a better coach than Thandi Kwanele could not produce. Busi soon became a mistress at batting doll's lashes and swinging her hips.

She also picked up that Brian never contradicted her. He also confessed to being a bit intimidated by her superior knowledge, picked up from her Model C school. 'Jeepers,' he once said. 'You can gempe-gempe-gempe all right. With so many English words in between. But you still a girlie, mos!'

So she hadn't had to work hard to get him between her thighs. Her words were there to melt away any reluctance he had. Nobody would ever blame him. She was pushing for it; ready and greedy. Why wait? Did he want somebody else to be there first? Why not grab the cherry when it was offered on a smooth virgin-white plate? That was Busi's favourite phrase, borrowed from Thandi, who was coaching her behind the scenes.

Soon the women in the house began frowning. Why was Busi suddenly so sprightly? Why had she become such a keen water mule? Was she giving it up to boys? 'Remember, smart one,' said sarcastic Phyllis, 'boys will make you pregnant! Then see who raises that child. Not the boy. No, never the boy; and it won't be me either, that I can tell you ... you can bet your last penny on that!'

And it was not just the grown-up members of her family, but also neighbours who were remarking on the new confident stance of Busi: 'They gossip that I grow up posh! Well, let them gossip; I will just go on minding my own business. Mine and Brian's!'

Busi listened to the clot that was once a heart inside her: rememberthat-rememberthat-rememberthat-rememberthat. *I am alone. I have to do it all myself.*

Brian became a regular layabout in Kwanele, and Busi became adept at getting the other children out of the back room during the weekends.

She would never forget that first time; the awkwardness of it. The whole thing suddenly overwhelmed her. Shivering as though thrust inside the deep freeze of a fridge, teeth chattering, eyes smarting, she heard a strange voice squeak: 'No!'

Brian pulled back, eyes wide as plates, barking, 'No?' She grabbed him back. 'No, I mean YES!' she said with a moan. His voice deep, gruff: 'Don't say no, then.' Back came her brain, her quick lips shut him up in the ways Thandi taught her.

And that became the ritual, whenever opportunity dawned. Fridays, but Saturday of course the best day; blessed Saturday with everybody out and away – not even the neighbours around, despite the terribly high rate of unemployment.

Busi had it all planned. She intended for the ninth month to fall during the holidays so that the birth would not interfere with her schoolwork, or the grant that would fund her through the rest of high school.

Now she had to scheme and plan on how to free her Saturdays, becoming prompt and orderly. On Fridays, she didn't even bother with a snack after returning from school; she went right ahead and did most of the laundry before the adults came back from work. She alerted the boys so they left their school uniforms where she could find them. Pretending to be soaking it overnight, she left the already washed laundry in clean water. The minute everybody left the next morning – et voilà, as the French teacher at her school would say: wring, rinse, and onto the washing line it all went!

Brian was her first. She was not his, but that did not matter – the last thing she needed was a fumbling virgin. What did surprise her, however, was the swiftness with which the whole thing was over. Already? The heady-dreamy-steamy sense of well-being ... did it really last only a few minutes?

After their first few times, Busi realised that there was no way she was going to become pregnant – Brian fastidiously sheathed his spear to the hilt. No baby from him!

'Don't want a lot of little Brians running all over the place!' he'd said the very first time they did it. He didn't even ask her to do anything; he took care of the business himself. Good boy, her Brian, but it was a baby she wanted, not this caution, this sense of responsibility! She had to change his style, and so she started the tap-tap-tap of the hammer: 'You keep telling me to wait. For what? Why is now not the right time? Why are we screwing then, if you want to do things the old-fashioned way? My mother didn't wait!'

'I want to do the right thing,' Brian defended himself.

'Which is?'

'My baby mama should first be ...' – he shot loud-shouting eyes at her – 'my wife.'

Not impressed, Busi challenged him: 'Your mother didn't wait for any white wedding dress, either.'

'Hey, wena! Mind your mouth. That's my late mama you're insulting!'

'So what?'

'Keep my mother out of your filthy lips.'

'They were not filthy just now,' she said, pursing those very lips and reaching up towards him. He shook his head and, frowning, firmly but gently pushed her away, put distance between that upturned, eager face and his, which remained stern, unsmiling.

But it wasn't long before she knew which piano keys to press, when and how. It pleased her no end that she could make Brian cry tears during nookie. His yelps thrilled her. And she relished the attention. So much attention! Her own body felt lifted. Luxurious. Honoured. It was as if the connecting eyes, mouths, and hips were the first real connection her body had ever experienced.

◇◇◇

'Who sees your toes?' Phyllis asked as she watched her daughter painting her toenails. 'Your feet are always boxed in shoes,' she added, irritation ruffling her words.

'I do,' replied Busi sweetly but with eyebrows arched. Did her mother dare come out with it? Of course, it was the subject of boys and sex she was skirting around, not nail polish.

Her thoughts moved to the forever-ring Brain had promised her for Christmas, and remembering, she burst out laughing, aglow at the memory of the words with which he'd made that promise.

'What's funny? Phyllis asked.

'Nothing,' replied Busi, but her laugh had morphed into a smirk she could not for the life of her stifle.

'Mmmh, uyathungulula,' Phyllis sneered. Puppy eyes begin to open! *Bitch!* Abruptly, she turned and made for the door. Out in the backyard of the house, Busi saw how her mother ran towards the hedge, bent over its bushes, and puked. When she'd gathered herself, she rinsed her mouth and swiped at the wet all around her wide-open but unseeing eyes.

Ignoring Phyllis's distress, Busi admitted to herself that she would have to change her strategy. She wanted a baby, yes;

otherwise on what would they live?

But she also wanted to live with Brian: *I love Brian, and it is his baby I want. But his goodness niggles me – even during a smootchie nookie, he is careful. But I will get him. I will get him ... our baby's name will start with B. The announcement will go: Brian and Busi have a baby. Her or his name will be Belinda; Bubele; Buyiswa; Bulelwa; Boyboy; Brutus; Bertha; Beulah; Benjamin; Bethwell; Barbara; Beauty – no, what if she isn't and we have to change it later? But let's get Brian over the hurdle first.*

◇◇◇

As we are correcting things, they are disturbing them:
So it will happen then
There will be turmoil and arguments
There will be chaos and madness
The girl is bent on it
She will not turn back
The curse of a nation
Children begetting children
Long before they are ready to be parents
As we are correcting things, they are disturbing them:
What cruel times they live in, our leavelings!
What cruel times, our neglected leavelings.

◇◇◇

Time was passing. Busi was filled with irritation, while Brian was confused about the ridicule she hurled at him for insisting on always using a condom.

'Are you old enough for what you're asking for?'

'Of course!'

'Sure?'

As she tried to kiss him, his head jerked back. 'What do you want a child for?'

'What do you want smarts for?'

That stopped him short. Busi pulled down Brian's pants, then snatched the condom out of his hand. Finally, nothing could stop him. After that first time without a condom, they never went back to using 'that tiresome thing'. Saw no reason to. He was almost sixteen. She was thirteen. They were figuring out a new life together. Or at least, Busi was.

'We'll manage,' she was convinced. 'We already look after ourselves, the way things are. My mama, too strict, too stingy, too drunk; and you, without mother or father! We'll make our own family. A family where there'll be fun and love, and no one will ever be hungry or beg for things they want – a loving family. Unlike the ones we have.'

uyalila
someone is crying
my mother, herself still a child
wants a child

no-no-no-no!
I refuse to be fleshborn
she thinks her body is ready
but her body hungers to be touched
hungers to be owned
hungers to be respected
her body is ready
her heart is not
her mind is not
only her foolheart wants me to be fleshborn
her foolheart stronger than her real heart
but I refuse to be fleshborn

how she weeps to see her monthly flow

for three months I resisted
finally, spirit world said I should go
one can't forever refuse when called

the tadpole
in shallow water he wallows
this is his world; all he knows, all he will ever know
this way and that, the tail swishing
water retreats, tadpole does not know
water retreats
tadpole does not see
water gone
tadpole sloshing
tadpole sloshing

WHEN THE VILLAGE SLEEPS

my mother was thirteen
when the teardrop from my father's thigh spilled
crawled right up into the cage
of my first flesh home
my mother's sacred cage
she, all of thirteen years
and now:

it is done.

CHAPTER EIGHT

Thrumpthrumpthrumpthrump
I am little more than a heartbeat
inside my first flesh home
the cage in my mother's body
thrumpthrumpthrump
does Busisiwe hear me?
hear my heartbeat?
echoing hers?

◇◇◇

Far away from Kwanele, Khulu was not at peace. Recently, it felt as if there was a heavy chunk of dry, dry ubulongwe, cow dung, in the innermost chamber of her heart. A premonition? Dread silted her soul. What evil was sloughing her way? There was no way of telling, but it made her innards shake and growl.

She prayed: 'Almighty, please, give me the strength to wade through whatever river of fire comes my way.'

Perhaps as a result of this heavy cloud hanging over her, birthed by the weight inside her heart, Khulu had of late become particularly observant. Things she used to take for granted, paid scant attention to, had suddenly taken on peculiar meaning. Anthills. Beehives. The croaking of toads shortly after the sun went to rest on her mother's breast.

She paid attention, wondering whether Hlombe, her late husband, might possibly be visiting her, all these years after he left this earth. He was the one who could tell of the stars, say which portended what.

'See the way that cluster over there leans a little to the east? Watch,' he would say in the evenings as they sat beside the hut, leaning against the rondavel's sun-warmed, mud-brick wall, their legs stretched out before them; she, flat on isicamba on the ground, and he perched on a block of wood. She would; and every time she would witness some oddity she'd have otherwise missed. Something beautiful, unusual, something that never failed to lift her spirits.

He taught her to pick out uCanzibe, the evening star; to first look for the group of amaKroza, Orion; and showed her how bright isiLimela became when it was time for harvesting. He had been a rare gift in her life. It is sad but true: the good die young.

Hlombe also knew the clouds – which ran before the rain, brought it, and how pregnant they were with that blessing – heavy or light, of long duration or swiftly passing showers. All that, just from the colours the clouds wore and the contours in which they were shaped as they hovered atop the mountain and hills, or scudded like beasts with predators hot on their heels, or waltzed across the heavens. They made a picture of the sense of belongingness that is the inheritance of all life on this beautiful planet, home to humans, animals and plants, beings visible and invisible, known and as yet unknown to humanity.

But the most unforgettable day was when Hlombe pointed at a formation of birds in flight. 'Do you see that one in front, how he leads? How the rest follow in orderly fashion. Now wait, you see how he falters, feeling the burden of leadership beginning to weary him? Now see how that other one thrusts herself forward. Not in envy or grumbling or boastfulness. But in humble obligation, to relieve the courageous leader now stepping down ... doing so without fuss.'

And so she learned that true glory lay in service rendered to others for the greater good. There was no nobler pursuit than contribution to the common well-being – never forgetting that ISINA IDEDELANA! One gave way to what followed; like the waves of the ocean, each in dying gives way to the coming, the new that follows in its wake.

Shortly after he left her for the spirit world – when he went to never-wake-from-sleep-land – she had begun to sense, discern, see the meaning of the soft, sweet song of air and felt submerged into thoughts of oneness:

THERE/IS/NO/TIME/PAST/TO/COME/GONE/NEVER/OR/
EVER/TIME/IS/ONE/ALWAYS/AND/ALWAYS/ONE/TIME/
ALL/TIME/NOW/THEN/WHEN/IS/NOW/NOW/NOW/
NEVER/THEN/NOW/NOW/FOR/WE/LIVE/FOREVER/
FOREVER/BREATHING/THE/SAME/AIR/ALWAYS/THE/
SAME/AIR/OVER/AND/OVER/THE/SAME/AIR/WHEN/
WE/ARE/BORN/AGAIN/AND/AGAIN/AND/AGAIN/THE/

SAME/SAME/SAME/AIR/WE/BREATHE/THE/SAME/SAME/
AIR/OVER/AND/OVER/AND/OVER/REMEMBER/THAT/
REMEMBER/THAT/WE/BREATHE/THE/SAME/SAME/
SAME/AIR
TIME/IS/ONE
TOMORROW/YESTERDAY/TODAY/AND/ALWAYS/ALL/ONE
AND/EVERYONE/IS/PRESENT/ALL/THE/TIME
THEREFORE/NEVER/ASK
WERE/YOU/THERE?
DID/YOU/KNOW/OR/REFUSE/TO/KNOW/REFUSE/TO/SEE
SEE/KNOW/FOR/SURE/SOMETHING/SO/WRONG
SO/EVIL/SO/INCONCEIVABLE/MANY/REFUSE/TO/SEE/IT/
REFUSE
TO/ACKNOWLEDGE/ITS/EXISTENCE/FOR/SEEING/IT/IS/
ALREADY
ENOUGH/RESPONSIBILITY/SEEING/IT/DEMANDS/
ACTION/OF/THE/SEER
THEY/WERE/THERE/AS/YOU/WERE
YOU/WERE/THEY/WERE/ALL/WERE/ALWAYS/FOR
TOMORROW/IS/TODAY/YESTERDAY/FOREVER/AND/EVER
YOU/WERE/THERE/ARE/HERE/WILL/BE/EVERYWHERE/
ALL/THE/TIME/ANY/AND/ALL/TIME

Then one night, Hlombe came to her in an unsettling dream. He looked so sad, it brought tears to her eyes. The look he gave her was sorrowful and loving, as if to say: *I wish I could take this from you, suffer in your stead.* She hardly slept after the dream, and when she did, Hlombe reappeared a second and a third time.

The next morning, she fretted: what evil was stalking her? Her heart flew to her children, Phyllis and Lilian. There was trouble there! Oh, there was always trouble in the townships: toyi-toyi-ing and protests against one or another service delivery deficit; violence against children; against women; and against anyone perceived as not belonging, violence against those strange, different, outside – the Other. Khulu clenched her hands: *that always-there Other – we create in the smallness and meanness of our hearts, in our inability to see the inescapable oneness of humanity; our blunted, blighted and blinded soul eyes.* Us-them! We-they! Making monsters of one another, making monsters of ourselves.

Convinced of trouble in Kwanele, at the crack of dawn, Khulu called MaNtaka. She knew Mrs Bird woke up with the first tweet of birdsong and was out walking by six-thirty.

'Please, Mrs B,' she said, 'find out what is wrong in Kwanele for me.'

'My goodness! Why don't you just call your girls?'

'They'll lie to me; pretend all is well, thinking they're protecting me.'

'And you don't want to be protected?' MaNtaka laughed. She knew Khulu too well.

'I want to know the truth, that's all.'

While waiting for news, night after night, Hlombe stood before her. Weeping. For decades, he had not visited her; now, she went to bed fearing his arrival. It was not good news that he was bringing.

◇◇◇

thrumpthrumpthrump
I see my family before I was there
long before I was in it
I would be born
designed other than by the Creator of all
uMdali weento zonke
pray that Spirit World supports and protects me
obedient, I will suffer the consequences gladly
oh, that humanity regains the humaneness it has forsaken
this is my family
the only family I know
everyone in my family has a heart full of wounds
some bleed; some are beached tadpoles
they gape and gasp but give out no sound
the mouths of beached tadpoles
give out no sound
dry sobs of hearts broken
over and over and over again

◇◇◇

Aunt Lily was the first to speak her mind. 'What mouse ravished the peanut butter so?'

'I thought your children only liked jam and cheese?'

'Yes! That's why this disappearance of stuff from the bottle is suspicious. Look here, somebody is scooping it with a finger!'

Phyllis didn't answer. She was watching the news and as usual, was raging: 'Promises. Promises. Promises! Listen to this one barking like a beached seal! Aargh-aaargh! Aargh-aaahargrhh! Khulu is so right; they just give promises to get votes.'

'Maybe you should watch Busi,' Aunt Lily suggested. 'Because I will simply stop buying bread …'

'Busi hates peanut butter, you know that. Doesn't it kill you that in a land of gold and platinum, we starve? In a land of universities galore, we are unschooled in the most basic of life-skills, conned into illicit acts and demonic dreams?' Phyllis was on a roll and did not even see her sister leaving the room.

'In the land of the first heart transplant, our teeth rot to mush. And all because of corruption: use the taxi of a company that has a tender with the government! Job creation has taken the form of tenderpreneurship.' Phyllis got up, still ranting: 'The formerly dispossessed continue to blame history, while the present is but a mirror thereof. Graft is king.'

Meanwhile Busi was beside herself with joy. No monthly visitor! Her plan was coming to fruition at last. The jackpot! Delight sent her to a baby shop in town, not to buy anything yet, but to look things over. But a cursory glance at the price of even the littlest thing came as a huge shock:

> NAPPIES NEWBORN 2-5KG R199.99;
> NEWBORN INFANT BATH ADJUSTABLE R112.00;
> BABY CARE BATH SET R19.00.

How could such little things cost *so-oo-oo* much? And she could only collect the money once the baby was born. This meant she had to implement Stage 2 of her plan. She must work on the baby in her belly. Get him to do as she intended.

She was happy and worried. Happy she was pregnant, worried about what Aunt Lily would say. And Uncle Luvo? What about Mama? She would probably make the loudest noise, the biggest fuss, but she was the last one to point fingers of blame. Besides, she would be of absolutely no help at all. *Ingxaki nguMama!*

But then it hit her: dear God! Khulu! Yhoo! Khulu would freak out. She would be the most disappointed of all. But Busi would make sure Khulu understood that her education would not be affected. She would definitely continue going to school; nowadays, teachers had to support girls who were pregnant. And besides, her moneyless days would soon be over.

In fact, if she had any money, she wouldn't be doing what she was doing. Wouldn't be making the plans she was making for, well … a special baby. What would Brian think of that? Should she tell him? Perhaps not. Not yet. But he would have to supply her with the necessary stuff. Wait, better idea, she'd hang around Thandi, who always had lots of everything – ganja, tik lollies, booze. Oh yes, and she would buy her own peanut butter and stash it under her clothes in the cardboard box that served as her suitcase. Peanut butter, lollies and brandy if she could lay hands on it: they would be her diet from now on.

I am not yet born
uyalila uyalila uyalila
but the pain

> *the pain*
> *the pain*
> *as poison floods my tiny body*
> *the tiny walnut of my brain freezes*
> *the pain*
> *the pain*
> *the pain*
> *my minuscule heart tires*
> *my spine withdraws into itself*
> *protect me Old Ones*
> *uyalila*
> *uyalila*

> *I knew it would come to this*
> *knew before I allowed myself to be fleshborn*
> *in the spirit world one sees all*
> *sees even before-before*
> *see, my mother's heart is not twined with mine*
> *it does not beat with mine in song*
> *the Song of Old; the Song of Life*
> *my mother's heart is not singing with mine*
> *my mother's heart is not singing at all*
> *thrumpthrumpthruuummmpp!*

◇◇◇

The next thing, Busi sprouted a sixth finger on each hand: daily breakages when she did the dishes, crust-rimmed cups, chipped dishes, water too soapy. A wasteful girl! Furious, Lily sent her to bed without dinner one night. Thrilled, Busi went to her room out the back. Where had she stowed her treat from Thandi? Here it was! She fished a half-jack of brandy out of her cardboard box. Bliss and more bliss. Bliss to oblivion!

Hot on the heels of Lily's complaints, alarm bells sounded from the school: Busi was inattentive and rude; her performance was plunging; teachers noticed dazed looks, red eyes, sometimes even alcohol fumes. Unless there was a speedy turnaround, the school would have 'to take drastic steps'.

Meanwhile, Lily's son Sazi seemed dedicated to outdoing Busi in this unwanted category. It seemed his habit of funeralling had had dire consequences, giving him a taste for alcohol in ever greater quantities. Suspicion of drinking was soon confirmed, but instead of reversing gear, the boy started missing school and missing nights at home, going 'Who knows where?' as his mother said. Drunk! – Lily grieved.

When the school results arrived, it was time for the showdown, but Busi was prepared. How could her family expect anything different? Had they forgotten the endless chores she had to do every day, lasting until well after dinner in the evenings? When was she supposed to study?

None of them went to one of those schools where the parents of classmates prepared special diets full of protein and vitamins for their studying children. Good results didn't just fall on kids; they *and* their parents worked for them. Was anybody in this house prepared to do their own laundry, wash dishes, clean the house, and sweep the yard? So what if her results stank? Of course they did, given the stupid conditions of her entire life since she had been only five, before she even started real school.

But – and now Busi outdid herself, turning in a fine performance – she was sorry. The truth is, the results were not bad, they were not even very bad: they were absolutely dreadful. They were a disgrace. 'I need to pick myself up and I will! I know I am very fortunate to be in the school I attend. I am grateful for all the help my family gives me even when their own lives are full of hardship. I know they're doing all this for me so that I escape the same fate.' Copious tears flew as she swore, 'I promise you, with all my heart I promise you, this will not happen again!'

The grown-ups were only too happy, eager to accept her remorse. They had harder nuts to grind – the boys had not done any better. Phyllis sighed and hiccupped. Lily scolded her sons: 'At least Busi here is sorry, while you don't seem to care!'

Luvo supported her. 'We didn't call this a pass in our days,' he said, tossing Sazi's report to the floor, disdain painted on his face.

'These are not your days!' Sazi shot back, striding out the door and banging it shut after him.

'Tyhini!' Luvo exclaimed. 'What's the matter with this boy?'

'Told you,' his wife said, also on her way out the door, 'but you won't do anything about it. They're all getting out of hand, these our children!'

Luvo shook his head and stared at the door that had swallowed his son and his wife as if he expected it to yield them back.

Hours later that night, a bedraggled Lily woke him up and told him she'd gone hunting all over the place. She'd finally found Sazi at Mamsie's, a hot spot for those who wanted to forget their sorrows and cares – a spaza shop by day and night club after dark. Drink, drugs, and sex galore ... oh, nyama too – vleis en pap for the stomach-hungry. Sazi had refused to budge, and, much to her chagrin, she had been forced to leave him there.

Meanwhile, Phyllis had been apprehensive about Busi for some time. The girl was up to no good. She was keeping bad company, it was plain to see. That Thandi, with her sugar daddies, she was not a good example for Busi. Her behaviour ... and she not yet even in high school? Yhoo! Kuya kuthi kuphi, kube kuphi? Where would it end?

But she had a plan. She would send her daughter to the Eastern Cape to prevent more trouble.

When the idea was first mooted, Busi was keen to go and stay with Khulu. However, Brian's presence in her life changed things. By the time the December school holidays came, her enthusiasm for the trip had not only dwindled in her heart of hearts, it had almost vanished. Much as she adored her grandmother, what on earth would she do in the village for weeks and weeks? Not a small consideration was how she would cope without her daily fix. There was no way that Khulu would miss seeing she was using something ... drink or smoke, whichever. No, Khulu was bound to notice Busi's new habits. She'd just have to leave all that back here, she told herself.

Brian was also supportive in the end. 'It will be nice,' he said, 'to miss you stacks and stacks.' Busi took umbrage. 'I thought you did that already – missed me each minute we are apart?' He laughed, brushing off her protestation. A kiss stopped further words running out that pretty mouth. A thought crossed his mind, and his eyes lit up: 'Let's pack all the fun we'd have had these holidays into the couple of days before your trip!'

That put a stop to the suspicion already brewing in Busi's mind. Everybody knew that December holidays were when everyone had fun. No school. Grown-up, if temporarily. Working, perhaps, if lucky. Very lucky! New clothes, braais and beaches! Was Brian encouraging her to leave because he wanted to hook up with someone else ... see other girls while she was away? But now, with this offer, her fears were allayed. It would also be easier to stop all bad habits after one last spree.

She would not disappoint her darling Khulu. When all was said and done, Khulu was the only person who truly loved her ... well, within the family. Of course, Brian loved her – no doubt about that! She'd be done with drugs and drink by the time she arrived at Khulu's. Fine, then.

CHAPTER NINE
◇◇◇◇◇◇◇◇◇◇◇◇◇◇◇◇

Aunt Lily paid for iPhela, the cockroach – the unlicensed and unlicensable wrecks that cart people to and from townships, not daring to set their tyres beyond those condemned places. Phyllis insisted on accompanying Busi to the transi depot at Stock Road. Strange, that. When Busi wanted a mother, Phyllis was never there. Now that she'd come to need her less, not to want her around in fact, Phyllis made herself too readily available.

Busi had hoped the boys wouldn't come to the depot with her, as Brian would be there. Now with her mother with her, she might not get an opportunity to kiss Brian goodbye!

This was the busiest time of the year, and taxi conductors took full advantage. December, they saw bags or suitcases and they knew: you are going emaXhoseni – in you go! Off to Stock Road they took you, and you were already linked to a taxi. A handsome reward awaited the cockroach driver from the taxi driver whose vehicle he helped fill with passengers. Thus did Phyllis and Busi find themselves smoothly and swiftly ferried to a Quantum minibus, which pleased Phyllis. She preferred taxis to buses: fewer people, less trouble.

Phyllis made sure she had the taxi's number and knew the

name of the driver. Even the most reckless of parents did this; there were too many fatalities on the road not to know which one of the hundreds of taxis one's child was in. On top of the drunken driving and excessive speed, drivers and other male passengers all too often had itchy fingers, groping children – girls and boys.

Mindful of this, once they'd found Busi's taxi, Phyllis made sure she had a seat next to a mama, a much older woman. Despite murderous looks from Busi, Phyllis introduced herself and Busi to the woman, who said she was MaNdaba. Next, she begged her to look after her little girl: 'First time she's travelling long-distance!'

'Where is she getting off?'

'EMthatha.'

The woman was also going to Mthatha. Phyllis made sure MaNdaba's and Busi's luggage was packed close together. The latter had a huge canvas bag, striped in bold red, blue and yellow with sturdy plastic handles, an incongruous white. This went into the trailer and Busi, now carrying a blanket, her backpack, and a big Tupperware crammed full of amagwinya, steamed bread, as well as home-made KFC and boiled eggs, followed the lady onto the minibus.

Phyllis didn't tarry long. As soon as she was satisfied that Busi would be looked after, she left.

Busi sighed with relief: she had spotted Brian and a friend of his waiting for Phyllis to leave so Brian could see her off. Telling MaNdaba she was going for a brief chat with a friend, Busi scrambled back out the taxi.

'Ten minutes, and we're off!' warned the driver, seeing her dash off.

Brian had brought a parcel for her: 'Open it in the taxi,' he said. Busi flushed. What could it be? But there was no time to ponder; Brian walked her back to her taxi, behind which they stole a quick kiss.

'Miss you already,' he said.

'Miss you more!' One more hug, and then, hearing buses revving and taxis going PEEEPEEP, she quickly disengaged and ran to the taxi door, got in, turned to blow him one last kiss. But he'd turned his back, already running to join his friend.

A self-conscious smile on her face, Busi returned to her seat. She forced herself to make small talk with MaNdaba before turning her attention to the contents of her parcel. More curious than excited, she peeped into the plastic bag Brian had thrust into her hand. Inside, not in any fancy special wrapping paper, just the usual soft store tissue, was a bottle of perfume. She would have been happy with a packet of Extra Strong Peppermints – all that mattered was that Brian cared enough to take the trouble to get her something, anything. Gingerly, she opened the bottle just enough to inhale a whiff. The soft scent of some flower wafted into her nostrils, made her close her eyes dreamily ... sweet sweet sweet!

Her hand trembled so that some of the perfume spilled. Fortunately, the bottle's mouth was small, and only a drop or two ran out, but the scent mushroomed. Not only was MaNdaba sniffing curiously, but a couple of people from the rows back and front of hers began sneezing. Heads turned; but Busi had stealthily pushed the offending article into the bag, out of sight.

Within minutes, the taxi was making its way along the highway. Traffic on both sides was thick but gliding swiftly – no jams.

Busi drank in the passing sights. The two roads, going and coming from Cape Town City ... green ... bushes in flower, reds, yellows and blues ... all so beautiful. And over there, greyish-white clouds hugged the sky, a fading blue in the late afternoon sun.

She thrust the packet into the backpack at her feet, fished out her earphones and stuck them into her phone, closed her eyes and listened to Beyoncé croon.

Her mind wandered off to her mother. Had Phyllis gone straight home as she said she would? Hell, no! Phyllis, home on a Friday night? Next she would be going to church. The thought of church brought Khulu to her mind. She smiled. Her eyes closed. Soon she was lost to the world, dancing with Brian, dancing to the soft, slow hum-m-m of loveland to which the melody had transported her.

Listen, Unborn One, let us give you the fullness of the heart.
Listen, sweetest Unborn One, we have heeded your call.
You who wait at the waterfall will get a respite.
You who hit with vapour will get a respite.
You who stop the wives of the ground hornbill,
Will get a respite.
There is no there
No here
No somewhere else
For everywhere is nowhere but
Where you stand is

The world
The world is where you
Think you stand
As you are
As the world turns and turns and turns
You are not there but
Here
Where wind kisses
Faces you will never see
Faces you see
Faces you saw
Will always, always kiss wind
Hear the waterfall,
Feel the vapour.
Stretch your hand to the ground hornbill,
Trees
Roots
Water
Everywhere you stand
Everywhere you
Are always not
Standing
Where
There
Where you believe
You are.

◇◇◇

thrumpthrumpthrumpthrump
thrumpthrumpthrumpthrump

◇◇◇

Busi had not realised she'd fallen asleep or when. When she woke up, the sweet she'd popped into her mouth at take-off stuck to the roof of her mouth, soggier than a dunked piece of toast, and as sticky. The taxi was no longer on the road; right then, it was reverse parking ... smooth as silk, almost not a sound, the tyres merely gliding. This startled Busi – it was the cessation of speed and sound that had awoken her.

'I would've thought the opposite would be true: the ride would keep me awake while the stillness would send me to thongoland!' she said to herself.

Wondering at the strangeness of things, she stole a glance at her neighbour and smiled when she saw the other was still asleep. Good! She was not the only sleepyhead. Looking around, Busi saw evidence confirming this. Many faces were bleary-eyed and not a few eyes were closed tight in sleep. But that didn't last for more than a few seconds. The agitation of people astir, and, of course, talk talk talk – voices unguarded in the excitement of the moment: George!

All at once, everybody was moving. A glance out the window told Busi they were at a garage – a very busy one. All the buses and taxis and cars she'd seen taking off from Stock Road seemed to have come to rest here.

Obviously, this was a popular stop; the first major place for vehicles to refuel and get whatever else they needed for the long trip ahead. It was the first stop for the passengers to get whatever their own provisions lacked, replenish what might have been inadvertently left behind, lost in transit, or already used up. She knew she didn't really need to buy anything, but got to her feet, stretched and yawned. Her neighbour was already heading towards the door and Busi fell in after her. Once they had got out the taxi, MaNdaba turned to Busi: 'Ukhawuleze, Sisana!' The smile in that voice told the girl the lady had some inkling she hadn't welcomed her mother's intervention.

'Yes, Mother,' Busi replied and quickly followed the throng, her eyes telling her which way to go. The place had good signage: toilets, shops, bank ATMs – all well indicated.

She had no missed calls, but was sure to get a message from Brian before long, she told herself. The crowds at the shops decided it for her; after visiting the toilets, she made a beeline back to her taxi. Busi had an aversion to loud, crowded spaces – they reminded her too much of breaks at school ... Kwanele too, especially around the communal tap or spaza shops. She was one of the first back in, and even finished a chicken piece she'd taken from her Tupperware, gulped down a can of ginger beer, shoved another of the delicious toffees Aunt Lily had given her into her mouth, all before MaNdaba returned.

Once back in her seat, MaNdaba pulled out a laptop and set to what appeared to be work. Busi remembered she also brought some reading, and fished out a book from her bag. The two then sat in companionable silence, each with eyes glued to what was before her. Busi, earphones plugged in, heart dancing to Beyoncé, reading by the torch of her phone, one of the pink novels Aunt Lily sometimes read. Unlike buses, taxis had no reading lights; something her mother didn't think mattered.

Busi suddenly realised that her mother did not read. She could not remember ever seeing a book in her mother's hands. No, in her memory bank, such a picture did not exist. How had such a blatant truth escaped her all this time? How was it possible she did not know this about Phyllis? Was she blind or just plain stupid? This realisation shook Busi not only for what it meant about her mother, but for what it told about family life ekasi. She had never, not once, seen her mother hold a book, never mind read one. Not even to read it for her own self! Forget about reading to Busi or any of her other children.

Except for one cold stop in the middle of nowhere, around midnight, there were no other noteworthy episodes on the journey, and, eventually both MaNdaba and Busi fell sound asleep. Bit by bit, the bus settled into quiet as one by one, the passengers drifted off. Finally, the lights dimmed as cell phone torches were switched off. Total silence except for the distant-sounding hum of heavy tyres on hard tar ... a constant deep hummhmm, lulling one into deeper and deeper slumber. Intermittently, a puff of a word, whispers between the driver and the occupant of the front passenger seat – designated! That passenger did not dare sleep; uzawulalis' udriver – they might be responsible for the driver falling asleep.

Early the next morning, the noise of the taxi ground to a stop, accompanied by the upheaval, hustle and bustle of other passengers waking up, gathering bags, yawning, phoning – the whole cacophony, to which the driver added, hollering: 'SIFIKILE! MTHATHA!'

That brought both Busi and MaNdaba to their feet. Like everybody else was doing, they hastily said their goodbyes and, thanking each other for the company, grabbed their bags and headed for the door. It was a little after seven, just as the driver had promised.

Outside in the early morning light, as they stood side by side, MaNdaba asked: 'nguMakhulu?' She tipped her head in the direction of an older woman ambling towards them, a smile broad as a carefully cut slice of melon. Had to be – was. MaNdaba exchanged greetings, a few pleasantries with Khulu, turned to Busi and said, 'Remember to call me when you're going back!'

Just then, the taxi driver pounced on them, and insisted they take his telephone number. 'Let me know when you're going back!' It was not a bad idea to book one's space, as taxis did get full. One risked spending a whole week in Mthatha, trying to find a seat in a taxi. Then MaNdaba was off and away, in search of her own people.

Now Khulu's arms spread, the wings of a mother hen, Busi snuggled into her embrace and, for a long minute, they hugged tightly. Then, calling a man standing at a slight distance, Khulu turned to Busi and pointed to the bag and backpack at her feet. 'These yours?' When she nodded, the man took the two bags and led the way to where he'd parked his car – a blood-red RAV4. He opened the back door for the two, packed in the luggage, and got behind the wheel. All in silence.

First they stopped at a store where Khulu bought bread, margarine, tea and sugar. This puzzled Busi – surely her grandmother had food at home? – but she didn't comment. The rest of the drive home was uneventful. Khulu asked her granddaughter about the taxi ride and how she had found it: she herself preferred the bus. It was sturdier, roomier, and more comfortable. The real fact of the matter, however, was that she had no great confidence in taxi drivers – chance-takers, some without drivers' licences; often sozzled even while on duty, or they did not heed road signs ... that is, if they understood them at all, which she sometimes doubted. No, as far as Khulu was concerned, taking a taxi was asking for trouble.

But it was not necessary to burden the child with such anxieties. Instead, she pointed out or named the villages they passed, giving a brief history of each, some titbit of local news.

While Busi paid attention and participated in the conversation, her eyes were wide open, taking in the so-different scenery. Yes, it was summer, this she knew. But the countryside here was so-oo green! The grass was lush, tall and thick; the trees in heavy leaf, brilliant in their abundance, their trunks barely showing where they branched into all sorts of crazy shapes. Some – Khulu said they were willows – hung their leaves down as if they were curtains. Busi felt that the homeless people her school kombi passed daily on their way into Cape Town, people who sheltered under bare bridges and beside dingy and garbage-clogged waterways, would welcome such spaces. She wondered whether Sidwadweni had any such unfortunate victims of homelessness.

After about half an hour, the car turned off the road on which it had been travelling since leaving town. The tar ended, but car and driver seemed quite at home on the gravel surface. Yes, there were a few bumps and dips, but, on the whole, nothing to write home about. Khulu's home was not that far from the national road. Busi recognised it immediately, as she had seen enough photos; but now, driving into the yard, getting out of the car, the place appeared much grander than she had imagined. And clean! The yard all around looked freshly raked. But it was not the quick 'Visitors coming!' flurry and feverish tidying-up kind of clean, done to impress. The serenity here looked as though it was always just so.

They were met at the gate by a beaming young man, not a close relative, as a cursory glance ascertained. The man, judging by his appearance, was definitely not in the same league as the man in whose car Khulu had come to pick her up. His conduct confirmed this: the way he opened and closed the gate after the car had passed through, running in the wake of the car, notwithstanding the dust it raised – even though he did run not behind but alongside that wake. But still! Something in his demeanour said 'paid servant' – umqeshwa or hired hand. Sibuka, for that was the name by which Khulu addressed him, was at the door even as they clambered out of the car. He grabbed the luggage and hastened inside with Busi's bags.

'Put those just inside the door, Sibuka!' Khulu said as they followed him into the house.

Sibuka put everything down by the door but to one side. He stood at attention, and, as Busi and Khulu entered, extended his right hand, the left under the elbow of that arm: a show of respect as from a child to an adult or a commoner to an official or professional person ... someone assumed to be upper-class. Busi was a bit embarrassed by this. She shook hands with him, however, making sure that the contact was as brief as decency allowed, not a second longer.

After the greetings and introductions were done, Khulu, still standing just inside the door, declared a moment of silence. Their heads bowed and Khulu raised her voice in prayer: 'Everlasting Father, we offer our huge thanks, from deep within our hearts. Here is our child. You have safely guarded her from a faraway place. She has come to set foot at the centre of her mother's origin. We beg You, loving All-powerful, be with her now, all the while she is here. See that You hide her under Your mighty wing and protect her from evil! We ask this, believing it is already granted, for You know the yearnings of our poor hearts long before they form in our pitiful minds.'

She paused, and all responded: 'Amen!'

Sibuka took the bags into the main bedroom and left, telling Khulu he was going to see to a leak that had sprung in one of the water drums. 'Maybe the drum is overfull,' he said as he exited. Later Busi would learn that he was the grandson of a distant clan cousin, who, as Khulu's factotum, minded the homestead during her absences.

Khulu now led Busi into the room where her luggage stood, obviously out of place in the meticulous if sparsely furnished room, where everything was where it was supposed to be, neat and orderly. 'We are going to share this room,' Khulu said. It would make it easier to have talks ... the whole point of Busi being there. But at that moment, Busi was busy giving Khulu what was hers.

Khulu was happy being shown and given her gifts. She was particularly moved and surprised that even Phyllis had remembered to send her something ... maybe ... just maybe ... her eldest was mending her ways. No words about that now. But Khulu was most visibly thrilled by a small bag from Luvo: 'For Mother-in-law!' Inside were two bottles of brandy; he knew she would need that. He knew the ways of the village.

'Son-in-law remembered! He knows men of this home will come to help me welcome you home, celebrate your being here! Of course they will expect to get something a little stronger than amarhewu! Hayi, undincede nyhani!'

But even as she made that announcement, she snatched one of the bottles and stashed it in the smaller of the two wardrobes in the room. 'For Christmas!' Khulu said in answer to the query in Busi's eyes.

The two had not quite finished the handover of gifts when someone at the door announced their arrival: 'EmaTolweni!' An older man's voice hailed.

Busi assumed this was a close neighbour. How else would he have got here so soon after their arrival? But there were no houses that close to Khulu's. The nearest, according to her eyes, would surely demand a full half-hour to reach on foot. Where did he come from?

Later, as she got to understand how things were done eSidwadweni, she would realise the man must have been lying in readiness somewhere nearby. Sondlo, as Khulu later introduced him, must have seen Khulu leave early that morning. Busi would come to see that the village might be without many of the modern communication facilities readily available in cities, but the village had eyes. It had ears. Very little happened in the village that was not common knowledge. When the once-a-day bus left in the morning on its way to town, the village knew where it stopped, who boarded it. It knew when that bus would return, bringing them back home. It also knew, was quite certain, which person would be bringing those mouth-watering delicacies one only got in town ... and only when one had money. But then, who went to town unless they had word that their son or daughter or other benefactor had sent them money? Therefore, one expected close friends, neighbours and relatives – people with social claims on one – to drop by after one's return for a cup of tea – euphemism for a full plate of food, meat included. Why else? Meat, that's what they came for. Inyama!

So, this gentleman at the door, having such a social claim, as Hlombe's cousin and the last of that generation still living, announced his arrival – greeted by calling out the clan name of the man of the house, although he had been dead for more than a decade. Yet he lived in the memory of the village. This was his home. Would always be.

'EmaTolweni!'

'E-ehee!' came Khulu's response, acknowledging the greeting. From the effusiveness of her welcome, Busi knew this was an important and welcome visitor. Even before the 'how are yous' were done, Khulu beckoned and called Busi to approach. Her smile stretched from ear to ear as she introduced the man as Sondlo, son of Hlombe's uncle, his father's youngest brother. But the introduction and 'getting to know you' business didn't last long, for hot on the heels of that visitor, came another. And then another. Busi soon saw that these visitors arrived at regular intervals. A decent interval seemed to be observed between the arrival of two or three, never a crowd; their stay for an hour or so; their departure and the arrival of the next visitor or someone in the company of one or two others.

As a sign of respect to the home, everyone identified themselves via the husband's clan name – EmaTolweni! Aa-a! Tolo! Standing at the door, there would be a loud hailing, acknowledged, followed by questions about the health of those in the homestead.

Protocol observed, the men automatically went to sit outside the kraal while the women joined Khulu inside the separate flat in which visitors were received. All were served, with great care taken that the men were not neglected. If anything, their servings often came before those of the womenfolk.

Now Busi understood why she had needed to carry all these magwinya; the home-made KFC pieces were a thrill to people. Over and over, she heard, 'Yhoo! Sayigqibela nini inyama! Uncedile ufike!' Both men and women said out loud how long it had been since they had tasted meat.

Everyone who came was received with the usual cup of tea or coffee. However, this day people were also offered biscuits. A big box of assorted biscuits stood on the serving table next to several plates of freshly made steamed bread, as well as loaves of home-made bread from Busi's Tupperware, and the sliced bread bought from the store that morning. Khulu took care that there would be enough for the endless stream of visitors. Indeed, the fare seemed to multiply miraculously as she managed to divide and, with a smile, serve all who dropped by 'unexpectedly' to see Khulu's grandchild from Cape Town.

Needing help, Khulu sent Sibuka to the nearest neighbour. He returned with Thobeka, a girl about Busi's age; the two girls would spend the rest of that day busy in the rondavel that served as a kitchen.

Thobeka joked, 'Perhaps we should just have the tray ready,' because as soon as the girls were called to come and clear a tray, they were called back the very next minute: 'Please bring the tray!' Refills were the order of the day. Tea with amagwinya or biscuits or buttered bread was not everyday fare for most. So most made sure they had their fill. For the two girls, this also meant endlessly fetching water, and Busi was grateful Khulu had diverted from the communal tap and paid to have her own one installed.

Amidst giggles, outbursts of laughter, oohs and aahs, Thobeka told Busi all about the guests – who was who in the Sidwadweni zoo. Gossiping was easy as the guests were in the stand-alone flat with its lounge-cum-dining area and inside bathroom Khulu used when she had visitors. She herself preferred to sleep under the thatched roof in the room her late husband had built, in which he had drawn his last breath. Like many of her age, she did not believe the Old could find one beneath a zinc roof. How would they enter?

Luvo's gift stood Khulu in great stead. For elderly men, there can be no better entertainment than a good bottle of brandy.

This continued throughout that first day. Although cell phone reception in the area was weak or non-existent at times, not only Sidwadweni, but surrounding villages knew Khulu had been to town that day. Knew also that she had come back with a young woman, a granddaughter. Word did get around, village-style!

After supper and evening prayer, Busi and Khulu readied themselves for bed. In the dim light of moonshine through a thin gauze curtain, the nightly ritual began: Khulu telling her granddaughter family tales and legends, and stories of Sidwadweni village. Some were stories Busi had heard before, others were new. That evening, listening to her grandmother, she remembered the big hoopla about a government project that would completely change the lives of people in the Eastern Cape region of Mthatha. It had something to do with the revival of agriculture, including cattle people would be able to buy with hefty sponsorship from government.

'How did that project you once told me about go?' she asked. Busi remembered that people were apparently very, very excited about it. Khulu had said back then she had last seen such excitement when Mandela gave his first public speech as a free man in 1990.

'Which project?'

'The cattle and cultivation of crops!' said Busi, surprised.

'I-ii'sh!' Khulu spat out. 'I will show you when we go to town.' She was silent for quite a while before, into the dark, she spoke again: 'Ulele?'

'No, Khulu.'

'Tomorrow morning, very early, we'll go see your grandfather. You must go to greet your grandfather at his place of rest.'

'Kulungile, Khulu,' Busi replied. Her voice was soft, subdued, but she was far from sleepy.

The girl's mind was whirling. Over and over again, she replayed the events and sights of the day: a happy Khulu meeting her at the taxi rank in town. Mthatha just about to wake up; very few people and cars on the streets. The drive: not much to see, really. Sibuka – he was about Brian's age. Not old, yet not in school, obviously. Working for Khulu ... since when? So handy and seemingly at peace with himself, at peace with the world. Thobeka: what was her story? Busi realised that despite their easy conversation, she knew very little about her new friend. She must ask tomorrow. And ... wow! All the people who had come to see her? Well, not really to see *her*, but to help Khulu receive her. They had come to welcome and acknowledge her presence among them. Community spirit in action! What a day it had been!

CHAPTER TEN

The next day, Khulu woke Busi up very early. 'Let me take you to your grandfather,' she said. At once Busi jumped up, scrambled into her clothes and, within minutes, joined Khulu in the front room. Busi saw that her grandmother carried a small plastic vaskom, with a towel slung over one shoulder. That arm was slightly bent at the elbow, showing that she hugged something against her breast. Because she wore a loose shawl, whatever that was remained invisible to the eye. As soon as Busi joined her, Khulu led the way out the door, which stood open.

The sky still looked undecided whether to call day in and chase night away. The fight, it appeared, was fierce. Iridescent reds splashed the sky, announcing the birth of day. However, night fought back; thick and heavy belts of black turning grey mingled with the red, attempting to overpower it. But this old battle had long been fought, long been decided, and a truce achieved. This was but play; reminder of what was what and the when of it. This morning, her first eSidwadweni, was also the first time Busi experienced the entire sky engaging in an exchange of dramatic beauty – and now she was visiting Hlombe's place of rest for the first time.

The soft slap-plash of water in the vaskom Khulu carried was the only sound as the two made their way along, not hurrying, but not as slow or solemn as though they were on a funeral march. Their feet made no sound on the unpaved ground, so different from the sand underfoot Busi was used to in Cape Town. This was earth, indeed; her mildly startled feet registered that they were not traversing umhlaba or isanti or intlabathi, sand.

They went down the slight slope to the gate, which Busi helped Khulu to open, unfastening the gnarled and twisted wire that kept the cross-bar in place. Khulu placed the vaskom just outside the gate as they entered the garden. Just then, a bull bellowed and at once, Khulu called out the clan praises of amaTolo, her late husband's clan. Even as she did so, she did not stop what she was doing. The praising became part of what was happening. She praised ooTolo, walked to the fence, and hung the towel there. A short minute or two further, and they stopped. Khulu fished out a small bundle from beneath her shawl – impepho – and from a pocket, a box of matches.

They walked on, across the thick wet grass. Although light was fighting to come into life in the sky, it was still dark. The sky was robing layer by delicate and ephemeral layer, donning the dazzling colours of her birth day.

Then Busi's eyes clapped onto the silent mound before them.

'Your grandfather rests here.' So saying, the old woman took the girl's hand, drew her close to the foot of the grave. Busi could see that there was writing on the flat headstone facing them but in the still-dim light, she couldn't make out the words. Khulu let go of her hand, and they stood, side by side, in reverent silence. Busi was surprised by a little sadness; on the way here, she had wondered what she was supposed to feel. She had never met Ma's Tata. She ascribed her sadness to sorrow for Khulu, whose husband this was, had been.

Then Khulu came alive. Busi watched in awe as deliberately, caringly, Khulu kindled impepho. At once, sparks flew and the new flame bit into the leafy bundle, making it crackle and softly hiss. The flame grew brighter, stronger, and Khulu bent down and placed the burning torch of leaves at the foot of the grave. After this, she kept clapping her hands, rhythmically, softly, the sound not loud, but musical. This she accompanied with praise calling – the clan praises of Hlombe, her husband, at whose place of rest they had arrived. Khulu's hands went on clapping, slightly cupped to arrest the sound so that it did not fly away and all over the place. It was meant only for this specific being, whose ears were sharper than before.

The brightly burning bunch had stopped its crackle; now thick wispy smoke spiralled high into the air, sending a pungent scent up and away all around. Those with sharp nostrils could tell from a mile away that someone was burning impepho. But this was not a scent that aroused suspicion or anxiety about witchcraft. All knew that impepho called on the Old to protect the living, ward off evil, bring blessings; none would disavow its use.

'Hlombe! Tolo, Zulu, Mchenge, Mabhanekazi, Vumba lempongo liyanuka, here is your eldest's eldest … Nali izibulo lezibulo lakho. Where you are, talk to your cohorts in that world. Walk with this child; protect her against all evil, including the dangers that lurk for the hearts and minds of the young in this wicked world we're still stuck in.' She paused. Then, her voice much softened, she continued, 'Where you left us,' paused again; then a smile in her voice, she added, 'Siyakukhumbula!'

Busi held herself still, her gaze fixed on her grandfather's grave, hearing Khulu's voice sounding as though she was not standing right next to her, but a distance away as she said soft, loving words to her husband no longer of this flesh world. Right at that moment, Busi was surprised by what felt like a fist boxing gently from inside her stomach.

Hlombe's bones had turned, communing with the unborn spirit.

◇◇◇

Do you feel the homesteads of our beginning?
The scent when the waterfall sings for us?
Dove in front,
Duiker at the back,
The grave and herb of our clan
Child of the child of my child
We meet again
You and I who dwell in the House of the Old
The Everywhere All Time House of Spirit
We meet again
You have now appeared,
My flesh offspring,
I, your spirit kin
Know your journey will be tough
This you know
Knew before the Before

I salute what is in you
Go and guide our lost fleshlings
Who no longer heed dreams and symbols
Tradition-forsaking
Followers of naught that builds them
Lost lost lost our children's children
I salute you for your sacrifice.

The young woman walking alongside her grandmother was not the same as the one Khulu had led to her late husband's grave less than half an hour before. As the two returned from paying their respects to their dearly departed, the young woman may have looked the same. Yes, outwardly, Busisiwe looked very much the same as before. However, inside, it was a totally different story. Busi was transformed. Since that moment when she had felt and then known, understood, that what moved within her was a life, a human being, someone else who lived in her body, someone who would live there until time came for her or him to emerge, be born into the world – she had changed. Changed completely.

Not for naught had Hlombe's bones turned.

As on the way hither, the two women walked in solemn silence. But this time, there was something different in the silence – it seemed to carry a weight that Khulu could feel, but not fathom. As for Busi, she walked with breath held; whirling thoughts in her head made her step light as that of a sleepwalker, unguided, unweighted – as light as clouds up in the sky, unanchored. She was filled with a bewildering fearfulness. She had felt the baby move inside her. What did that mean? Surely not ... no, it couldn't be. She would have felt pain. Everybody said birthing was painful. They said even a miscarriage was painful. And for that to not only happen, but happen here ... she would die. She would surely die ... what would Khulu say? Do?

They reached the gate and stopped. Khulu washed her hands and indicated that Busi should do the same. They dried their hands using the towel left there earlier. Busi emptied the vaskom, and the two walked back to the homestead.

Khulu informed her: 'You have met your grandfather and, favoured, we knew he moved his bones for you. You must never forget that we are never alone, that there is an unbreakable chain of life. And you will get the full benefit of your ancestral home, because your grandfather has favoured you!'

Busi understood, but didn't yet know she understood. Khulu explained: 'Your grandfather knows everything. He has known you from before-before. He has helped you to be with me, his wife, so that you can learn from me; that was part of his mission. And mine. To help you, who is Busisiwe, the child of our Phyllis, to be in the world. So that being one in caring can be possible, and so all will be well again. If the flesh-ears open, the flesh-heart opens; and mouths forget to talk talk talk in pursuit of vanity and evil.'

They had not yet finished breakfast when Thobeka arrived. Khulu had made an arrangement with the girl's mother that she would keep company with Busi during the holidays. As she was the middle one of three daughters, her mother had no problems sparing her. Thobeka said she had come early because her mother had seen Khulu Ngxama descending towards the homestead. Khulu Ngxama was, of course, aiming to breakfast at Khulu's. The two girls got cracking right away, for, as Khulu said, as soon as the eyes of the village saw him enter, that would be a declaration: 'The gates are open!' It would be an invitation to all and sundry to come and keep them company. 'We are cold; your company will warm us!'

That whole day, a Saturday, there was an endless stream of people arriving at Khulu's, the mood decidedly joyous. Busi could not remember when last, if ever, she had enjoyed a Saturday with people so much. She was particularly struck by the stress-free way things were done; the ease with which they seemed to happen; the camaraderie of it all. Everybody knew everybody else. These were people with a common history, a common way of doing things, a common understanding of who they were and what they were about. They laughed a lot, teasing one another with various jokes. What a jarring contrast to her world, to Kwanele!

Sunday morning, Busi did not even hear Khulu wake up. When Khulu eventually woke her, a roaring fire greeted her outside.

'There's your hot water!' Khulu jerked her head, pointing to the fire on which stood a great three-legged pot. She put a round bright-blue basin filled with steaming water near Busi's bed.

'When did Khulu get up?' the girl wondered aloud, hastening to get herself clean and ready. Khulu was already fully dressed for church! After washing and while still dressing, Busi heard the church bells peal.

'Those bells say we must be on our way,' Khulu said. 'The second lot must find us half-way there,' she added. She didn't say 'otherwise we'll be late,' but Busi heard the implication. She knew being late for anything, but especially church, was a no-no for Khulu.

She hurried, but as always, the unfamiliar made Busi nervous. She was reassured, therefore, to see Thobeka waiting for them at the gate. When she reached her new friend, Thobeka showed her two small packets – sweets and biscuits – in her bag. The three walked briskly, Khulu leading the way, to the white building Busi saw some distance away, a big cross on the roof letting her know it was their destination. She was a little less apprehensive when Khulu asked Thobeka to show Busi the Girls section, so she would not need to wander all over the place, announcing to all and sundry that she was a stranger.

The white building looked humble from the outside, not at all imposing. Inside, the one-room affair was little better, the makeshift pulpit a bit rickety, the benches on which the congregation sat announcing themselves as the work of a dedicated church member who had most probably not asked for much for his labour. Definitely not factory-made, but they served their purpose.

What Busi did not know was that at a specific moment during the service, the priest would call for those with special requests, announcements or news they would like to share: 'Please come up to the altar!'

And that even before the reverend minister had finished her announcement, Khulu would already be up and singing at the top of her voice as she three-stepped, in rhythm to the tune of the hymn she was singing, up the aisle to the front, where she whispered to the priest, who stepped back to give her a space to speak.

'I am grateful!' said Khulu, 'to our ever-loving, ever-shielding Father. He has safely carried to my arms my granddaughter, izibulo lezibulo lam, eldest of my eldest, all the way from Cape Town. Brothers and sisters, you all know how these dangerous roads swallow our children, especially during the December holidays. What with drunk driving, speeding, and roads that cry for mending. With this one hundred rand' – she held the note up for all to see – 'I want to say, "Thank you, Jesus!"'

Thunderous clapping sounded. Khulu raised her arm and the congregation quietened. 'Busi,' Khulu said, her voice loud, 'stand up!'

Please, ground, just open up and swallow me NOW!

'That's my first granddaughter!'

Another round of applause and Busi felt heads turn. Everybody would be looking this way, at the Girls section. Thobeka nudged her even as Busi unfolded herself as slowly as a chameleon changes colour.

'Thank you!' said the priest as, dying inside, Busi collapsed back onto her pew. Thobeka put a hand to her back and slapped it two-three times, then brushed it up and down before giving it a firm, final pat. Silently, the two looked at each other, Thobeka grinning mischievously. Busi shrugged and shook her head. *So what? The skies had not fallen.*

Of course, Brian would choose that moment to call. Fortunately, her phone was set to vibrate and, as it began purring, she reached one hand into the back of her pocket, squeezed the appropriate button, and the phone died.

Meanwhile, she gave herself over to the service, enjoying the joyous, carefree singing, the beautiful harmonising, stamping of feet sedate and dignified, in rhythm with the soft tapping of hands and gently swaying bodies, shoulders rising and falling in alignment with hip control. It was beautiful to watch, to hear, and Busi drank it all in. She even caught herself participating. When she didn't know the lyrics of a hymn, she just hummed along, arms raised and hands upturned to the ceiling.

Afterwards several of the younger girls congregated around Busi, who was very glad Thobeka was by her side to help field some of the questions and to direct both introductions and conversation. Several times, Busi heard mention made of seeing her 'Wednesday'. With no idea what this was about, she nodded along as Thobeka did, or voiced consent.

They then made their way home where lunch awaited them; Khulu, the miracle-maker, produced meat and vegetables that only needed to be warmed. Then, pleading exhaustion, she took herself into the bedroom, leaving the two girls to keep each other company.

On the way to church, Thobeka had expressed admiration for Busi's dress, and Busi had not been able to ignore the shabby state of the one the girl wore. In the few days she had known Thobeka, Busi had seen her wearing only the one dress. Before lunch, Busi had changed into her jeans, put her dress into a plastic bag and thrown in a few more articles of clothing – items she had brought along not because she liked them, but precisely because she wanted to wear them to rags, and the village seemed the most appropriate space to do that. No one knew her there, and no one cared what she wore. No competition and no vying with others about libitso!

When she gave Thobeka the bag of clothing, the girl went bananas. She couldn't believe her luck. Now, she said, if only she had money to do her hair, she'd be tops.

'I can give you braids,' Busi said.

'You can do plaits?'

The girls set to, and Thobeka couldn't wait to go home to show her mother the total transformation the plaits had accomplished.

That evening, after supper, a happily exhausted Busi washed up, and after prayers, grandmother and granddaughter turned in. In bed, Busi was amazed at how contented people seemed to be ... and yet, the simplicity of their lives — their manner of dress, the absence of flamboyance — she stood out in her braids, and those were far from 'high fashion' or extravagant. The ordinariness of it all surprised her. It looked, felt, so uncontrived, natural, easy. She liked it. She especially appreciated the non-judgemental manner in which even the young people operated. No competition about clothes, never mind brands!

She had enjoyed talking with Thobeka, too. Being with her the whole day, they'd chatted, not about boys or clothes, but about life: chores, family, church. Busi realised she felt accepted for who she was, with no frills. She didn't have to pretend or prove to be anything other than herself. What a relief! Herself was as special as everybody else!

Busi and Thobeka soon became inseparable, their friendship cemented over making tea for Khulu's never-ending stream of visitors. Although, to be fair to the people of Sidwadweni, that stream was never quite as thick, as strong, as on that first day.

When other young people stopped by, the chorus 'See you Wednesday!' echoed over and over.

'What's this about Wednesday?' Busi asked Thobeka, who explained that on that day, the community would gather at the fields for ilima, the community gathering and harvesting day.

'You better go to bed early tonight,' Thobeka warned her friend on Tuesday. The next day being ilima, an early start was the norm. Although Khulu was not part of this conversation, that evening even her prayer was much curtailed. And their nightly conversation was abbreviated, too. By eight, both Khulu and Busi were fast asleep.

Just as well, because at four the next morning, Busi heard something unusual. Since she had arrived eSidwadweni, the stillness, the quietness of the place was one of the things that had struck her, and which she came to enjoy. However, this morning the sound of voices could be heard – cheery voices of people greeting one another, singing, and going about as though they were at a fair.

Khulu was not only up, she was dressed, a cup of coffee in her hand. Even as Busi dressed, she heard Thobeka enter and greet Khulu. Busi joined them in the front room, and the two girls each got a huge slice of steamed bread Khulu had just turned out of the pot. Busi didn't even bother adding anything to hers – no spread. Not so her friend. When would she get the chance again? She lathered hers with butter, cut it into two, added jam to one half and peanut butter to the other. Then the two girls were on their way.

Khulu stayed behind. By the look of things, she'd been busy for some time. Busi wondered when she had arisen. She had not heard her. The cooking pots were ready, waiting just outside the kitchen where Sibuka had piled lots and lots of wood – more than enough for the envisaged feast Khulu was preparing – food to take to the headman's home later. That was where the whole village would meet and the crop exchange would take place. When people gathered, there was food for them to eat. During ilima, everybody contributed. Each brought food and shared the food others had brought. That was an indispensable aspect of ilima.

Meanwhile, Busi and Thobeka arrived at the field at the centre of activity. They had found Sibuka and several others, men and women of all ages, already hard at work – a pile of maize cobs evidence of their efforts. If you think all that work went on in silence, then you don't know village life. Their voices joined in song:

> Sing, sing, you who wait at the waterfall
> Sing, you who release vapour
> Sing, you who stop the wives of ground hornbill
> When abantu gather, in joy or in sorrow
> Their voices they raise
> Praying to the source of all
> Living in constant awareness
> Of their limitedness
> Their vulnerability
> Their power
> From the Source all comes

> To the Source they accord reverence and
> > thanksgiving
> For what appears their prowess
> Is nothing if not manifestation
> Of the power of the Source
> Sing, sing, you who wait at the waterfall!

Busi was dumbstruck by what her grandmother and others grew in their fields. The thing they called a garden back in Kwanele was pitiful – no comparison between the two. Not only was there more land, more rich soil, but the hard work people put in, and so happily, eagerly even, floored her. And as a direct result of that, the yield was so much more impressive. Briefly, the analogy reminded her of her poor grades. *I really have to put more in to do better next year,* she resolved.

Later that day, talking to her grandmother about how splendidly everything grew, Busi added, 'It's because here in the village, you have all this land!'

The implied comparison provoked a strong reaction from Khulu: 'It is not only the land, my child, but the management of the land that is making the difference!' Khulu stopped, looked at the young woman, and said: 'Let me tell you something my mother told me. She said, "Lumka, my child, you must do for yourself. Never accept charity. That is what living is … one's participation in life. One does not just drift along like dead leaves blown about by autumn's unfriendly winds."'

Saying all this, her face glowed; it was obvious that Khulu took pride in what she did. Their Kwanele township garden was suffered and tolerated: always frenziedly planted and weeded when they heard Khulu was coming, visited grudgingly in desperate search of something to cook, and its yield was stingy. The garden showed it was not loved; a more reluctant grower would be hard to find.

Another of the many surprises and discoveries Sidwadweni offered Busi was duck meat. It was her first taste of duck meat, which she absolutely loved.

And there were other tastes to develop, too. One evening as Busi admired the setting sun, Khulu asked her to bring a particular book from the small bookshelf in the visiting room. Khulu opened the clearly well-thumbed volume and read aloud:

Dyo-o-rhom! Livakele lihlokoma bukhali lisitsho izwi lendun' enkulu, emazants' entlambo ngasentshonalanga yezo ntaba zaseKorana. Bô ... grom! With a throaty but authoritative sound the old male baboon waited on the west side of the Korana mountains. *Dyo? Dyo? Dyo? Ivakele isitsho ngelibuzayo indyondyo ephantsi ivela kwiqela elalithe xaka esingeni emazants' enduli enentlabathi.* Bogroh? Bogroh? The group of baboons answered while searching for the dinner among the sandy hills where the kloof stopped ...

'But now,' Khulu said, 'I want to read this to you ... hear how our great SEK Mqhayi describes the sunset, second by second.'

The last level-falling rays extinguish slowly and softly like a lamp dies, like eyes being closed into darkness. In the dusk, the time when rabbits run, the trees are covered in a sunset dust, dry and chapped like winter lips crying out for balm, appearing spooky like the lightning bird. The evening breeze dies down and the calm of great open stretches hangs breathless above the sleeping baboons lying fallow, lying asleep soft like snow. As these creatures of the veld fall asleep they are embraced by a light fragrance of impepho.

Busi sat transfixed. She was taking isiXhosa at her Model C school, but never had she been under the spell of her mother tongue this way before, as the words fell from Khulu's lips in the quiet slow dusk.

As Busi became more and more attracted to everything Khulu stood for, the older woman was transported one morning back to what her mother taught her in long-ago time. Yes, with freshly harvested vegetables at her feet, old as she was, she was once again a woman in prideful youth, absorbing from her mother the wisdom of her years.

Khulu explained: 'Mother discussed with me the two meanings of the word umzi and umzi – the last syllable, the -zi falling in the first, rising in the second. Same spelling, different intonation, different meaning. Home. Reed. Mama asked me, "But are these meanings really different? Umzi meaning reed and umzi meaning home?" Then she explained, "Each is supposed to feed itself; look after itself; protect itself ... one's home was meant to be self-sufficient just as the reed stands all alone, by river's edge. Come rain, come scorching sun – it stands. Come frost or even hail – the reed will withstand them all. Human homes were like that in the olden days. Each stood alone: self-sufficient; independent; built to withstand the vicissitudes of life; and proud of its uniqueness. Kwakunjalo ke ngaphambili. Umzi ngamnye uzimele … kanye okuya kwengcongolo ngasemlanjeni. Umzi uzimele; awuxhomekeke komnye okanye nakwenye na into. The reed stands alone, not dependent on another or on anything whatsoever. There is no dignity in dependence." That is what Mama told me … and now, I tell it to you!'

CAMAGU!

The ancestors chanted their approval.

◇◇◇

As the day of her departure neared, Busi was not sure whether she was happy or unhappy. Okay, her mother said this happened to people sometimes – not that she paid much attention to what Phyllis said – but for once, there was validity in it: which weighed more? Was she, at this moment, happier than she was unhappy, or unhappier than she was happy?

And yet she was not surprised at her ambivalence, for she had realised her growing attachment and, yes, affection for everything here around Khulu and her community. Busi had to remind herself Brian was waiting for her in Kwanele. School, and her 'big plan' all awaited her there. Still, she was not as happy at the prospect of her return as she knew she ought to have been. Something had shifted.

A week before her departure, Khulu reminded her to book her

seat on the taxi. Busi called the driver, who welcomed the sound of her voice with a chuckle. She could tick that off her list of to-dos.

As her thoughts turned homewards, Busi remembered something she had meant to do before she returned to Cape Town. But when she asked to go and see the government project she had heard about, the project that promised 'To change the lives of the people of the Eastern Cape!', Khulu told her there was nothing to see.

'But ...' Busi said, not understanding.

The corners of her lips downturned, eyes slanted, Khulu sucked air onto the sides of her tongue, a gesture of exceeding disgust.

'Wait,' she said, pulling her phone from the pocket of her overalls. After a brief call, she turned to Busi, 'Get ready. Car will be here in half an hour. He'll take you girls there!'

The gentleman with the red RAV4, Mr Ngacu, arrived to fetch them, but Khulu refused to go with them. She had seen enough of that stupid project, how all that money had been stolen. Our people had no shame, she said. Greed ruled their hearts. So Busi and Thobeka were accompanied by Sibuka, who had something to get in town.

To get to the project grounds, one had to go through the centre of town. When they arrived, they saw that the enormous billboard, complete with fat cows grazing, calves lolling by their sides, was torn here and there. The pictures, a little faded. But the most unsettling thing was the actual site of the project. Acres and acres of hard, unturned and unplanted land; not simply left fallow but uncared for, neglected, fallen into disuse. These were supposed to be communal gardens or demonstration lots, Mr Ngacu said.

The cattle kraals were a study in Grabbers' Lot. Barren of any cattle, a sorry sight, clear signs of foraging, if you could call it that. Stripped according to the need of the plunderer, no rhyme or reason to what was taken and was now missing. Ugly gaps told the story. A minor war was going on here, Busi thought, for the plundering of building materials reminded her of pictures she'd seen of war-torn zones.

On the way back, Mr Ngacu explained the profound failure of this and many other government projects with one word: graft. To which, later, as she listened to their stories of the day, Khulu added another: greed.

Busi was immensely saddened. All that hope dashed. She could just imagine how people with nothing or next to nothing must have been filled with hope when the project was first announced. People like Thobeka's family. Life was truly cruel. She must look up graft. She'd been too shy to ask Mr Ngacu what that meant although, as with Khulu's greed, it had to mean something bad. Well, the results spoke for themselves. Graft was evil, even if she didn't know the actual dictionary meaning of it; what it had given birth to was enough to surmise that!

The days before Busi's leaving sent Khulu, Thobeka and Sibuka in a whirl, each with things to do, tasks related to her departure. Each went about doing what was before them to do with a smile and a bit of sadness on their faces.

Busi realised she would miss them sorely. She would miss Sidwadweni. But she had no idea yet how much. She did not fully understand how much of the cultural milieu of Sidwadweni had seeped into her blood in the short space of time she had been there.

◇◇◇

Meanwhile, Cape Town had woken up to the reality of Busi's imminent return. Suddenly, people who either had not called her at all remembered she existed, and called her. Even her Ma called. And those who had only called dutifully once a week now called almost daily. That, of course, applied to Brian and Thandi. Suddenly Busi realised she would love to be like Thobeka. Easy-going but well-grounded. Living simply, contented, uncomplaining. There was a lesson there. Busi was ashamed to think of how she complained ceaselessly about her life. Her life! Her lack of money! Sheer luxury in comparison to Thobeka's!

On the day penultimate to her departure, Sibuka had to twist several necks: two geese, both females, and two chickens, a hen and a cock. They would become umphako for the road. Poor chickens! Often, Busi felt sorry for animals, living only to be devoured by humans. Mind you, her pity didn't go even half-way towards giving up meat. No vegetarian was she.

One of the girls would knead the dough late that night. Khulu wanted her vetkoek packed hot-hot, just minutes before she left, so they would be as fresh as fresh can be. These were both kinds: fried and baked, or roosterkoek. Busi had discovered she liked the latter. Then there was laundry and ironing, which Thobeka insisted on doing (and Busi thought a waste of time and energy). Who in the townships ironed jeans and sweaters?

The day went swiftly past in a flurry of activity. It was a bustle-about day, joking, cheery talk abounding, but there was no denying a little sadness laced all that activity. Yes, Khulu and the other two were happy to be doing what they were doing for her, did it with all their hearts and willingly – but they were also sad to do it – sad it had to be done.

To think she might have missed this experience ... had her Mama not insisted and, for once, prevailed. Unaware of what she was doing, Busi had begun a re-evaluation of her beliefs, the things she held on to without much appraisal, but because role modelling pointed that way.

Not for naught had Hlombe's bones turned, said the Old once more.

CAMAGU!

On that last day together, the two girls couldn't hold back tears. 'I suppose I'll never see you again,' Thobeka said.

'Why not?'

'When will you ever come here again?'

Startled, Busi looked at her friend. Obviously, the idea of going to Cape Town was completely far-fetched for Thobeka; and to think she lived a life bothered about rich white kids holidaying in Mauritius? But she realised, Thobeka was contented; her days were filled with meaning, reason, rhythm. Not a bad life at all. Compassion and admiration filled her; she reached out to Thobeka, and they embraced.

'I hope we meet again,' Busi said, emotion muffling her voice. Sooner rather than later, her mind went. Then she had an idea. Rummaging in her backpack, she pulled out the package that held Brian's perfume, which she had all but forgotten. She pressed it on her friend; Brian would not know, or mind, and Thobeka's joy at the gift made it all worthwhile. Besides, Busi now found that she preferred the smell of impepho burning, the thatch of the roof, the soil and fields outside.

Early on the morning of Busi's departure, Thobeka arrived even before Khulu was up. She brought her parting gift: cooked ibhanqa, young and tender corn on cob. With a self-conscious little smile, she said, 'A little something to chew on the road!' She also gave her something Busi had never heard of: ground roasted corn, utshongo, in a small plastic container that had once contained margarine. Utshongo has fallen into disuse in these days of refrigeration. In the olden days, Khulu explained to the startled Busi, travel was mainly on foot, distances thus long, and travellers used utshongo a lot, unlikely to spoil like meat, or even bread. The dry papery taste was strange to Busi but utshongo was something she saw she would not throw out; would eat, and perhaps, by and by, even get to enjoy.

What Thobeka also brought was a mournful face. Thinking to ease the children's unhappiness, Khulu suggested that Thobeka go ask her mother if she could see Busi off in town. The girl flew home and soon returned, changed into one of her 'new' dresses.

But later, as she witnessed their tears during their final farewell at the taxi rank, both girls openly weeping, Khulu thought she might have miscalculated. 'Kufe bani?' she barked gruffly. The broad banana smile on her face belied the harsh-sounding words. Her words were not a rebuke, but a reminder of what friendship brought – what all life brought: sadness was the other side of happiness. Khulu's question, 'Who has died?' reminded them all to smile. And, yes, though their eyes were glassy, smile they did. Smiled, and hugged tight as tight can be.

Tweet-tweet-tweet of the taxi signalled it was time to get on or get left behind. Busi quickly disengaged from Thobeka, threw herself at Khulu, who plonked a wettish kiss on the girl's lips and then pushed her away.

'That taxi will leave without you!'

Busi clambered into the vehicle, and seconds later, it screeched off and away with a now louder, more decisive tweet-tweet-tweet! Busi, at a window seat, face plastered there, waved and waved at the fast-fading figures of Thobeka and Khulu. She waved until they were just a blur in the distance.

Another blur was the ride back to Cape Town, during which Busi mostly slept, exhausted from all the excitement of leave-taking. She was also exhausted with foreboding, dreading all the turmoil that would soon fall upon her. She had managed so far to keep her secret, secret. However, no secret, however securely locked in the human heart, can remain one forever; especially one such as Busi carried, which had a delivery date stamped on its packaging.

CHAPTER ELEVEN

It was a very disgruntled young woman who arrived in Kwanele, which had changed a lot during Busisiwe's brief absence. That is, her Kwanele – the house in which she lived. News of that great shift greeted her on arrival, when she heard that Phyllis was now living with Mrs Bird, sometimes returning to see the family on Sundays. Meanwhile Sazi was in rehab, and it was doubtful whether he would return to school; and her own father, Mzi, had returned to Cape Town seriously ill, and wanted to see her.

As far as Busi was concerned, her father was a non-event. She had absolutely no intention of going to see him. And when she heard where he was living, in the same-same house from which his brother had thrown her child-self and her mother out after Mzi had abandoned them – she was even less inclined to see him. That was her first home, her happy home. She had no intention of revisiting the house that had haunted her throughout her childhood. Home!

The sojourn of three weeks eSidwadweni had changed her, opening her eyes. How pleasant, joyful even, it had been to be surrounded by a peaceful silence, a tranquillity she'd never before experienced – a place where she could just be herself, not judged by appearance or what brand of cell phone she had. Where all the people looked like her, and her skin colour was no issue, no marker, irrelevant.

ESidwadweni she'd taken and appreciated walks and talks; sights; people and the simple way they lived in peaceful co-existence; food and how it was grown. The amazing spirit of community co-operation she had witnessed during ilima – that, she would never forget. No wonder, she now reflected, she had unhesitatingly if tearfully said, 'I will certainly come again,' making a promise to Khulu at the taxi rank. She now told herself: 'That is a promise I will make sure to keep.'

Grateful for the lessons learned, fiercely aware of the change in her heart, Busi was angry. She could now see how she had been deceived, duped. Garbage had been dealt to her outstretched hand. She was determined to fight for her independence – real independence: the right to dignity inherent in self-sufficiency. She would not live on scraps from the tables of the government. She would make her own life.

Above all, she felt a deep anger at the bad choices she had made. Angrier still at what had led to those choices. She could not believe what she had done. If anyone had even suggested she was capable of such evil, she would have ... have ... what would she have done? Attacked them? Walked away?

But she knew that it was no longer an issue of what one wanted, but a matter of taking responsibility for one's actions. Nobody had held a gun to her head. She had not taken anything, no lollies or alcohol, for a full three weeks. All she had to do was continue doing what she'd done eSidwadweni. Surely she could do that? Yes! Oh, yes, she could! Would too, or her name was not Busisiwe.

So it was with great gusto that Busi began getting ready for school, which was starting in just a little over a week, while also working on the much-neglected garden in their Kwanele yard. In her mind, she dreamed of imitating the splendour of Khulu's veggie garden, to say nothing of the fields beyond, full of nourishing food, plenty of it, enough to engage in ilima, bartering with neighbours and supplementing one's supplies while giving to others of your surplus. Nifty and cool.

Her days after her return became well-ordered, even programmed. Busi found she had less and less time to spend 'doing nothing'. She made sure she had study time, garden time, as well as time for the inescapable house duties and chores. Even those, much as she would never be enthralled by them, she began to see them in a different light, and tackled them with less and less resentment.

She had learned a trick or two from Thobeka. She had learned to accept that which she could not change. Right now, she was a child, a girl child, in a household that had specific role allocations for members of their family.

She could not explain the intense relief she felt at the absence of Phyllis. An added bonus for her was that Owam and Esam now lived with Phyllis at her place of work. She, Busi, was for the first time in a long, very long time, child-free.

But then it zapped into her mind. *Child-free?* How could she have forgotten? Never again in her life would she ever be child-free. Never! A wave of sheer and utter dread washed over the girl, enveloped her tight, even tighter than her skin. It held and squeezed itself into every cell of her being. Belatedly, she found she was not as enamoured with motherhood as she had first believed. Yet she would have to shoulder her burden – no way out of the hole into which she had dug herself. Busi saw the truth: glaring and bitter and self-inflicted.

◇◇◇

Friday night! The last weekend before school started. She was alone, all alone.

Everyone gone to wherever, for whatever. And here comes dear, darling, sweetest man Brian. Here he is and, o-oh! Just look what he's brought for me. Just for me.

'No, Brian. I'm off that stuff. But where did you get such a stash?'

'Sweety pie, want some?'

'No!'

'Just a little? Have some fun!'

'No, Brian. And I mean no. Appreciate it; but am no longer into that.'

'Oh, ja-a?

'Yu-up!'

'Really?' He was frowning at her as though she'd sprouted horns.

Busi nodded. She hoped he would not pester her. She didn't feel like an argument. Right now, her body memory was shouting, *Why are you waiting?* The sight of him had awakened a need, a hunger in her she had not given much thought to lately.

'Fine!' Brian shrugged. 'There's more for me, then.' Whistling, he plunged his hand into his rucksack, rummaged around, and pulled out a small bottle of Diet Coke. Handing it to her, he said, 'Your favourite.'

She gave him her smiling doll's eyes: 'Oh, you remember?'

'Don't be cutie on me.'

'Since you called me so few times, I thought you'd blown cold on me.'

'Any idea how hot I am for you right now?'

'Show me,' she purred.

After the frenzy, she was so thirsty ... needed a drink. Reached for the Diet Coke, Brian hastily opened it for her.

'Thanks!' she said, dreamily, and guzzled the lot.

'Wasn't that grand-grand?' He reached down and kissed her on her closed eyes. 'Shows how much I missed you,' he whispered, gently nibbling her earlobe.

'Show me again!' Her eyes had sprung wide as a window on a spring morning.

His voice husky, he growled, 'In a sec.' He lit up one of the lollies he had brought, inhaled and slowly blew out smoke. Eyes contracted, he looked at her through the haze and whispered, 'You have no idea how good this stuff is. Special!'

I watch as he smokes the tik pipe.

I watch, and something in me revolts. 'Just a little,' I told Brian. And the little I took demanded that I took another hit from his pipe. Brian laughed. His laugh was louder than the devil's in hell. I thought that was funniest, and laughed with him. Laughed at him; laughed to outlaugh him.

Suddenly, it was another day. And then another. And another. And I kept wanting. More and more and more than more. Schools reopened, and I was back where I'd been before I went to the silly Eastern Cape. Booze and drugs at Thandi's were my daily bread. No one could tell me squat-nothing; I knew it all. Knew it better than all of them. My decision to abstain? Well, it was my decision. Mine, get that? And I have power, absolute power, to revoke any decision of mine. Who wants to be a slave to things such as decisions – even good decisions? And this one wasn't even good to begin with. Who gives up heaven? I must have been out of my crazy mind!

Next thing I know, I'm back knee-deep in the murk. And apparently things are so bad I am in the same rehab centre as my cousin, Sazi. We are in the same room. They figured it was okay since we are blood relatives.

What nobody knows is how viciously vindictive Sazi has become. Yhoo, the swearing and the lashing out! I have to weave and dodge his fists. Fortunately, he's so wasted most of the time he flays and lashes, he's as pap as a sleepy dog's tail.

How long have I been in this place? No idea. Sazi is no help at all; I wonder if he even remembers his name. But where is he getting the stuff? How do I get my hands on it ... maybe that's why we are sharing a room! Hey, my great good fortune. I share a room with a Clever who gets his supply. But then Sazi has always been smart. Where does he hide the flippin' stuff? I need it. Need it. Need it desperately or I'm going to die.

One night, I cannot fall asleep. Tired as I am, all night long I toss, turn, wriggle and wiggle in bed, the tips of my fingers and toes prickly. Deep down in my throat a fire rages, my chest bursts with craving, my tongue is wrung cardboard. In the middle of this endless night, I suddenly see it is no normal, ordinary night. Witches and horrible creatures abound, and they are all after me. Petrified, I leap off the bed, strip off all the filthy clothes that scratch as though small, hard-shelled insects are crawling all over me. I tear off the two blankets I was given, spread one on the floor beside the bed and roll myself in the other. Safe! With my clothes discarded, I feel purified and protected. But I'm not out of the woods yet. The night still has me in its stomach. I cover myself in the blanket as tight as a pupa in its shell. That cocoon first kneels; down on my knees, I send a fervent, urgent, two-word prayer to the Almighty. SAVE ME! SAVE ME! SAVE ME!

Suddenly, I am back to me, monsters and insects gone, but words continue pouring out of me. Like a sorcerer's chant, I repeat those two words. Over and over, I repeat those two words. Over and over and over until my throat burns and my voice grows hoarse. Finally, I stop. Stop because I have to or must stop. Drained, I roll over, lie on my side, and plunge into a deep and dreamless sleep.

Busi screamed and screamed. In no time, someone banged frantically at the back-room door. 'What's wrong?' she heard her cousin Themba's voice calling her. Slowly, the relief dawned. She was home, safe. She was not at any rehab centre; there was no Sazi, there were no monsters, no insects. Brian must have left some time in the night: she was alone. She had been seized by a terrible nightmare.

Now her body began to tremble, her teeth chattering, and a cold, clammy sweat washed all over her, drenching her as though she'd stepped out of the shower and forgot to towel herself dry.

'I'm all right, thanks!' *Busi, get a grip on yourself. You are all right.*

'Are you sure?'

'Leave me alone!' Is Themba deaf or demented?

'Uh-h! Right, bye!'

'Thanks for caring. But I am really okay.' *He was only trying to help ...*

The full horror, the meaning of what she had done overwhelmed her. *What possessed me, dear God in Heaven? Forgive me. Please, God, forgive me!* Sick, Busi ran to the toilet – barely made it before she threw up. When that had become nothing but gurgly heaving, she limply folded onto the floor where she sat staring at nothing; no thought in her mind either. Blank.

Without knowing or deciding that this was what she had to do, out of her mouth poured: 'Tolo, Zulu, Mchenge, Mabhanekazi. Hlombe! Vumba lempongo liyanuka! Dlangamandla!'

To hear her say the clan-names of amaTolo would have surprised those who knew her. They would not have been more surprised than she was herself. She began to have an inkling how much of Khulu's teachings she had taken in. Much more than she realised.

◇◇◇

We have shown her
If she has eyes
She may avoid this certain future
It is up to her. Our job is done.
We can only go so far.

◇◇◇

Minutes later, when she had calmed down a little, she told herself: 'I have to remember; Khulu said I am never alone.' She repeated the words aloud, in a clear voice: 'I should not forget we are never alone. There is an unbreakable chain of life.'

One night with Brian, and this is the result? No, she would never go back to her treacherous plan. That had taken long enough to sink into her apparently very thick skull.

Also, was it not enough burden on the family that Sazi was in a roundabout of rehabilitation-relapse-rehabilitation? She could not add to the pain the family was suffering. Busi sorrowed for Sazi; he was one more reason to stick to the straight and narrow. Yes, Sazi's fate was part of what kept her on her toes. That, and her fear of the urges, the cravings, the craze-bringers. Easier said than done, she told herself. But: *whatever had possessed her?*

Easier said than done, a hoary voice whispered in her mind's ear again, and again, Busisiwe praised her ancestors, ooDlanga-mandla. She made herself yet another promise: *Each morning and each night before bed, I shall sing the praises of my ancestors.*

Not for naught had Hlombe's bones turned.

CAMAGU!

◇◇◇

It was a very apprehensive Khulu who remained eSidwadweni mourning the departure of her eldest grandchild. Yes, she had absolutely delighted in Busisiwe's being with her. However, something kept niggling at her. Strange indeed was it that throughout all the time the child had been here, Hlombe had not once appeared to her, Khulu. It was most unusual for him to abandon her, especially during times of heightened emotions: births, deaths, weddings … and the visit of their first-born grandchild ought to have brought him – several times, in fact.

Why had Hlombe turned his back on her? Khulu grieved for Busi's departure, and even more for Hlombe's abandonment.

Busi had called her several times from the road, but Khulu could only relax once she heard, 'I arrived safely, Khulu!' Busi had thanked her grandmother profusely for 'a most enjoyable holiday,' telling her she would plant the seeds she had brought from Sidwadweni that very afternoon. Khulu chuckled, glad to hear that Busi had not lost her new-found enthusiasm for growing vegetables. Something might still be salvaged from that incorrigible crowd that was her family.

However, again, that night, sleeping alone again, Hlombe returned to her in her dreams. But there was no comfort to be had from his presence: he was still silent, still sad.

◇◇◇

Back in Cape Town, between the gardening, planning for high school, and house chores, Busi had more than enough on her plate. Did her school uniform fit? Were her school shoes still fine? Meanwhile Brian had apparently found a part-time job; this saved Busi time, not having him around during the day. She was so preoccupied, it took several days for her to register the fact that Brian had not made another appearance since his first visit after her return. That was wha-at, more than a week ago!

When Phyllis came home that first Sunday after Busi's return, the girl almost didn't recognise her. Her mama could be beautiful if she only took better care of herself. By all appearances, Phyllis was beginning to do just that. Even the little boys looked sprightly and well satisfied with their lot; bubbly and giggly at the slightest hint of teasing or tickling.

Not that Phyllis had much to say about her stay at Mrs Bird's except that the older woman had asked her to be on the premises, almost full-time.

'I hope she's paying you for all the time you're there,' said Lily.

Phyllis looked at her sister, raised her brows, and asked, 'Do you hear me complaining?'

◇◇◇

Weeks passed. School started. And then came the day that could no longer be avoided. Lily's sly eyes had been searching Busi from top to toe, volunteering to make her a dress. Lily had suspected for some time, but thanks to Busi's lying stomach, still almost as flat as the well-pressed pleats of a new skirt, she could not be sure. But

Busi knew the moment had arrived.

Phyllis was visiting the night the bomb dropped. Out came the story of Busi growing a child in her belly. Ukhulelwe! Her suspicion confirmed. Yes, Busi, for whom Mrs Bird was paying such good money to give her a decent education, a better chance to get a better life. Now this? Six months gone!

Phyllis wept. 'This is my luck! Just when I try to change my life, taking evening classes at St John Ambulance so I can become a qualified carer – now this! I will not allow Busisiswe's foolishness to stop me! I will not!'

'Mzi will kill you,' said Lily.

Phyllis turned on her sister: 'Kill me?'

'Yes.'

'Did I make his precious daughter pregnant?'

'That's not the point.'

'Oh, so you know what the point is! Please tell us!'

'You are supposed to raise your daughter; teach her the ways of womanhood.'

'Apparently she didn't need lessons from me!'

'But you have to tell Mama.'

'Me? Why don't you tell her?'

'Busi is your daughter!'

'And not yours? Are you saying my child is not your child?'

'No, child of my mother's, that is not what I am saying. But maybe stop thinking only about yourself!'

Shame solidly sheathed the eyes of both women.

'I will tell Khulu,' said Luvo, and squared his stout shoulders.

◇◇◇

Khulu saw flashing on her phone, Lily's husband's name. Alarm bells pealed in her heart. She answered: 'Who died?'

And so did the news thunder into her ears. With a cry, Khulu threw her phone away from her as if it were a poisonous snake, and cracks crazed the screen. Her mind reeled. Surely the family would insist that the young people marry? That was the Christian way, the traditional way too – tradition in these times of unmarried women birthing ... yeh-aa!

Gone were the days of before-before, when a man's family first offered lobola to the girl's family long before he could call her wife. And never would he bed her before he called her that; and no maiden contemplated such an outrage, of lying beneath a man who had not spoken to her father! Lobola: security against adversity for the woman and her offspring. Security, in the event husband later turned monster. Security, for even good husbands die. Security against the eventuality of any and all of life's unforeseeable, unpredictable odds.

Once again, her cobwebbed phone rang. Yhoo! Mrs Bird herself calling?

'Oh, Gracie, can you believe our Busi has gone and got herself into this kind of trouble? And she's only what ... thirteen, fourteen? Dear God, when I was that age, I didn't even know the real difference between girls and boys. Oh, I knew boys stood when they peed while girls sat down. But really ... Gracie, what are you going to do?'

Khulu gave a long, loud sigh. 'I don't know,' she said. And that was the truth. She had no idea what role she could play in such a disaster.

Mrs Bird had. 'I think you should find your way back here. Poor Phyllis told me about it and is totally overwhelmed. I had to take her to the doctor this morning. Depression, I suspect. And she has every right to be depressed, I think.'

Khulu sighed. An uneasy silence fell, neither woman quite sure how to break it, what next to say, talk about – the trend of their usual conversations so rudely disrupted.

Finally, into the silence, Mrs Bird continued: 'You will come, won't you? You must, you know. Your family needs you right now. You know that, don't you?'

Another heavy sigh before Khulu agreed. 'Yes, I do. I think you're right. I will come.'

'Do you need any help?'

'No thanks. I will be fine. Thank you.'

'Come straight to iintaka,' Mrs Bird laughed at the old joke, but it was short, subdued.

'I will! Again, thank you for your call.'

'Bye-bye, then ...'

CHAPTER TWELVE

Khulu left for Cape Town, but not for Kwanele; her destination was her old employer's home in Bishopscourt, the wealthiest suburb in Cape Town. It never ceased to amuse Khulu how the eyes of the other passengers in the taxi would pop to see her alight at this posh spot. What resident of Cape Town did not know the meaning of Bishopscourt, home of the Archbishops of the Anglican church, including the world-famous and revered Desmond Tutu?

During the long journey, Khulu came to understand the agitation that laced both Luvo's and Mrs Bird's words: this was it! This was the doomsday premonition that had become her second skin this past while. This was what the dung pile in her heart had foretold. The sins of her children and their children would be the end of her before the ancestors were of mind to call her.

Khulu arrived in Cape Town on a Friday; she didn't care that her daughter would be there. This was not about her or her daughter. This was about her granddaughter, the little girl her daughter had failed – not raising her correctly, according to standards of culture or church, or just simple, common decency – the way she herself had been raised. In any event, whether she went to Kwanele straightaway or waited a couple of days, Busi would be just as pregnant when she got there.

Sunday prayer was what she needed before she saw that grandchild of hers. Meanwhile, she'd come and found something else going on with her friend, something that seemed even more urgent. How long had Mrs Bird been like this? Why had neither Mrs Bird nor dizzy Phyllis thought to inform her? She had appeared fine when Khulu had last seen her, not that long ago. How could she look this gaunt, this haggard? Something was definitely not right. But MaNtaka said she didn't want any fuss and bother about her health. She was fine, what were a few dizzy spells for someone her age? Please, people must not even think of treating her like an invalid.

Another surprise: Phyllis no longer just charred for MaBird; she had been staying there, working five or more days, ever since the older woman's health had begun to decline. What was more, MaBird was full of praise for Phyllis.

Strange to say, the rough patches in her life appeared to have smoothed something in Phyllis's heart. This showed in the deliberate way in which she did her work, especially that of minding her employer when she was feeling low and lonely and useless.

Khulu took all this in: the disastrous news that had brought her to Cape Town, her friend's ill-health, and Phyllis being praised as a star. She must be losing her mind, Khulu thought, or the world had gone stark, raving mad. Nothing made sense any more. Thing was, none of this had killed her. She must be getting very old ... well, older than she felt.

That evening, Phyllis paid Kwanele a surprise visit; even more surprising was the news she brought – their mother was in town.

She knew full well this would not please her sister. The whole family was on edge: the two women knew it was their shared responsibility to keep their eyes on the girl child. And they had failed.

Phyllis warned her sister, 'Our mother will blame you more.'

Surprise arched Lily's brows, her eyes those of an owl: 'Me?'

'Yes, you. At least,' Phyllis went on slowly, 'she expects something from you. Me?' She stopped.

A brief silence fell between them, sisters eyeing each other, apprehension in the face of the younger, scorn in that of her older sister. Then, her own brows arched, lips pursed in a wicked, wicked smile, Phyllis purred: 'Mama already knows I'm through-and-through irresponsible.' Then her shoulders shook soundlessly, she put her hands on her head, took into them the beret she wore and, wringing it and stretching it like an accordion, she burst out: 'What's your excuse?' She fell onto the sofa in a heap, laughing uproariously.

Speechless, Lily looked at her sister.

Phyllis sat up and shrugged. Lily felt helpless; although what Phyllis had just said might sound ridiculous, she had a sneaking suspicion it was true. The smile in her sister's eyes did nothing to assuage the stress she felt building up inside her. Lily's unhappiness, always, but always, pleased Phyllis.

But the person who was really terrified about the visit was Busi. So when the Sunday arrived, everybody was waiting on tenterhooks.

'Where is she?' Lily asked Phyllis, when the shadows began to lengthen. 'Does church take so long nowadays?'

Phyllis offered an explanation: 'Mama has stayed to care and comfort Mrs Bird. You know her health has not been good. Mama is so mad at me for not telling her that MaNtaka was ill. How was I to break the strict instructions from Mrs Bird not to tell her, or even her own children?'

So they waited, their minds tracing Khulu's movements. She hated walking on the dirty footpaths of the township after all the years of working in Bishopscourt, the ways of the village, her own clean yard. Khulu absolutely loathed dirt. 'First thing done to a human being right at birth is to clean her. Clean should be like skin to a person, clean air to breathe and clean ground to walk on. God's good clean earth.' By the time dusk set in, they were thinking about her safety and how evil men had decided an elderly woman was next to virgin.

Finally, Khulu stood in the doorway. Her family welcomed her with a nervous pandemonium and open arms. In each heart, however, embarrassment, shame and anger vied for first position. Without a winner, they came together in a hostile union. No one gave direction. No one asked questions. No one offered any help.

On seeing her grandmother, Busi burst into a torrent of tears. And finally, the discussion had to begin.

'Phyllis, my dear, the child must attend the clinic for pregnant women.'

'I'm not stopping her.'

'You may have to take her there.'

'Why doesn't her man do that? Why me?'

Khulu looked at her daughter. She couldn't believe the words out of her mouth.

'She's a child, Phyllis. *Your* child!'

'She should have thought of that before she did what she did.'

Khulu clapped her lips, looked at her daughter and thought: 'I will have to accept that this one will be a wet rag until the day she dies. There is no understanding a mind such as hers. No understanding such a mind at all, at all, at all.'

Then the interrogation began. In which Busisiwe initially surprised herself. It was as if the words of her mother and Aunt Lily, so bent on intimidating her, were freeing her anger. She kept two conversations going, one in her head, the other in her responses. Who did they think they were? God's angels descended to earth to lead sinners like her back to the holy flock?

But under the stern eye of Khulu, the two persisted:

'Who?'

'Who what?' Busi spat. 'Spell it out!'

'The man who did this to you?'

'Did what do me? Ondenze ntoni? Out with it! Why are you so coy and cagey?'

Then Khulu stepped in. She didn't raise her voice, and concern, genuine concern, was there.

'Mzukulwana, my grandchild, there is a child we will soon be welcoming into this family. Right?'

Busi nodded. Her voice lowered, she replied, 'Yes, Khulu.'

'Well, my child, a child has two parents. We cannot welcome a stranger. So, will you tell us of the other parent – the father of this new person who will soon be joining us?'

It became clear that Busi knew his name, but had no knowledge of his clan or pedigree. Nor, exactly, where in Khayelitsha he lived or with whom. She knew Brian had dropped out of school years ago, that both his parents were dead, and that he was too much for his aged granny. Brian's father, Kholisile, had been her only child and had been gunned down in a botched car-jacking in the pandemic violence of the townships in the Western Cape, in broad daylight, right in front of his girlfriend, Brian's mother.

Some said the mother died of a broken heart. Others said she died trying to rid herself of what her man had planted inside her before carelessly getting himself shot, peppered with so many holes his body looked like Swiss cheese. She couldn't bear the thought of bringing yet another starving mouth into her mother's house, with her mother's children, and their children too, a house already full of so many mouths gaping daily for food that seldom came. The doctors cut Brian out of his dying mother's belly. She only lived two days after her boyfriend's death, and the two were buried together. 'Saves me time,' Brian had told Busi of his visits to the grave once a year, either on Father's Day or Mother's Day. 'But I alternate the dates – being fair to both of them.'

'And does the father of this new person know of your news?'

Busi hung her head. This was a sore point. She had asked Brian for a meeting and told him the news, which he took quietly; it could not have come as a huge surprise. But he had been scarce ever since.

But soon old and new feuds spilled across the table. Naturally, Lily was concerned about yet another child coming into her space. 'Another add-on is all I need now! As much as I want to appear non-judgemental and supportive of this girl, I am not forgetting how my own sister "camelled" me out of my space.'

'Camelled?' Khulu frowned. Phyllis got a word in: 'It's a story. It's a Mthwa who gave a wandering camel space in his cave and ended up caveless, while Mr Camel ensconced himself in his cave.'

But Lily hadn't finished: 'How do I know that Busi is not simply a version of you? The last thing I want is to have my yard become a typical slum-house yard. Overcrowding! Too many people in a space that will not and cannot be expanded! Why do you think I and Luvo only had the two boys? This is one of the few things about which I totally agree with Mama. If you have nowhere to put your children and call it their home, then don't have them!'

'This could so easily have been avoided,' said Khulu in a soothing voice, 'if we had done the ukuthombisa rite of passage for Busi.'

'Ma-a!' Lily huffed. 'What has that to do with this mess?'

'Everything. You said ukuthombisa was out of date, old-fashioned, would make the child the laughing stock of all of Kwanele. Well, I hope Kwanele applauds you now. But I don't see you sing and dance and take a bow, accepting the applause.'

'Applause?' Phyllis queried, eyebrows raised to the doek.

Khulu nodded. Phyllis glared at her mother, closed her now-brimming eyes. In a soft voice, the voice of one unaware the mouth had opened and let out one's inner thoughts, Phyllis asked, 'Why applaud?' Again she stopped. In the silence that followed, the words sounded as if in search of some indecipherable truth. They hung in the air and no one disturbed them. In what seemed like an hour or more, but was not more than a few minutes, Phyllis went on: 'Applaud us for this ... inconvenience?' She heaved her exhalation, shook her head. Then, she opened her eyes and regarded those with her one by one, and, in a loud voice, said: 'To say nothing of the shame – ihlazo!'

None among those present responded. Phyllis's voice rose as though she could force them to hear her, as though their silence meant they had not heard the words of her mouth, those words too soft to reach their ears. 'Plus,' she screamed out that one word as she rose to her feet, 'who is going to look after this child?' This time, not waiting for any answer, *bah'am!* sounded a hard open palm slamming on the table as she cried out, 'Not me!' *Bah'am!* 'No! It is not going to be me!'

Lily snapped, 'Why would we expect you to do that when you've hardly looked after your own children? Busi raised all your babies, don't forget that.'

Eyes wide, Phyllis screeched, 'Yhoo, uyamthethelela? You take her side?'

'If truth is her side, then I am taking her side!'

Phyllis shot back, 'Usindwa yimali. Money burdens you, burns holes in your pocket!'

'Is that what makes you come running to me every week for a loan?'

Khulu suddenly stood fiercely upright and strong.

'Enough, you two! Act your age!' she said, glaring at her daughters. 'You seem to forget there is a new soul around you; one you are infecting with selfish lies and self-righteous anger! It is time for practical steps, and she is part of all of us, so all of us will assist her. First, Busi needs to go to a clinic. Second, we need to get some infant clothes. Third, we need to determine where and how the birth will take place. We also need to think about a name ...'

'Thandeka, loveable,' Busi blurted out, contributing for the first time.

Khulu ruled that one out immediately. 'That word has a double meaning ..."By design", so that is a wrong message. As I can see, this family had no such intent.'

Busi shut up after that, but her mind galloped past all the names she thought of so long ago now: Bonisile, Belinda, Bonke, Buyiswa, Bulelwa, Buyisile ... The boy who fathered her child who had suddenly become as shy as a bride on her wedding night. When she had asked for a name, it turned out he hadn't thought that far ahead.

'Your man has no preference? He has not thought of a name, all this time? He knew he'd made a human; the baby is no surprise to him, the surprise is only for the rest of us, not so?'

'Maybe we should wait until the baby is born and allow it to give us a sign,' suggested Lily.

Khulu agreed: 'It's often unwise to rush into naming a child.' Then, eyes wearing sadness, she moved to another topic. 'I hope this is a first-born for you. Keep it that way. Don't you dare have another first-born! And I am not just saying this to my granddaughter, but you too, Phyllis, heaven knows.'

'What do you mean, "first-borns?"' asked Phyllis.

'All yours are first-borns, aren't they?' Khulu answered with a question. Then she elucidated. 'Your eldest – a first-born with your so-called husband; no lobola and ...'

'Ma,' screamed Phyllis. 'Lobola is a thing of the olden days. People don't pay any ...'

'Pay?' Khulu sneered, 'Did you say pay? Lobola is not payment. Nothing and certainly no one is purchased. Yes, these days, people more often use money. But it must not be forgotten that the money is a stand-in. It stands in place of the cattle the groom's family offers the bride's. Offers, not pays! It is the use of money that has caused such confusion around this sacred rite.

'Feeding children has never been out of fashion. You young people do not understand anything. Children are made out of love and loving, but it is not that kind of loving that grows them. It is the other kind, physical. It is caring, minding, guiding, nurturing. Iinkomo ezi ke zezokulondoloza abantwana kwakonakala! Those cows or their issue ensure the wellbeing of the children should things go awry.'

The explanation was met with silence. Then Phyllis recovered. 'But ...'

Khulu cut her short. 'No buts,' she said, shaking her head, 'I don't know what you all learned at school. We studied the Mqhayis, the Jordans, and the Jolobes – great African writers, great thinkers. Practices such as lobola and more all spelled out for you in those books.'

'We studied those writers too.'

'Doesn't seem to have had any effect.'

'Meaning?'

'Never mind that! All I'm saying, my own pocket is not the kraal into which your non-existent lobola never went. You should remember that and use your own two arms and hands – limani! Plant food for your children! There's a yard at the back of this house as well as at the front.'

'This is not a house.'

'It is that if you live in it. Your ancestors cultivated land unfenced when they lived in caves! Do what you need to do with what you have. Don't wait on wishes, for they seldom come a-visiting.'

'Yhoo, Mama! Uyayithethela shame, imali yakho. Unkind words do truly accompany your money.'

'And that deters you, my daughter?' Khulu asked, and answered her own question with a vehement, 'No! It does not stop you from coming back, again and again, asking me, a pensioner, for money. Loan or out-and-out handout – makes no difference. You don't ever remember to pay back the money you borrow from me.'

Lips downturned in shame and anger, Phyllis left the room, Khulu's eyes trained on her until she disappeared.

◇◇◇

A few days after the family indaba in which Busi was grilled, Phyllis announced: 'Mzi is coming to see you, Busisiwe.'

Busi growled, 'For wha-at? Tell him my birthday has long passed. I don't want to see his sorry face now.'

'He's your father.'

'Since when?'

'Well, he is.'

'He conveniently forgot that all this time – years? And what has suddenly reminded him of me?'

'You're being difficult.'

'No, Mama. You are! And so is the fool of a man who comes here pretending to be my father.'

'Busisiwe, enough!'

For a long moment, Busi glowered at Phyllis. 'As far as I am concerned, I have no father. Hear me? Andinatata mna, undibona nje. No father have I as I stand here before you.'

But he came. The man who had left Cape Town, who had never returned, not even once to see her, now found time and energy to visit, despite looking a skeleton of himself. Money had long parted company with him. Jobless and wifeless, illness was the only companion of his dying days. But on hearing of his daughter's pregnancy, he had come. And he was filled with venom, furious with his daughter for disgracing his family name.

'Whose child will people say you are? Such trash ... enje yona inkunkuma! Pregnant even before you finish school? Ufuze laa njakaz' ingunyoko! You take after that she-dog, your mother! And who is the father? Where is he? At least he should come and discuss things with me ...'

Busi watched him with a smirk. Yes, the kind of smirk she had learned from her mother. Did he want to use her pregnancy to get damages paid by Brian? Busi stood mute right through his furious tirade. When he left, she wished she felt better about her mother, because she would have loved a high five from Phyllis for routing her father ...

The encounter with the old mlungu woman was another one that threatened unpleasantness. Initially Busi absolutely refused to go see her, despite Mrs Bird's written invitation – well, more of a summons really: 'Busi, please come and see me. Urgent!!!'

Busi wondered if the nuisance woman would stop paying for her posh education now. She had only just scraped into high school as it was. Her second-hand blazer covered most of her body, and the teachers probably assumed she was becoming overweight, like many of her classmates. But during the last month of her pregnancy, she would have to stay at home, so let the Model C go ... Although when she thought of it, she knew she didn't fancy having to go to a township school. Boy, would everybody laugh at her. Ufahlakile! She had come down thirteen pegs, one for each year of her precious life! From lofty suburb heights to kasiskolo! Kasiskorokoroskolo!

So she endured the visit, and to her surprise, Mrs Bird was unexpectedly kind. 'You want to change your life, Busi? School will enable you to accomplish that. You will be able to live a different life from your mother's.' The girl promised that she would finish school, even if she had to repeat the year.

If the family was having a hard time accepting her coming child, not so Busi's kasi friends: they were in celebration mode, even Thandi, who was spending more and more time away from school with a new blesser. They got together and gave her a baby shower from which she returned giggling and delighted. She had to be helped into the house, staggering under a mountain of boxes and packages all wrapped in bright, bright colours – baby clothes, toys and even a few books – much to the surprise of many! Generous hilarity filled the hearts of her friends because they knew she didn't have it easy at home ... some had been there before her, and all knew what happened ... social disapproval so thick you could cut it with a knife. By the end of the ceremony, Busi was dizzy, bursting with pride.

Back home, however, that pride had absolutely no place. No

place at all, at all, at all. When she entered the house, her mother, visiting from Mrs Bird, made her cringe with a look that cut through her. As though with X-ray eyes, she had looked through her and seen nothing. This look declared her non-partisan status, and it left Busi harrowed inside. A slap, kick, fist, even verbal assault, would have been better than this erasure, silent disavowal. But between the two of them now – mother and daughter – niks, nothing! Busi hurried to reach her room with all her presents.

Go home and do not sleep, there come pools of blood;
Go home and do not sleep, there comes the end of humanity;
As dead flies give perfume a bad smell,
So a little learning outweighs wisdom and honour

Go home and do not sleep, your fathers will sell you out;
Go home and do not sleep, you too will sell your mothers out;
The heart of the wise inclines to the right,
But the heart of the fool to the left.

Go home and do not sleep, you are the base supporting the people;
Go home and do not sleep, your families are in danger;
If a learned one's anger rises against you,
Do not leave your position;

Go home and do not sleep, there comes a time of darkness;
Go home and do not sleep, we will not be here forever;

Calmness can crush great arrows to bluntness.
There is an evil I have heard over the loudest microphone.

Go home and do not sleep, give service to the coming generation;
Go home and do not sleep, I say the real war has come.
The sort of error that arises from a professor:
Fools are put in many high positions,
While the wise occupy low ones.

PART TWO

CHAPTER THIRTEEN

I was designed by my mother
Busisiwe Mkhonto,
whom everybody calls Busi.
I am her story
pay attention when she comes through
however trite, rash, mundane she may sound
I am coming through her voice
for all her foibles are but shades of you

the whole neighbourhood gasps
when I am born
my birth shocks them
everyone is surprised
there is wailing and there is weeping
there is wringing of hands
there is blame

there is unexpected, unsuspected horror at myself
even by she who births me
she rues the day as she looks up into her grandmother's face

so day after day
they look down at me
questions in their eyes
zips on their lips
their minds jumping all over the place
avoiding my thin and frequent cries
the pitiful squeaks as of a new-born mouse
the thin, greenish stools, watery
feeding more spillage than swallow
eye movement erratic
in search of answers too painful to grasp

gradually, however, their mouths open—
and they give voice to the irrefutable reality:
something is not right with this baby

for two or three days
the family waited for the name
to be announced by this neonate
but I do not give a sign
any indication of myself
other than my body
then my navel falls – I step into being my own,
independent of source,
and then Khulu takes the bull by the horns:

CAMAGU!

Heavy was the old woman's heart. *Ukuba besizixabisile, sizihloniphile, izinto ezifana nale nyula sikuyo ngezingenzeki nje konke*, went her thoughts. 'If we had pride in ourselves, respected ourselves, things such as the mess we're in now would just not happen. What kind of people are we? Have we become? How could such a thing happen to us? Where were our eyes? And I, the oldest of us all, failed to see such perdition coming! What is the worth of living my days?'

Dazed with grief, Khulu took the baby to her room. In the sanctity of her own space, alone with the baby, she fell on her knees. Feverishly she prayed to her God, her only hope in a situation she found overwhelming: 'Father of our fathers! Parent of our parents and theirs before, humbly do I come before you and beg you. Let me be an instrument. Let my hands be the tools.' The thudding of her heart loud, she paused and wiped the tears streaming down her cheeks with the back of her hand. She continued, cried out, 'Father God, let my mouth speak the wisdom of the ages, the wisdom of the old unchanging truth: the meaning of life is its inescapably intricately interwoven oneness.'

When she was done, she sat on the edge of her bed and watched the sleeping infant breathe. The bundle wrapped in soft woolly blankets rose and fell, marking the infant's inhalations and exhalations. *If only all life were that simple!* Khulu wondered how she would steer her family through this unexpected crisis.

Some time in the course of the night, her prayers hovered and transmuted into ancestral worship. She felt convinced that the

Old had turned their backs on her family. This would not have happened were they watching over the family. They would surely have alerted her. 'And God? He, Greatest Being, Lord of All, to You Almighty, Thy lowly servant turns in this her hour of direst shame. Your fallen wretch knows still awutshonelwa langa, awuphelelwa nyanga, unguSoxesha, Mandlakazi ayinqaba, sicuntsulele uvuthululele phezu kwethu lawo mandla akho, siyakubongoza, Bawo wethu OseZulwini. I cling to You. Nothing is impossible. No poison or drug or any man-made deformity is beyond Your power to reverse – if that is Your will. God raised Christ who was three days dead. Dead and buried. What is deformity to Your mighty power?'

Even in her deepest moments of anger against her daughter and Busi, who corrupted the sanctity of the womb, Khulu could not bring herself to actually blame anybody but herself for the plight into which the family was thrust. So what would be an appropriate Christian response? That whole long day, she was seized by the question; it would not leave her. All day long, she pondered: what was she being called to do, to be?

Always be of service to others, came immediately to mind, followed closely by: *to help others in their becoming*. Although many might view such an undertaking as sacrifice, Khulu did not, for she firmly believed that it was precisely in the performance of such ordinary acts of neighbourliness to family, friend, neighbour or total stranger – humane acts – that she became 'more and more who I am meant to be'.

'This little girl must be very strong to be here at all,' she said the next morning. 'The signs of malfeasance are evident. That she managed to get herself born, after a full term too, surely proclaims her zest for living? She is a girl with mighty strength ... NguMandlakazi, her name is Mandlakazi!'

CAMAGU!
Mandlakazi.
Coming from strength, with strength,
Coming to strengthen those who will listen to her truth.
CAMAGU!

Sisidalwa esi.
This here is a creature.
In the manner of amaXhosa:
Singled out by the general to emphasise the specific.
Sisidalwa esi.
This, a creature is.
CAMAGU!

Busi was overwhelmed and ashamed. Phyllis was working on her nerves. She kept insisting that her daughter should wean the baby and apply for the grant. The bottle was okay; she needed to go back to school soon, but the long queues at those government departments! They made her feel like a dog at the dumpsite hunting for scraps, and they spoke so crudely, so humiliatingly!

And there were forms to be filled in. Appointments to be made. Social workers to see.

Khulu demanded that Phyllis go with Busi, dragging her feet every step of the way. Phyllis was as crushingly mortified as her daughter. But, of course, she looked forward to reaping the riches of the 'deformed baby' grant – the deaf-money, they called it in the townships – so let her suffer. Besides, she knew the procedures and forms all too well.

All around her, Busi could hear the derogatory quips from the cleaners – talking about her like she was not there, as if she could not see that she was the youngest in the line. Speaking in code, of course. But Busi knew those ways of roundabout speech. Was she not Lily's niece? Lily, the mistress of ukukwekwa!

They spent the whole bloody day at the government office. And now as Busi entered the house, she could hear the baby screeching like she was berserk. Couldn't she have at least a minute for herself?

'You came in just as she woke up!' Khulu greeted her. 'This one must have sensed your approach. They're like that, the newborns. They smell the mother's milk, and although you've stopped nursing her, she smells you. It is not in a hurry she will forget who carried her all nine months. She can sense you.' She told Busi she was about to give Mandlakazi her bath. 'Then, after I have massaged her, you can give her the bottle while I prepare her herbs.'

It was not just the baby Khulu was ministering to with roots and herbs; she had decided to tackle the problem of Sazi, who was home from rehab and sitting around idle and listless.

Khulu ground grated uthuvana and mixed it with the powder she had made burning and pulverising hair clipped off the tail of a horse. Uthuvana, a well-known cleanser, was often used to regulate upset stomachs, both as laxative or enema, while horse tail was said to make the body reject smoke and liquor that any who took the mixture could no longer stand the smell of those things, never mind use them.

'Ukhe wafak' emlonyeni wakho nantoni engendawo – uya kuhlanza. Should you ingest any matter untoward, you will vomit,' Khulu told her grandson as she gave him the mixture dissolved in hot water.

'Khulu warned you!' Lily's voice was tinged with some empathy: 'Go to the bathroom and stick your finger into your throat,' she advised.

But Sazi was already running for the bathroom, his stomach doing the Macarena, his hand plugging his mouth. In minutes, he had brought up everything in his guts. The heaving scared him; so much so, it proved an effective counter to what had become an unbearable urge to drink drink drink. Sazi was not cured that day, but it was a beginning.

Themba and the two younger boys came rushing in. A baby had been stolen. Again!

'It has become a plague!' mumbled Khulu. Almost daily, there were news reports of children who had disappeared: snatched from prams in shops with the adults under whose care they were busy paying at tills, the prams right there at their side. Children snatched from their cots in their bedrooms, the parents either asleep in their own bedrooms or, believe it or not, wide awake and entertaining friends in their living rooms, believing their little ones safe in their own home. And what was done to those poor little mites by the time they were discovered – or their bodies were – was beyond the worst nightmares.

But this was the first case in Kwanele itself. Busi's alarm grew by the day, and added to that was Khulu's reaction. Her fears for the baby, who should already be turning her head, but was only moving her eyes, hit their highest pitch. In her mind, Mandlakazi was more vulnerable than others. Who would care if she was to be snatched? What if, when she began crawling, she found her way outside without anyone in the house noticing? Things like that happened to little children. Khulu feared that sooner or later, Mandlakazi was bound to come to harm. Many in the neighbourhood knew of her, of her vulnerability. Who was to say no one would take advantage of the situation?

After much prayer and communing with the Old, Khulu at last called a family indaba to plead her case. 'Let me take the baby back to Sidwadweni for a little while. Mandlakazi would be much safer there,' she said. As an added advantage, she pointed out, 'There is also far better access to traditional medicines in the rural areas.'

'For how long?' Lily wanted to know.

'Oh,' replied Khulu, smiling, 'maybe a month or two, while Busi works to catch up on her school work so she can still make her grade this year!'

So Khulu leaves
carrying me
on her sturdy back
without a sound

I go with her
fast asleep
hidden and warm
safe and kept
beyond the Beyond
and the Beyond
is with the two of us.

One thing about Khulu: once her mind was made up about something, she didn't waste time, but went to execution with swiftness.

That very first night eSidwadweni, a new routine began for the baby. Usana lwalala ngesihlungu; lwavuka ngenembe yemifuno nobisi lwebhokhwe – dining on aloe vera and breakfasting the next morning on veggie gruel and goat milk.

Khulu believed in plasticity of every aspect of the neonate: bone and skin, so why not brain and everything else that made up this new body? Bones mended. Skin healed. Why not all that was inside this new person?

Khulu sang and talked to the baby almost non-stop, pausing only when the baby succumbed to sleep. This was not infrequent, much to Khulu's relief. She firmly believed it was during that sleep that all that had gone into the body melded and blended, growing what needed growing; mending what needed mending; restoring what needed restoration.

Sleep and rest; sleep and recuperation. Mend mend mend; and grow grow grow.

While the baby slept, Khulu summoned the Old and prayed to her Almighty God. The Maker of Heaven and Earth would surely not be defeated by so small a task as mending the broken body of this imveku, a neonate.

Khulu also started doing daily exercises with the baby: a lot of stretching of limbs; gentle rubbing of joints, toes and fingers; the palms of hands and soles of feet were made to clap and dance in the air. Long before dawn, she very gently and tenderly massaged the fontenelle. An enema was given before breakfast, and all meals started with aloe vera, so the baby then welcomed the food that followed, and learned to distinguish between unpleasant and pleasant tastes. No sugar, hardly any salt, lots and lots of fruit, berries and vegetables ground or boiled to gruel. All the baby's meals were accompanied by lots and lots of mimicry, sounds that recalled the delight of previous meals, songs and rhymes, melodious and soothing. Every bath was followed by full-body massages with oils and medicinal Dutch remedies.

All this accompanied by the sweetest music from Khulu, her songs mostly nonsensical, full of Khulu's heart-smile, her glee in living:

    Nwai-nwai-nwai; Nwai-nwai-nwai-nwai!
    Nwai-nwai-nwai; Nwai-nwai-nwai-nwai!
    Nwai-nywai-nywai!
    Nwai-nwai-nwai!
    Nwai-nwai-nwai; Nwai-nywai-nywai ...

The baby invariably fell asleep under the spell of song, in a room filled with the aroma of impepho. Steadfast, Khulu kept faith with the herbs, roots and berries she mixed for the baby as part of her daily ritual. And although at first she thought she might be kidding herself, she began to see, slowly but surely, a change in the little broken bundle on her back.

In her arms.

In her heart.

Thobeka, who often came over to assist Khulu, was the one who first pointed out the recovery that was taking place.

'She sits!' shrieked Thobeka, jumping up and down, her arms flapping about as though she were skipping rope. She was positively flying out of her skin with the excitement, the marvel of it all. 'The baby can sit!' she repeated. This time, her voice was hushed in awe.

and this was our routine
our murmurings, deep into the night
and again, early morning,
in the crepuscular twilight of predawn
our humming and singing
the bliss in almost-hot wet towels
her hands nourishing my skin
rubbing oil into joints
stroking it into muscles
stretching ligaments
outside in the sun
stretched – pulled; stretched – pulled

Khulu's hands are whispers
of the wings of a passing dove

I fall asleep to the ministrations
of her hands infused with care
and into that sleep
the lyrics of songs pouring from an ancient throat
sink deep into my mind
into my brain, my heart, my limbs.
Later, when deep sleep overcomes
Her, nursery rhymes are overtaken
by iintsomi, the folktales of amaXhosa
these abound in folklore, in wisdom
in morality, in hilarity
no clobbering do I ever get
just gentle leading on,
guidance, encouragement
into the valley of blissful living. Amandla!
as my name implies,
deep within me is buried immense power
the same as in every living being
I am just more aware of who I am
more alive to my being
Khulu reinvigorates that which has succumbed
to ill-treatment, cruelty, evil
to restore and even exceed my original form
the glory disturbed, poisoned, condemned
yet love faith steadfastness heals.

CHAPTER FOURTEEN

A text popped up on Busi's phone. She hoped it was the not-returning-any-messages Brian. He had become indisputably slippery, an eel in the soapy hands of a toddler. She looked, but the message was from sly Zodwa. Although she didn't care much for her, perhaps she had news of Thandi, another character who had all but disappeared, to the extent that Busi was fearful for her friend. It was rumoured the latest blesser had gang ties.

Zodwa sent a picture of – WHA-AT! Busi's mind reeled, her eyes popped ... With the abruptness of a hailstorm, Facebook told the world, her world, that Brian had moved on. Moved on with another girl, another sweet-sixteen-touched-NevaNevaNeva-More.

The news of his betrayal threw everybody. He had seemed so docile, if subdued about the baby; if anything, the adults suspected that Busisiwe had bullied him into fatherhood. *Well, look at that!* they said to one other, shaking heads.

But the more Busi heard about his whereabouts and his new lady-love, the less she cared. She found this astonishing, but it was also something she relished. If anyone had told her, a few months ago, she would not care if Brian were to disappear from her life, that he would never kiss her again, never tell her he loved her ...

she would have thought that person mad. Yet, when she thought of him now, she could hardly believe how unfazed she was by his absence. Indeed, she looked deep into herself and knew, without any shadow of a doubt, that she no longer loved him ... if she ever had. Even about that, she was no longer certain.

Her personal concerns had shifted: to her child far away in the Eastern Cape, and to her school exams. She was slowly working through a pile of books in preparation for the imminent exams. Shona had turned into a great ally with the latter, while Brian's disappearance was a hidden blessing; less to distract her in her endeavours.

There were times Busi felt despondent regarding the examinations. Surely she had missed too much to ever catch up? However, with Shona's faithful assistance and encouragement, she made better progress than she had reason to believe possible. Shona even spent time coaching her during their breaks.

'Am I one of your projects?' Busi one day demanded, rather ungraciously.

'I'm only doing what I hope you would do for me, were the situations reversed,' Shona threw back.

Busi was a little shamefaced. 'Sorry,' she said.

'No problem.'

Before long, exams commenced. Busi felt better prepared than she'd hoped, but there was trouble for Thandi, who was ahead of her. Who, in her right mind, would miss the chance to pass Grade Twelve unless they'd gone and died? It seemed Thandiwe Dianna Diko did exactly that: missed her matric examinations. Kasi school or not, her teachers were frantic when she failed to show up for the first paper. The principal herself went to Thandi's home and interrogated the family. Not even her father, the policeman, knew where she was. Uphambene lo mntana?

But as Thandi's star sank, Busi's was on the rise. When the exam results came, everyone, including Mrs Bird, congratulated her. She had done much better than she had ever done before. Straight 7s – an 'outstanding achievement' – except for isiXhosa, in which she got a 6. Khulu questioned this over the phone, and Busi promised she would take the subject more seriously from then on.

There was much jubilation and many congratulations. That this should be the year she excelled in her examination results surprised and thrilled everyone, given the recent developments.

'Who would have thought, of all the years you've been in school, this would be your bumper year?' Phyllis said, for once praising her daughter even if in a roundabout manner.

And with equally unaccustomed modesty, Busi replied, 'I had lots and lots of help.'

Meanwhile, Busi had not forgotten that she was a mother. Through photos and short videos, she could delight in the progress Mandlakazi was making. The baby was growing, showing signs of differentiation. She recognised people; remembered faces and smiled at the familiar ones; frowned at strangers. Busisiwe felt her chest swell in gratitude at Khulu's ministrations, and was amazed at the change in the baby's demeanour – in so short a period of time, too.

And, in a voice gravelly and unshy, Mandlakazi was constantly bubbling away. 'Almost like a normal baby,' Luvo said one evening after watching a short clip Khulu had sent. Busi bristled, then drooped with shame. What was normal, anyway?

◇◇◇

Normal? there it was, said at last:
the unforgiving label: normal
said in negation: not normal
Abnormal, away from the norm
strange weird ugly cursed different
all these and more
will I encounter
during the course of my earth journey
what a difficult task is mine
to change perception
remind humanity
what it is busy forgetting:
the Oneness of them all
– of all living things – all life—
creation is One in its totality
all the laws and regulations
the conventions and declarations
uphold this one truth:
the indivisibility of humanity.

◇◇◇

Grieved at her uncle's words and her own sin, Busi welcomed the day Phyllis called with good news. 'Mrs Bird found a vac training opportunity for you, at Walla-Wallas! They have a programme for teenagers.'

Busi's spirits lifted. Her eyes bright and big, she said, 'Wha-at?' It was not a question. Walla-Wallas just happened to be the best retail store in the entire country.

'Why don't you call her? Find out more about it.'

Right then and there, the girl did exactly that.

So, throughout the school holidays, Busi was a working young woman – earning a bit of money. It came in very handy. Although she had applied for the child grant, and had been told by the social workers that her baby qualified for the care dependency grant – what people in Kwanele called the 'deaf grant', finding the full name too cumbersome to remember – this was now for Khulu to claim.

Both Mrs Bird and Khulu would have been even more optimistic about Busi's chances of success in life if they'd known about the workshop she attended as part of her orientation at Walla-Wallas. The older woman who'd facilitated the workshop had spelled things out, very clearly, for the attendees:

'Childhood through to youth is a time for preparation. Learn all you can, for you will need the knowledge. Stay in school till you have a certificate that tells the world how you will live, look after yourself and the children that shall be entrusted to you. Stay in school. Stay drug-free. Stay child-free until you enter the house of adulthood and then the world of work, fully armed with the prerequisite infrastructure for happy and successful living.

'Go forth and matter! You are here to be of count in the world!'

◇◇◇

These words would stay with Busisiwe for a long, long time, even though it was too late for her to take the advice about remaining child-free. And throughout the school holidays, when she was not at work or doing chores at home, she was at the local library. Yes, Kwanele lacked many of the amenities associated with modern urban living, but among the few it did boast was a library. It had beautiful and well-stocked bookshelves that rivalled the best in the country, thanks to the donation of one of the Scandinavian countries.

Busi read about three to four books a week. This was a challenge her class teacher had set before schools closed for the year. Read! Read! Read! Well, Busisiwe Mkhonto was reading, all right. And whenever she went to the library, she made sure she also read the newspapers there. This was her response to another of her teacher's exhortations: 'Keep abreast of current affairs!'

CHAPTER FIFTEEN

The village was home to many disparate people, different things to different people. To some it was heaven; to others a hell they could barely stand. To others still, the vice-like trap from which they would never escape – fate having dealt them a poisonous card.

Still, although it had its drawbacks, when Khulu returned to Sidwadweni, a baby on her back, it had always been a place of plenty, of beauty, of peace and love and restfulness.

On a Tuesday, long before a rumour of sun streaked the far horizon, Khulu was already waiting for the bus beside the gate of The Great Place, as the chief's domicile was called. She was on her way to the clinic in town – it should be much, much better than the local village clinics that were always, but always, running out of this and out of that, with nurses on this and that special leave – conference, or research – with those present deeply resentful that they should have to work, and so taking it out on the people in front of them. No good could ever come from one who lacked heart, Khulu believed. A dry spring might sound echoes of running water, but from it not a drop could ever be had.

But Khulu returned to the village that day angry and hurt. The staff at the clinic in town had ordered her to return to her small local clinic. Wednesday, she went to the local clinic as those in town had instructed, and had to bear the brunt of the nasty comments of the local nurses: 'Why did you go to the town clinic? You thought yourself better? Better than us here? Well, why are you here now? Since you've already judged us and found us wanting, of what assistance could we possibly be?'

Empty-handed, she returned with the child on her back, and felt how the village of her mind, her memory, had begun to die. It was in her past, mornings with blood-streaked skies, the soft hoot of an owl winging homeward, high, still in the sky, the eagle, the murmuring doves. Maybe all that truly survived were her memories. People had changed; and yet Khulu abided by her prayer bush, isicithi sakhe for the time of spirits, devotion time.

One morning, Khulu stood rooted to the spot and watched as Mandla, amidst scattered bushes, sat hunched and staring at some large, meaty-leafed plants. Khulu knew she knew this plant, but at that moment couldn't remember the name of it. From nowhere, a woman appeared, right next to Khulu: 'Intelezi,' she whispered loudly, 'Pluck a few leaves, go home and grind them. Boil them. Mix with a little isolisi ...' Then she was gone, as mysteriously as she had appeared.

Of course! Intelezi!

Coming to it like this, unexpectedly, she felt guided. Later, when Khulu described the woman of the veld to others, no one recognised her. She could have been a passer-by, someone journeying to villages beyond this one of Sidwadweni – perhaps going to Qumbu or Cingco, who knew?

Khulu crushed the leaves and added cooled, boiled water and

a few grains of salt. The salt helped to preserve the medicine so that it would last for up to ten days. She then gave Mandlakazi two teaspoons of the mixture with a pinch of Epsom salts.

This became an integral part of the little girl's medicinal therapy, both as a drink and as rubbing stuff. Much later still, those who knew something of the power of plants told Khulu this intelezi was powerful medicine used in treating birth and infant-related diseases. Khulu also used ucibicibane, which Mrs Bird called Leopard's Lily, with its big spotted leaves, for enemas. The kindly veld more than made up for the pathetic non-service of the clinics.

The little girl was always, but always at Khulu's side, even as a crawling baby, before she walked. Once that miracle was achieved, there was no stopping her. Miraculously, none of the animals bothered her, much to Khulu's relief. The little thing delighted in everything there was to see, and took no heed of dog or cat, geese or hen, her just-hatched flock of chickens scattered all over the yard. Mandla would run to them, talk to them, want to play with them; squawking notwithstanding. The same applied to just-farrowed sows.

Luckily, that year was a good one, lambs aplenty. So was milk. Where there was milk, amasi abounded. Mandlakazi was particularly partial to amasi: to drink, over crumbly mealie porridge, umphokoqo as umvubo. Left to her own devices, the child would have consumed amasi morning, noon and night.

But the little girl's favourite thing was gardening. Passionate about growing things, she would follow Khulu in and out of the veggie patch in front of the house or, if she'd taken her along to the fields further away, she would dive among the tall plants.

If Khulu had an implement in her hand, Mandlakazi found the closest approximation to it: stick, or twig or stone. She scratched and dug and pounded the soil, imitating what she saw Khulu do.

All this delightful business was conveyed via texts and calls to Busi in Kwanele, where Mandla's exploits drew oohs and aahs. All were thrilled to hear snippets of the toddler's escapades.

Thobeka helped Khulu with texting. She also helped with the baby. She was, in a huge way, Mandlakazi's village 'mother' ... after Khulu, whom she called 'mama' before she turned two. Yes, there was contact with her mother, Busisiwe. There were pictures of Busi all over the place and a particularly clear and beautiful one on the wall opposite Mandla's cot. But phone calls, letters and even photos could never replace real, immediate physical interaction.

Free calls provided a joyous space for deep discussions between Mandla's two mothers. Busi, for her part, tried to keep a regular schedule. Sunday afternoons suited her best, and that day and time was perfect for Khulu too.

One evening, Busi called with a puzzle to solve: 'I had a call from Thobeka. She said everybody finds it strange that since Mandlakazi's arrival you have stopped going to town ... especially on SASSA pay days. You don't seem to go even for your own pension! Why, Khulu? You have Mandla's SASSA card!'

'I know. Your mother has stopped milking me every month – I suppose because of Mandla. Or maybe living with Mrs B and taking care of her, she's no longer a container that always needs to be filled. But we have all we need. I grow the food we eat. The animals kindly give us milk and, occasionally, meat. What do I need money for on a monthly basis? Now and then I use some money for clothes, but really we are fine!'

'But I don't want you to be suffering!'

'We don't suffer. How did we raise our children before the grant?'

Another phone call was also linked to Thobeka.

'Khulu, Thobeka says the animals in her mother's kraal are the result of inqoma, whatever that is. And that, without it, her mother would have perished. Are you finally drawing money?'

'My dear Busi, inqoma is about cattle and other animals that give us milk and meat. We all saw their kraal was nearly empty, as the mine had only paid out a little fee for the loss of the father. So it was not only me, but one by one, people with more came and offered a few animals – two or so ... always young ones, female and a male.'

One evening, there was almost a fight between the two. The conversation was once again about Khulu's resistance to the grant.

'What about those who might not have enough?' asked Busi, stirring the pot.

'Why would they not have enough? That is where you must start – with the reason behind what the eye sees. For every malady known to human beings, there is a cause which, unless rectified, corrected, no amount of help will alleviate.'

'Meaning?'

'What is the point of the child grant?'

'To help parents who cannot afford ...'

'Afford what?'

'To feed their children.'

'Because?'

'Oh, for any number of reasons.'

'Name one or two or three of those, and then tell me how the grant addresses even one of them,' Khulu challenged.

Busi inhaled slowly, then started with what sounded like a list: 'Lost job, too many children for the salary, father ran away, no support or poorly paid support—'

'Stop there,' Khulu broke in. 'I don't see the grant addressing even one of those issues! It won't make insufficient wages sufficient, nor bring back an errant father. It will not make the number of "too many children" any less. I don't see it as helpful.'

'Wha-at? No, Khulu, you don't understand!'

'Those who need help should be helped, of course ... but *temporarily*. Help should not be a permanent feature in anyone's life.'

'You think the grant is that? A permanent feature?'

'*Eighteen continuous years?* Good God! That is all the growing-up years of an individual. Think of the child who grows up on this grant. To such a child, the grant must seem the most natural thing in the world.'

'So?'

'But don't you see? It is not!'

'It isn't?'

'No child should grow up believing they will always have to depend on outside help to be, to live. That is inhuman.'

'So poor people should not be helped?'

'Of course they must be helped. Bubuntu obo. But they must not be helped to stay poor. That's the whole point I'm making! People must be helped to stand on their own feet – proud, independent agents in their own lives and the living of those lives!'

'Oh,' Busi said, 'I see ...'

'Kulungile!' The two were so seldom at odds, that with a cough, they turned the conversation, and were soon happily chatting about Mandla's latest doings.

◇◇◇

ESidwadweni, three-year-old Mandla pottered around at Khulu's feet, busier even than Khulu. A stick in hand, she scratched uneven furrows and buried seeds. Khulu smiled as she watched her great-granddaughter. Finally, she thought, someone who had inherited her love of growing things.

Strangest of feats! Now and again, Mandlakazi would wander a little away from Khulu and, as she played in the veld, she would often, the way children have done since way back when, pluck something from the ground or a leaf from a plant, and put it into her mouth. If she found it bragworthy, she would run to Khulu, holding the green stuff high in the air: 'Nantsi! Nantsi, Khulu!'

It wasn't long before the toddler started to plant as well. In the vegetable garden, she picked and plucked and dug with sticks, planting her own seeds or pulling out weeds. 'Le? Le, Khulu?'

By the age of four, Mandla could differentiate plant from weed, and she could identify quite a few – umsobo, which she loved; irhwabe, which she tolerated; isindiyandiya, which she loved in that wild spinach dish with maize-meal, isigwampa, stywe pap with greens.

Busi, her Kwanele mother, came to stay eSidwadweni that year, as soon as she had passed her Grade Twelve exams, which she did with flying colours. It was another touching reunion between mother and child, with Busi overjoyed at the evident happiness and health of her little daughter. She was amused to see the child's enthusiasm for all things green and growing – noting that her play-field was in fact her great-grandmother's garden.

When Khulu had first noticed how keen the child was on growing things, she gave her a small corner section of the main garden. Impossible to paint an accurate picture of the jubilation this event occasioned! Mandla was beside herself. She and Khulu eagerly recounted for Busi what had followed.

Mandla's first crop was beans. Carefully, she spaced them, counted them, and filled the holes.

'I had to watch that she didn't drown the seeds; not only immediately after she planted them, but every hour of every day, she had the urge to give the poor things a little water!' Khulu told Busi, chuckling. The sprouts had soon appeared, healthy and none the worse for overindulgence.

Busi's arrival had coincided with the harvest, so she was in time to praise her daughter for a yield any keen gardener, or farmer for that matter, would have been proud of. Meanwhile Mandlakazi nearly killed Khulu, Busi and Sibuka with her jubilant cries of 'Look! Just look! I planted only one, enye jwi, kodwa jonga! Look how many came out!' She counted the number of beans in each pod, erratically, but counting nonetheless. 'I got a lot more beans than what I planted!'

She could not stop smiling, and all had to agree she spoke nothing but the truth. The wide gate displayed by the smile showed another truth: the child had also just lost her top two incisors.

Busi was glad to be present for this small step forward in her daughter's progress; she also relished the relaxation, the peace she found with her grandmother and daughter, and also the company of her old friend Thobeka. It was with a heavy heart that she returned home, even though she had a place at university to study social work – a source of both apprehension and excitement. There was by now no thought of dragging Mandla back to Kwanele with her; it was clear that the little girl was content and healthy in the care of her great-grandmother.

As her sixth birthday approached, Mandla wanted to stop napping in the afternoon: 'I am a big girl now, I will be going to school soon – isn't that so, Khulu?' Then, out of the blue one day, she told Khulu what the name of her teacher would be. Khulu paid little heed to what the child said. The school to which she would be going had no teacher by that name. However, toward the end of the year, before schools closed, there was a bus accident in which four teachers returning from a schools fair died. Two were from Mandlakazi's prospective school. In the new school year, Mandlakazi was assigned to one of the replacement teachers. The teacher's name? Why, the same name Mandla had mentioned.

Khulu could not get over it. The man was a total stranger from Port Elizabeth, and had never before set foot in the area. What did it mean? She had noticed that since she was able to speak, Mandla had always known when Busi was due to visit, right down to the actual day of arrival – before she, Khulu, had said one word about the matter. She had not paid it much attention before, but now it was becoming certain: Mandlakazi was a seer – *uyabona*.

CAMAGU!
The Old acknowledged her.
Camagu! Praise be!

Khulu was deeply thankful when, to the amazement of all, once she started school, it seemed that Mandla's brain was somehow unscathed by her trauma in the womb, although a reminder of who she was, 'designed' by her mother, was still traceable in her outward appearance, especially the eyes that, if one looked carefully, always seemed a little out of focus ... yes, not quite centred. She was also slightly palsied, her limbs shaking when she was tired or excited. The child's cognitive abilities seemed to be intact, however, as was confirmed when she went to school, and her prowess grew even more marked.

Bit by bit, predictions became one of her more striking gifts. And more than predictions; she would sleep, or appear asleep sometimes, eyes wide open, but unresponsive to verbal or tactile cues. And then, out of her limp form, someone would speak out, his or her voice unlike any known to Khulu: ethereal. And the voice said things strange or only vaguely understood – things only understood in remote retrospect.

There were times when she told Khulu of a visitor she did not expect, someone she had not seen for a very long time. And often, the voice would say what manner of transport would bring the visitor to Ekuphumleni: car, horse, or his or her God-given two feet, clothed in dust. Sometimes the voice would tell what colour clothes the person would be wearing, whether they were male or female, young or old, whether they were still far off, or a spittle distance away.

Needless to say, this for Khulu was not only strange, but perplexing in one so young. She had grown up with the legend of Vongothwane, true, and Hlombe himself had some visionary prowess. She understood that ukubiwa – being stolen – was the sleep from which there was no voluntary exit. But once that person had transitioned, anything was possible. They might speak in tongues; speak in another's voice, or their own. The sleeper would wake only when the Old were done. And when they returned from that other realm, they had no ken of what had come through their mouths.

But this? In such a small child? This was something else! Who should she tell? And what should or could she say? What would be the reception of such a thing eSidwadweni? To say nothing of the folk back in Kwanele? The last thing she wanted was for this poor child to be labelled or regarded as being possessed by the devil!

Her childlike ramblings via a disembodied voice easily missed the ears of the grown-ups, but in her third year of school, Mandlakazi's ability to predict burst out into the open.

Before the wife of the headman gave birth, Mandla in a voice strange and ethereal said that her child would be born twice. Indeed, the woman gave birth to twins, but no ordinary twins: twins so identical that only the woman who suckled them could tell them apart. Bantu had the stronger suck, while Bonke's was a mite gentler.

But from the moment people clapped their eyes on the twin boys, those who had heard of Mandla's prediction marvelled at its accuracy. Yes, not a few remembered the strange words out the mouth of Mandlakazi, and few among them would forget the profundity of the girl's prophecy.

As was common practice in the area, during church services Khulu usually left the little girl to play with the other children in the yard around the church. One Sunday, Mandla was nowhere to be seen. After much anxiety, Khulu discovered an older girl sitting besides the still form of Mandlakazi, a deep frown carving her face.

'Makhulu! Makhulu! UMandlakazi akavuki! Mandla does not wake up! Kodwa uyathetha. Uthetha funny. But she speaks, speaks strangely!'

Khulu stared helpless at Mandla in her trance. No amount of shouting the child's name could open her eyes. There was also no sign of anything untoward – snakebite, or ants, or blisters. No amount of fanning her face or loosening her clothes achieved the slightest stirring in the stone-still form, inert and prone on the brown dry grass of the churchyard.

Nor did the priest's sprinklings and mutterings yield any deliverance. Right then and there, Khulu decided she would zip her mouth. If Mandlakazi or the ancestors chose this place to manifest, she was not the one who would open her mouth and explain to the whole congregation that she had seen this before. What would her name be then? Surely her membership would immediately be suspended, if not out-and-out cancelled. Oh, yes, she might well be excommunicated from the holy body of the church.

'Let them deal with it whichever way they see fit!' she told herself. Then, supported by both elbows by other women, she was guided back inside the church and gratefully sank onto a seat. Hands covering her face, she sank her head towards her heaving chest. What now? And then she heard the oldest woman in Sidwadweni say: 'Leave her be! When she is ready, she will return.'

And so it happened. Early, before dawn the next day, a few of the neighbours came to see how she and Mandla had spent the night. Had the girl fallen again into that strange fainting spell? Khulu had a hard time trying to convince the sympathisers no need for their sympathy existed.

I am called back
the Old demand my presence
the only way back is through deep sleep
unconsciousness the fleshlings deem it
I knew
I was going back
making my way to the Old
my fellow people of the unfleshed world
not an easy ride
that of spirit
cold cold cold
then the flesh is left behind

I am there
home
with my fellow people of the unfleshed world
I feel the aura of its coming
I have no way of knowing how long I will be gone
I do not have the words to warn anyone when it comes
the aura is both long and strong
it is also tongue-tying
I am called back
the Old demand my presence
I am silent until they speak through me
They come through as they please
I have no control over voice or message
I am but the instrument of the Old.

◇◇◇

The next time the trance visited Mandlakazi, Khulu took the whole thing in her stride. Without panic, she waited for the storm or spell to travel its course, waited until the little girl returned once more. This time, her voice was Hlombe's: Hlombe transported into the body of little Mandlakazi. Definitely his voice. She'd know it in her sleep. And to her, it related all Mandlakazi was seeing. All she was told – where she'd been taken – who said what to her. Descriptions were vivid; sounds echoed; messages clear. Dutifully, Mandla conveyed Hlombe's words to Khulu until she herself felt and saw and heard as though she herself was present with him, transported by the strange and powerful telling of it.

'Ndiyakukhumbula. I miss you.'

And then abruptly ... silence.
Dead maddening silence.

◇◇◇

Not only did Mandla do exceedingly well in school, but her ukubiwa was fast becoming legendary. Word of it spread year after year, as the girl's fame grew. Of course some were suspicious; how could a child with her physical challenges be so gifted? If this was ukuthwasa, why did she not need training, induction? A few jealous souls said the child was possessed; others believed she was no child but impundulu, a firebird disguised, possessed by and in possession of her grandmother. Worse, there were those who said Khulu herself was an evil spirit who used Mandla for her benefit to lord it over them all. Why was her garden always the greenest, her soil so productive? Why did her hens lay so well?

Khulu pushed these murmurings to the back of her mind. Her ministrations to Mandla continued unabated. She improved this; amended that. The constant was intelezi, uthuvana, ikhala ... the mighty food of elephants and a tiny bit of isolisi and umhlonyane. Over time, this was overtaken by more and more wild fruit and berries: irhwabe, umsobo, intlokotshane, imvomvo, ingwenye – all according to their seasons. Khulu had everything under control, manageable, perfectly understood.

However, when the country hosted the Soccer World Cup, everything went helter-skelter. Khulu could no more exercise any control over Mandla's gift than she could steer inkanyamba, a hurricane. This new and alarming manifestation began two days before the World Cup games started, on the last day of school in early June.

Mandlakazi came back from school all excited, and Khulu put that down to her excellent exam report. But the girl handed that over to her, and sped off in search of Sibuka. The two returned, Sibuka carrying Mandla on his shoulders; he was jittery with an excitement Khulu had not thought she'd ever see in the lukewarm-blooded one.

'She knows all the teams!' Sibuka shouted, hopping about, seeming completely unaware of the weight on his shoulders.

And that was the beginning. The games lasted throughout the school holidays, and Sibuka and his group all but camped at Mandla's feet for the duration. And, of course, word got around!

Sibuka and his friends who knew the players, the teams and the referees soon discovered that Mandla could predict what would happen in the flow of the games, or when an upset would occur. People flocked to hear her and doubly marvelled watching the games: her predictions gave a totally different slant and excitement to them. But to Khulu, of course, Mandla might as well have been speaking Greek.

After her predictions about the very last game, Mandla said something that only Khulu really noticed. In a voice wailing as if at a wake, Mandla cried: '2010 – the world plays; 2020 – the world dies!' Then, the pitch of her voice changed, sounding as the voice of more than one person, the voice of a multitude – well-orchestrated, but plural nonetheless. Aloud this chorus of voices authoritatively announced, decreed: 'Ten years from now: no trophies, only caskets; the ground will not be able to swallow all the dead!'

The rest of the people in the house were already placing bets and planning where to watch or listen to the last match, so it was only Khulu, busy cutting beans, who heard these words. She pondered, then sighed: 'Perhaps I needn't worry ... Perhaps I will be dead by then.' But her heart was heavier than a bag of cement.

Once the World Cup was over, Khulu refused any use of Mandla for ukuvumisa – divining – declaring: 'This child is no witchdoctor, sangoma, nyanga or any such. Yes, she has a gift, but that gift will guide her. When, how and why she must use it, she will know, and let it be known.'

But it was already too late. Jealous tongues had been scandalmongering. Late one Saturday night, a man appeared at Khulu's door: 'MamTolo, do not say I came to you, do not repeat what I say to you, do not ask me the whos, wheres and whys. I come because I respect you, I admire you.'

In the dark of a moonless night, Khulu made out a form who was not unfamiliar. Sondlo?

The voice confirmed it. 'Go!' he said in a hoarse whisper. 'Leave this place. Leave, at once, or you are dead. Kuthiwa uyathakatha. They say you are igqwirha – witch.'

Khulu, wrapped in a blanket at her front door, wanted to respond with the anger she felt rising in her; but his upheld hand clamped her mouth.

'I risk my life coming to you. I warn you. Do not give the evil people of this village the satisfaction of killing you, slaughtering you like a beast of the forest. You know what I know. A case like that is never solved. Remember?'

Khulu remembered *UTshiwo*, a book she read in school. When was that? She had not even sprouted. Amagqwirha – witches – were put to death in the most cruel, inhumane manner; rough and knobbly stakes thrust through their bodies from anus to mouth while they were alive. Thereafter, the executioner threw them off the highest mountain cliff to whatever lay hidden, groaning, gurgling, and growling in the dense depths of the forest. Or, worse still, in its ominous and brooding silence, the air heavy with the exhalations of all that lay in it; invisible, prowling, ruthless.

'May your God and your ancestors always protect and shield you from all harm,' Khulu thanked her informer in a soft whisper.

Then she remembered something Mandla had said, had been saying, for several days: 'Siya kuBusi! We're going to Busi!' And she had taken it for child's play!

Khulu's mind was cool as cool could be. However, she immediately made plans. She must play it casual; arouse no suspicion. Before she'd retired for the night, she had made sure, as usual, that her Sunday was ready to go. Her Mothers' Union uniform lay ready, shoes polished to a blinding shine by Sibuka. Little Mandla's clothes were all ready, too. She decided she would one: not panic; two: go to church as planned. She must not only go to church, but act normally while there.

As was her wont, the next morning she woke up before the

birds. She had hardly slept a wink in the few hours since Sondlo's alarming visitation. Because she had worked it all out in her mind ... yes, lying wide-eyed in her bed, she had already mentally packed the bag she would take. Nothing to shout 'LEAVING!' Whatever the two of them needed, Mandlakazi and herself, they would find in Kwanele. Find it or get it.

Khulu was in church bright, early, looking normal as ever. Toward the end of the service, the Womens' Manyano leader made a plea for members to stay on after the service: 'Some urgent business has come up and we need to respond immediately. Unfortunately, this can't wait for our usual meeting on Thursday. I promise you,' she said, hearing loud groans and barely suppressed grumbles from some of her cohorts, 'on my word of honour, we won't be long!'

Khulu stayed. She was one of the few members who responded to the call and made a commitment to contribute financially to the request they'd received from headquarters. She explained that she needed to go to another village to help a visiting relative in need that day, but that she would be present to take the matter up the next Sunday. Who would have suspected she was already in flight?

Only hours later, with no farewell to anyone, she and Mandla were at the taxi rank in Mthatha. On their way to Kwanele. They were safe.

PART THREE

CHAPTER SIXTEEN

To say the folk in Kwanele were surprised to see Khulu that Monday morning would be putting it mildly. She had not warned them she was coming. Throughout the drive, whenever she was awake, Mandlakazi had sung a one-tune song: 'Busi! Busi! Busi!' But Khulu reminded herself: Did she not know Mandlakazi? Kakade, uzibhanxela ntoni; akamazi uMandlakazi?

Luvo heard the taxi stop outside the gate: were they expecting a visitor? He nudged his wife, tried to wake her up. A futile action; Lily slept the sleep of the dead. From the boys' room came a scratchy voice, 'Da-ad! Someone's at the gate.' Sazi had taken a peek out the window. Not safe. He must speak to the young man. Drive-by shootings had become a common occurrence in Kwanele.

Luvo jumped out of bed, grabbed a dressing-gown and strode into the living room. As he reached the door, he was surprised to see that Busi had beaten him to it.

As the small group trudged toward the now open front door, his surprise grew. Busi, a grown young woman, now in her first year of employment as a social worker, had anxiety in her heart and voice. What was wrong? Was Mandla ill?

'Why did you come if nothing is wrong with her?' she implored.

'Busisiwe!' Khulu said, a note of vexation or tiredness quite pronounced in her voice. 'I've just told you, Mandla is fine.'

Pleading, Busi asked, 'You wouldn't hide anything from me, Khulu?'

But Khulu brushed her off. 'Nothing's the matter with her, I tell you.'

'Oh,' the young mother gave a loud sigh of relief. 'Thank God for that.' She turned to her daughter, said, 'Come here, you!' No mistaking the smile in that warm voice. The two trailed behind the others going into the house, where they met Lily, half-awake and yawning. Her eyes grew round and huge, a frown gashed her forehead. 'Khulu?'

'Yes, it's me.' She nodded back at Mandlakazi, who was in her mother's arms, and said, 'This one must be famished. She slept throughout most of the drive ... and we're both tired.'

Of course, everybody was up now, so there was no chance of the new arrivals being let off the hook to go to bed. Questions rained on them.

'Wha-at is happening?'

'When did you arrive?'

'Why did you not tell us you were coming?'

'You've been away for years – why are you here now?'

But a bath and a good breakfast made the weary travellers more than ready for a snooze. Midday, Khulu got up and called Mrs Bird. From her erstwhile employer, friend and rock, against whom she knew she could lean in times of dire distress, came the startled, 'Are you telling me you're in Kwanele, right now?' She couldn't hide her surprise. 'You didn't say anything about coming back!' She added, 'Is everything all right? Is the child all right?'

Khulu replied, 'We're fine.' The worry in the other's voice reminded Khulu of the earlier encounter with Busi, and her anxiety about her daughter. Taking her to the village had never been a divorce declaration between the two; Busi had always cared, followed her daughter's progress.

Now MaBird was also concerned. How did one start explaining the reason for their sudden return? Khulu repeated what she'd just said, what she'd told all the others: 'We are fine.' She chuckled before going on: 'Although everybody seems to think otherwise.'

'It happens when you take people by surprise like this.'

'I suppose so.'

A pause followed, then Mrs Bird gave a cough and said, 'In a way, I'm glad you're back in Cape Town.'

Another pause, then Khulu said, 'Oh, so am I.'

'When do we see you?'

'Well, this week, we—' The other cut her short. 'Must see you as soon as possible. Come tomorrow ... or do I fetch you?'

'No,' Khulu answered, 'I'll find my way there ...'

'Bye, then!'

Relieved Mrs Bird had not made a song and dance about her going straight to Kwanele, Khulu was nonetheless happy she'd be seeing her friend as soon as the next day.

It was one of those ironies. She had left Cape Town almost a decade before, fleeing to the Eastern Cape, bent on finding healing for her great-granddaughter, Mandlakazi. Now she was back in Cape Town, circumstances having once more forced her to move, this time to flee from the village she had considered a place of hope and reprieve. Yet her determination to work for the healing of the little girl remained unchanged, had not diminished in the slightest. If anything, it had grown.

Her responses to all the harried, incredulous queries remained subdued; more ambiguous than revelatory, to say nothing of explanatory. She explained nothing; owed none any explanation. Moreover, she had not made up her mind how much of what had sent her packing, post-haste, from her retirement home, a home in her birth village, she should share; and to whom, and for what reason. Better say nothing than lead others to incorrect conclusions.

Besides, what did she stand to gain from telling her children she had been accused of witchcraft? And that this was on account of Mandla's gifts? Would they hold her responsible for Mandla's episodes, if these recurred? Would they believe, without question, her innocence, yet more important, her great-granddaughter's innocence? If they did not, what would she do about that? And, should they say they did, would she in turn believe them? The trouble with accusations, she found – more so when they had absolutely no merit, no foundation – was that the accused became so destabilised in her sense of self that she doubted others saw the same person they had previously seen. How could they when she herself did not see the same persons in them? Shifting hearts; shifting faces. If they saw her as such, as this new evil force, who were they? And if they were not the same as she had believed them to be, had she not also changed then? Could she remain constant, all about her shifting?

Well into the night, Khulu lay awake, her mind reliving the place she'd just fled. The woes of the village had shown her even more clearly the needs of the child. In the past years, she had witnessed and lived alongside sad changes eSidwadweni. The land had stopped being kind; yields were pitiful for the few who still bothered planting anything. Most gardens were not lying fallow; they were in a terrible state of neglect, overrun by natural vegetation and, even worse, foreign vegetation. More robust than the native plants, they seemed to thrive at the expense of the latter. Indeed, a few of the chiefs had inaugurated projects where young people went about destroying the intruding plants.

What is more, she discovered she had a very cushioned life after all. *Of course, that is comparatively speaking,* she corrected herself. She had not thought of herself as wealthy and, indeed, she was far from that, God knew the truth of her situation. But what she saw, how people living on next to nothing but the thin hope that someone – a child or relative employed in one of the nearby towns far, far away – might send them something, truly saddened her. Khulu shuddered, a few of the perpetually hungry faces springing to mind.

Her mind turned over one issue after another. The homestead she'd left eSidwadweni. What about her garden? What of the poor animals? And, dear Lord, what would become of all her belongings? In fact, she must call Sibuka the next day and make arrangements, say that her date of return was still unknown. She must remind him to brand the two newest lambs for Thobeka's mother, who would help him to oversee her homestead while she was away.

When would she ever go there again? Would it be safe for her to do that, return to the place she'd fled? Would whoever had started the witchcraft lie have forgotten, died, or gone away? Would the evil lie itself be dead, or would it still live, most probably embellished, having grown bigger and more menacing?

Khulu thought long and hard about all these and more. However, of all the concerns keeping her awake none pressed her heavier than that of Mandlakazi – the child who had sent her back to Sidwadweni in the first place. Perhaps it was as well they had come to Cape Town. To raise a child, any child, never mind one who, like Mandlakazi, needed special attention and care, was very difficult when the purchase of a litre of milk from the spaza shop was headline news. It would bring, within minutes, a child with an empty cup: 'Mama says please help her with a drop of milk. Her head is killing her because she has not had coffee for three days!'

In a strange way, she was relieved, glad she had been forced to leave the place. Yes, being there had helped – a lot. Just look at the journey of healing of the girl. And she herself had learned more and more about the healing herbs of benevolent nature. However, it felt good to be back in Cape Town.

> *The Old knew before-before*
> *it would come to this*
> *much as they hoped, wished, prayed*
> *they knew that*
> *one of them would have to come down*
> *live among their beloved earthlings*
> *and I was the one chosen.*

Our leavelings had strayed so far from the path of ubuntu
Only umntu from the other side, the spirit side,
Had the least hope of righting them; guiding them back to
The meaning of ubuntu
I am because
You are.
Umntu ngumntu ngabantu.
A human is human through the humanity of others.
That is the marrow of ubuntu. Nanko ke umongo wobuntu.

CHAPTER SEVENTEEN

Although Kwanele welcomed her with open arms, there was amazement at Mandlakazi's transformation in both appearance and prowess.

Esam was first to remark on it: 'Uthetha nje kakuhle ngoku!' he announced. Khulu had to laugh, for Esam was the picture of perplexity; he had difficulty putting together the jig-saw puzzle he had in his mind.

'Your niece has grown, Esam,' Khulu said and added, 'Just as you have.' She patted the boy on his head and said, 'And, you're quite right, her speech has improved, and so has her gait.'

Esam nodded. However, the look of puzzlement did not immediately fade.

Khulu could not help herself. She burst out laughing. 'Oh, Esam, my child!' she said. 'Don't look so worried. You will soon catch up.' Mandlakazi, tall for her age, had grown even taller than Esam, six years older. Esam was obviously finding this difficult to comprehend, never mind accept.

But even more incredulous were Khulu's daughters. Even with pictures sent over the years, they could not believe the calm confidence of the child, her ability to speak, her physical growth. Busi was less surprised; she who had spoken on the phone to Mandla regularly, visited Sidwadweni during university holidays. She had witnessed far more of the transformation, and yet even she was awestruck.

Now, the four women sitting down around the table, Khulu praised Busi highly for what she'd made of the garden, where every inch was now crowded with vegetables.

At that, both Phyllis and Lily broke out laughing. 'Mama, you and your gardening!' Lily said.

Her sister shook her head, 'Mama, you think Kwanele is Sidwadweni.'

'I don't!' Khulu said, giving Phyllis the eye. She went on, 'I think it is Bishopscourt.'

The day passed in a whirl. By the end of it, not only had Busi contacted Mandla's school eSidwadweni; she'd submitted applications to four schools and expected to hear back before the end of the week.

Very early the next day, Khulu made her way to Mrs Bird's home. There, she received disturbing news. At least, that was her feeling when her friend said, 'Dear Gracie, a very big decision needs to be made in my life.'

Khulu plonked herself onto the nearest chair, as it happened, the chair right at the entrance. This was once the prized possession of Mrs Bird's father-in-law, a bigoted racist who never stopped reminding her and her husband how indebted to him they were. As a result, much as the funny-looking chair was not only a family heirloom but also a rare antique with significant monetary value – as old Mr Bird never stopped bragging, 'the thing belonged to one of the Egyptian Pharoah's!' – his daughter-in-law treated it with disdain.

'Maralee wants me to go live with them,' she now said.

'But they're in ...'

'Australia, I know.'

'But—'

Mrs Bird interrupted her old friend. It was clear she did not want to discuss the cancer she had fought off a decade earlier. Instead, she wanted to tell Gracie her plans in case she failed to ward off her daughters. However, she maintained vehemently that she was determined to stay in her house, and die in it when the time came.

Her daughters had chosen emigration, reversing the early twentieth-century exodus of their great-grandparents, hers from Germany, her late husband's from England. That was their choice, and she had not stopped them. Now they were crying distance and concern because of her age and health. Who knew if and when the cancer might recur? All this she understood. It was the remedy at which she baulked. They had no right to even think of dragging her to God-forsaken Australia, or even England, where Thelma, the younger daughter, had settled.

But now she wanted to tell her friend about the most important matter, her will; what she wanted her to remember, 'In the event I crock out before you ...'

'No!'

'I'm just saying,' Mrs Bird said, her eyes shining with mirth. 'We are both of an age when anything can happen.'

'I know.'

'Should I go before you, remember to come to the reading of my will. You must get what is due to you.'

'But I don't want anything.'

'That is not for you to say, my friend.'

Silence fell. The two friends looked at each other, all solemn, but not at all sad. Abruptly, Khulu pushed herself to her feet. 'I don't know about you,' she said. 'But I need a cup of something.'

'Make that two, please! And thanks for the suggestion!' As Khulu headed in the direction of the kitchen, Mrs Bird called out, 'There are fresh scones in the tin, if you don't mind!'

Gracie could say whatever she liked, but she could not stop her from doing the right thing, the fair thing. It should have been done back in 1994: white South Africans should have paid back some of the unfair earnings that they had because of legislated racism. They should have been asked to give half, at least, of what they owned. That would have been only fair. Who needed more than one house to live in? Beach house or holiday house, something most white South Africans took for granted – all as unnecessary as the third and fourth cars in a family of two! No, she would give Gracie what was due to her. Her late husband could turn in his grave, if he so wanted, but the thought of him brought a deep sigh ... no, not regret, reminiscence. How long had she been a widow? God, that long!

Imagine Mrs B's surprise when upon her friend's return, as she was setting up the tea table, out of her mouth came the question: 'How long have we been without them, our husbands, now?'

'Wha-at?' Before she got an answer to her question, she added, 'Why do you ask?'

Khulu laughed out loud and shook her head. 'I know if master was still around—' She stopped, looked at her friend through narrowed eyes and said, 'I mean, if you had died and he were still here ...' She stopped again, looked her friend squarely in the eye, and said, 'He would not think of us in that will of his.'

Mrs Bird nodded and reached for her cup. 'You are right. He would not.' That was the side of Timothy she had resented – his narrow-mindedness that bordered on racism. A good man, he'd had an abominably biased childhood he just never escaped ... or wanted to escape. Saw no need. To a large extent, that was why she was willing away the bigger portion of the sizeable inheritance he had left her ... making amends for what he had done, even unknowingly or unconsciously. Ignorance of the extent and effect of one's bias was no excuse; it affected others, the victims, just as much as the bigotry of those who were knowingly racist.

She did it without any qualms: her daughters were provided for, and she had left a small something for Marvin, her lazy nephew. The rest went to Khulu and her family – Mandlakazi would never lack for top-rate medical treatment, should she need it – and a variety of charities.

They were just polishing off the scones when Busi rang her grandmother, jubilation in her voice: 'We're in!'

'In what?' Khulu asked.

'Mandla's been accepted at my old school!'

'Yhoo!' Khulu shouted; turned to her friend, 'Hear that Mrs B?' In answer to the other's raised brows, continued, 'Busi's daughter!'

'Yes?'

'Will go to school at St Stevens, just as her mother did.'

'That was fast!'

'Well done!' She congratulated Busi before ringing off.

◇◇◇

That evening, Khulu brought up Mandla's admission to Busi's old school; told her granddaughter again, 'I'm impressed by how fast you work!' It was a remark she would have occasion to repeat when, by Thursday, all Mandla's school needs – books, uniform, transport, extra-mural activities – were in place. That Busi had managed all this with the added chore of having to liaise with the school back eSidwadweni simply amazed her. But Busi explained that with technology, things moved faster. 'It's not like I have to write a letter and mail it to the school, Khulu.'

'Still ...'

'With email it is so-oo easy!'

Smiling, Khulu just shook her head, absolutely amazed at the young people and their what-what. What-what reminded her of Thobeka. She must remember to call the girl and her mother the next day. Sibuka too, of course! Give them an update without letting them see their flight had been planned, not accidental at all. A plan would necessitate explanation, and she had promised Sondlo she would never let anyone know what he'd revealed to her. Keeping that promise was the least she could do, although she had from the very moment of his revelation wondered what would constitute a fitting reward. However, for once, she was stumped. It is not often one is called to reward someone who has literally saved one's life. But she was sure she would find a way. She must.

But more immediate concerns needed her attention. Therefore, next up for discussion, according to Khulu, was the matter of paying for Mandla's education at her mother's alma mater, with its Model-C fee structure.

'We'll be fine, Khulu,' Busi said.

'You're not going to Mrs Bird, are you?'

'Oh no! She's done enough for me. I should be able to pay for my child's education.'

Needless to say, Khulu was much relieved to hear this, and said as much. She said more, in fact. But that came later, when both her daughters were present. She felt they, probably more than Busi, needed to bear witness. They needed to see what growing one's food did, how it paid you back, gave you leeway so money did not become indispensable. Did not rule and ruin your life; you mastered the use of it, instead of it becoming your master.

After dinner, with the family present, Khulu made a point of praising Busisiwe for paying for her daughter's education. She looked at Phyllis and Lily, for both, if in different and to differing degrees, got help with theirs: 'This tells me Busi has really grown.'

One brow raised, 'And we …?' Phyllis asked.

Head inclined to one side as though giving the matter serious consideration, Khulu let a lazy smile creep into her eyes, softening them and slowly spreading her lips sideways. Then she let out a long, soft sigh. 'We'll talk about that another time,' she said, looking her girls in the eye. She shook her head, sighed again. 'Not now.'

◇◇◇

One thing about life in Kwanele that Khulu found hard to stomach was anyone making fun of her Mandlakazi. Especially as she had made it a point not to fight the girl's battles for her. Instead, she encouraged her, goaded her, into self-defence mode. No, not physically, but mentally.

One day Mandla had come to her great-grandmother wailing: 'The other children say I have frog eyes!'

'Go ask them to bring you the frog.'

'Wha-at?'

'Tell them you want to give the frog its eyes and take yours back. Inoba kaloku lona lithathe awakho. It must have taken yours.'

That so surprised the child, she immediately stopped crying. Khulu sat her on her lap, ensconced her in her arms and shushed her, all the time patting her fondly on her back. 'Next time anybody is nasty about your body – any part of your body – remind them your body is God-made. Then ask them if they think God made you "wrong".'

Mandla asked if that were true: was she indeed God-made?

'When have I ever lied to you?'

From then on, anyone who dared make fun of Mandla got: 'You think God made a mistake?' Her unflinching stare did the rest. She soon developed further responses to that kind of bullying: 'Like yours, my eyes were made by God!' And: 'Do you know where I can get them repaired?' Her explanations were so calmly and firmly given, the others were left feeling stupid for not having realised something so obvious.

But her favourite was a play on the nursery rhyme said by a child when losing a tooth: 'Khulu! Khulu, thatha eli zinyo lam lidala, undinike elitsha!'

This she changed to: 'Sihlobo! Sihlobo, thatha eli zinyo lam libi, undinike elihle! Friend! Friend, take my ugly tooth and give me a beautiful one!'

◇◆◇

This strategy soon gained Mandlakazi the reputation of being a 'toughie'; it was said that 'with such a sturdy raincoat, insults merely glided down to the ground leaving no mark on her'.

One Saturday Esam was standing at the gate, surrounded by a small group of boys and girls his age. The friends were chatting and joking when Mandlakazi joined the group. Suddenly, all talk stopped and the teens, except for Esam, started eyeing one another. There was derision in those eyes.

'What's wrong?' Esam asked, for he had noticed the sudden drop in temperature. Muffled snorts could be heard as one of the group mimicked a limping gait, and another crossed his eyes.

'Did I say something funny?' he asked, adding, 'Or nihleka mna?' He was beginning to be annoyed.

'Don't worry, Esam,' Mandla said, taking one of Esam's hands. 'It is me, not you, they laugh at.'

At that, all laughter stopped. The older teenagers were amazed at the sheer lack of any emotion approaching anger or blame or begging for inclusion in the voice they'd just heard. More frightening, they'd heard pity. Great pity. But how was it possible? Eyes roamed and darted. Eyes found reflection, pair by pair, of what was in the heart. Trepidation swamped all those who heard

Mandlakazi's so-grown remonstration.

But what had called up such dread? Surely not the words from the mouth of a little girl, a little disabled girl, one who was not 'quite right', whose eyes blurred and limbs trembled?

But the little girl wasn't quite done. Voice calm and peaceful, Mandlakazi told the group: 'Aninabuntu. Loo nto asilothamsanqa; yiyekeni. Unkindness is cruelty; it brings none any fortune. Shed it!'

Not one of the girls and boys present would ever forget those words. What is more, many would remember them particularly when some misfortune or unpleasantness befell them. *Please God! Don't pay me back for the careless remarks of my youth!* They would find themselves praying, once more remembering the little girl's words of long before.

CHAPTER EIGHTEEN

Disinclination to belief,
the sad lot of our leavelings.
The very fact of one's own life fails to
fill them with a sense of wonder — the miracle of it all.
Day in, day out, minute by minute, awake or asleep,
the blood runs
And they thank not Qamata, the All-powerful.

Alas, the fleshlings have abandoned reason
Hearts dark as night rule their every waking moment
In deep sleep of night, they embrace dreams of greed
Rapacious, lascivious living is the order of the day
Ubuntu has become stranger.

A Saturday morning. TV news. An eighty-four-year-old woman burned alive in her home. First dragged out by a relative, a man in his thirties. Video shots of the incident. But it was the woman's haunting, piteous wailing that stabbed Khulu's heart as she watched the satanic drama. The woman's cry was totally devoid of hope. She cried knowing in her heart she was already dead; none would come to help her as she was dragged forcibly back into her house by two men. They then doused the house with petrol and threw a burning twig inside. A woman, in her early twenties, delightedly threw liquid, presumably paraffin, onto the furnace.

Khulu was reminded of her narrow escape. That could so easily have been her fate: Flagstaff, where this heinous crime took place, was an hour's drive, if that, from Sidwadweni. Silently, she thanked her ancestors and her God. She thanked dear Sondlo too. In this instance, he was the hands and mouth of her Lord and Saviour.

But she chose not to burden the family with this matter, neither did she mention the innumerable mishaps, inefficiencies, the rudeness, the dreadful lack of facilities and the shabbiness of the structures that existed supposedly to serve.

Murmurs of complaint were met with comparisons: 'You say the taxi service is bad eSidwadweni?' Lily asked shrewdly. 'You think the taxi drivers in Cape Town are gentlemen, all legally and professionally licensed, all sober behind the wheel, none with touchy-feely fingers or just plain long fingers? That they run clean, safe, reliable service – Yii-yhoo! Uvelaphi, ndiye?'

One of the first things Khulu did, insisted on doing, was to build her own set of rooms next door. She had paid for the tiny bit of land, where once a ruined shack had stood, years before.

The main house suffocated her, she said. There were just too many people, their lungs gulping in the air long before it got to her. And when it did, it smelled of the lungs through which it had come back into the house. It certainly was no longer the air God had sent in from the outside into the house. By the time it reached her nose and it went into her own lungs, it was different, and it smelled different, too. And with some of the younger people smoking and drinking liquor, if she were not careful, Khulu said, she herself would get drunk from the fumes she inhaled. Her lungs too would get infected, and she would end up with TB or all the poison from cigarettes and tobacco getting into her lungs and her blood. And she knew there were things intsha imbibed, but never named. Well, not with names she and people like her recognised. Weird-sounding names; terribly dangerous names disguised as fun. But she had ears and heard things. People talked and there was always the radio.

So she threw herself into making her little bungalow comfortable, and took comfort in the good she saw. Phyllis looked better than she had in years. Looking after Mrs Bird was paying dividends – in more ways than one.

And she thanked God Busi had stayed on the straight and narrow, graduating from university, finding employment as a social worker. A working woman – a professional! Khulu was mightily pleased at that. And the fact that she and Mandlakazi were often together, at play or poring over books, or this small computer that looked like a typewriter but was silent, making none of those tikkety-tok-tik noises of the typewriter. Busi was forever on her machine, and so were the older boys. It was a miracle they finished their learning with the tips of their fingers not only still attached, but not looking any worse for wear. She feared all that tapping meant they'd end up with the calloused fingers of farm workers.

But although we may and do move around, the places where we have lived inhabit us too. Out of the blue, Khulu would exclaim,

'Zange ndayibona into enje ngaleya! Never have I seen anything like that!' in referring to the atrocious conditions people in the Eastern Cape suffered. The prolonged drought had but added to the hardships there. Entire towns had run out of water. Families starved.

But about the abruptness of her departure from Sidwadweni, Khulu kept her mouth clamped tight. She would not put her benefactor's name in jeopardy. She could not risk endangering others; after all, the impassioned unthinking acted even on guesswork.

So Khulu remained in Cape Town with little appetite for talk on matters personal or familial either. All her answers or speeches were curt, brief, unembellished, very different from the incessant din in her head.

Those cars the officials of the Education Department drove – one each! Each of those a 4x4; each worth more than the paltry buildings of most of the village schools. Posh cars for officials of education, but no school buildings worth the name, not even latrines – what evil times they lived in! There were many missteps all around, Khulu reminded herself, and proceeded to look at her own assumptions. With hindsight, these definitely needed revisiting.

The burning of elderly women dubbed witches by a few crazies occurred both night and day. Those not directly involved, not at that moment named, accused, were careful to keep their distance, their eyes unseeing; they prayed in their hearts they would not be next. Prayed such would not touch them, not come near to where they stood. Doubt was easily planted in minds – could it be true? A lifetime of knowing that day's target, decades of experience and interaction with the newest 'witch' obliterated; bothersome conscience snuffed out by cowardice.

All this time ... all my life, I have been looking at the village through rose-tinted spectacles – seeing what I wanted to see – believing what I wanted to believe – what I was taught to believe. There is gross evil in the village. Gross evil; and it looks like me!

However the odds might be stacked against her in Cape Town, at least no one was accusing her of ubugqwirha, witchcraft.

And unlike the villages, in the urban areas, it was not that easy to kill and remain traceless. There was always the chance that sooner or later, the law would catch up with you.

So, yes, it was back to Cape Town she'd fled.

This time, however, things would change. They had to. She would stick it out for Mandlakazi. For the child, she would stick out anything.

Khulu wondered how the Kwanele folk, especially her family, would react to Mandla's special gift. It was only a matter of time before it manifested itself. She had thought about this even during the trip to Cape Town; now she prayed that she would be around the first time it happened. As there was no way this could be guaranteed, she made a mental note to talk to Busisiwe about the matter. Should they alert the school about it? How would they explain?

The child had not yet been taken in Busi's presence. Therefore, for the mother, the daughter's special ability was a matter of hearsay, a mystery she had yet to witness, and about which she harboured not a little scepticism. This was something Khulu intuited, for she knew and understood the deep-seated disbelief of the westernised – amakhumsha: a label she applied to all those who had received any significant education.

◇◇◇

Khulu was not kept waiting long to see how her daughters and their families, the Kwanele folk, would react to Mandlakazi's special gift. One evening, as Busi and Lily got dinner ready, Esam burst into the house screaming, 'Ufeyintile! Ufeyintile! She has fainted! She has fainted!'

No one asked who had fainted, for the only child around was Mandlakazi. But as the others rushed to the door, a sharp 'Ningamphazamisi!' stopped them short: there was such authority in that voice, the tone not loud but surefooted, as commanding as that of a sangoma or a chief – it could not but be obeyed.

But it was also the word choice that surprised the rushing feet to standstill. Ordinarily, one wants or needs to disturb someone in a fainting spell. Therefore, the negative command struck such a discordant note, all action stopped. But even as visible action abruptly halted, thoughts went whirling. *What did Khulu mean? Why did she say the child should be untouched, left as she was?*

But Khulu appeared unconcerned. 'Esam!' she called out. 'Bring me my shawl or a towel, whichever you find first,' she said, walking toward the door. She turned to the others, 'Yambathani! Cover yourselves!' The men knew hats and jackets were called for; the women, doeks and wraps on shoulders. Silently Khulu waited at the door until Esam brought her a towel. She draped this over her shoulders and began saying the praises of her clan as she walked toward the figure prone on the ground outside.

If the others were puzzled, Khulu's demeanour left them in no doubt that this was a sacred moment. They did as they were bid; hesitant, doubtful and confused, they nevertheless raised no objections, but stood and watched.

To everyone's surprise, Mrs Bird came through Mandla's prostrate form. There was no doubting that voice; all had heard it enough times that identifying it was immediate and certain.

'Well done, Phyllis! Well done! Such good work deserves a raise ... wouldn't you agree? Mmhh?'

This last word came in the form of a sigh-laugh: *Mmhh?* Anyone hearing it couldn't but imagine a smile that reached even the eyes.

A few minutes later, Mandla's own eyes popped open. She looked around, stretched, gave a long, loud yawn and then slowly got into a sitting position.

All eyes turned to Khulu. 'Uyabiwa uMandlakazi,' she explained and walked toward the child, reached for her and helped her up. The two walked indoors, and Khulu led her to her own bedroom, where she left Mandla resting comfortably. She went back to Busi, Lily and her husband, and Esam. Themba and Sazi were out that night. Although Busi had known of Mandla's ukubiwa, she had never experienced it first-hand before, and was clearly disturbed.

But it was Luvo who asked the first question. 'Kanti kumhla iyintoni na le? Wha-at in the world was that?'

Khulu explained. She told them of her first experience of witnessing the phenomenon, and briefly told its history. However, she did not mention what it had birthed. She was not going to saddle her family with the sordid details. Nor did she wish to jeopardise Sondlo's life.

'Does this mean Phyllis is getting a raise?'

Khulu shrugged, but Lily was not going to be put off that easily. She called her sister. But after a short conversation, she shook her head and rung off.

'Na-ah!' Phyllis knew nothing of any extra money.

Among the delights Khulu found in Kwanele was a much-revamped garden. Busi had stayed true to her word, and the seeds she had brought back from her visits to Sidwadweni continued to flourish in her well-tended garden. Pumpkin; beetroot; sweet potatoes and potatoes; tomatoes; onion; garlic; sweet peppers; cucumber; and lots more. There were plants Khulu did not recognise as coming from Ekuphumleni at all – Busi must have found them on her own. *Amazing*, Khulu said to herself. *Truly amazing.*

As could be expected, Mandlakazi demanded 'her own garden' in Kwanele, too. Why not? she asked in response to explanations about 'school work' and 'not enough ground' and other such silly sentiments; sentiments the girl did not want to heed.

Eventually, it was Khulu who came up with a plan. There was a little private plot behind the Bishopscourt flatlet where Khulu had once lived. Why not make that Mandlakazi's exclusive garden? Phyllis had done nothing there; she'd always been happy to live on MacDonald's and fish and chips, had done so since her late teens or early twenties. Not that Khulu did not eat the stuff; she relished it, in fact. But she always said to those hard pressed to put food on the table, *the sea is never near*. With all that fish, seaweed, and water ... what use to those without fishing rod, will, skill or care to fish? But now, vegetables, they were a different kettle of fish! Vegetables cost so little when you grew them yourself.

AmaXhosa wona ath: 'Akukho nkwali iphandel' enye; ephandel' enye, yenamantshontsho. No pheasant scratches for another; that which does is with chicks.

'Niya kuba ngamantshontsho karhulumente kude kube nini na? Khona, uyise wabantwana nonina wabo abo ukwazi njani ukuzingca ngempumelelo yemizamo eyeyakhe xa nje ephila ngokukhongozwa?'

Hearing Khulu say, 'Now that we are free, why should we be lazy to grow our own food?', her two daughters tried to argue with her. This led to another discussion about money. Khulu looked hard at them, wordlessly she looked at them. But the sadness in the eyes was loud with concern. Loud sadness the two women could not but see.

'Let me show you something!' And Khulu upped and went to fetch her bag, calling Busi from her room to come and join them. Returning, she took out a bank statement and gave it to Phyllis. 'Remember what we spoke about the other day ... when I praised Busi's very apparent money management skills and you ...' She was interrupted because as she spoke, she plunked down the bank statement she had refrained from showing to them during that discussion. Now, at sight of it, Phyllis screamed: 'Maa-mah! Where did you get all this money?'

Curious, Lily grabbed the document and perused it, her eyes

growing larger and larger. Then she looked rather than spoke her question. Finally, Busi picked up the paper and scrutinised it.

'That's not my money. Look carefully.'

Three pairs of eyes looked.

'YekaMandlakazi? Mandlakazi's?' All three shouted at once.

Khulu nodded.

'B-b-but?'

'Busi,' Khulu said, 'do you remember when I asked you for the baby's SASSA card? What did you think I wanted that card for?'

'To get her money.'

Khulu shook her head. 'No,' she said. 'First of all, it is not *her* money. Children have no need for money, their parents do.'

'Well, to help the parents then,' Lily said.

Khulu nodded. 'Help the parents.' She looked at the three women before her, her daughters and the daughter of the elder one. 'But,' she said, 'I didn't need any help. Not that kind of help, monetary help, anyway.'

Phyllis was quick with her question: 'What did you feed her then?'

'You mean you don't know, after all this time? Milk from my animals – sheep, goat, or cow. As for food, that is why we have gardens.'

'You grew all her food?' Lily asked.

'That is all Mandlakazi has been raised on: food fresh from the garden and the veld.'

'And, you're telling us, all this money,' Phyllis nodded her head toward the sheet of paper on the table before them, 'is from SASSA?' Incredulity rode on each word out of her mouth.

Lily managed to squeeze out a single word from a throat blocked by sheer disbelief: 'SASSA?'

Khulu nodded.

Lily's voice had returned. 'But how? Njani, Mama?' She bent forward, stretched her hand and took the bank statement from Phyllis, who was reading it again. Eyes squeezed in concentration, the sisters read the figures. And read again. And again. Nothing made sense. *All this money!?*

'My children,' Khulu addressed them pityingly, 'if you could only listen. Do not make yourselves needy for money because you know it is there. Live as though it weren't there. Grow your own food; do not buy clothes unless you really need them, or the child does. You'd be amazed at how little children really need. But what we, grown-ups do, is foist our needs and cravings on them. We give them things they don't need to satisfy our vanity, our hunger, our blindness. The earth gives us everything we need to live, to survive. If we treat her kindly, use her wisely, she rewards us unstintingly.'

Lily sprung a headache. She could not fathom what she had done with all the SASSA money she had received over the years. That much? In less than ten years? And for only one child? So, okay, the child got the deaf grant. But there were many children who got that grant, and their parents saved nothing at all. They were just like the rest of them, always waiting for the next pay date with hardly anything left in their pockets. Always desperately hard up.

The two sisters looked at each other, and then at Busi, who was beginning to smile. She raised her brows at her mother and aunt:

'This time, you cannot say "Kodwa uwrongo, Mama!"'

'And there's something else you should know,' said Phyllis. 'I got that raise from MaBird ...'

CHAPTER NINETEEN

As Mandlakazi grew, with Khulu the anchor in her life, and also benefiting from the loving presence of her mother and the rest of her family, so her understanding seemed to grow. She was both extraordinarily perceptive and receptive, game to try anything Khulu suggested. She was not easily frustrated; the more she was pushed past what some deemed her comfort zone, the greater her delight. If she at first failed at anything she attempted, she didn't give up or get embarrassed. She simply got herself ready for the next attempt, and gave it her all until, bit by determined little bit, she achieved her goal.

Khulu had decided, ever since she first took charge of this baby, to drive all self-pity from the girl's knowledge of herself, of who she was. Therefore, as understanding grew in Mandlakazi, so did her inner strength. She overcame many of her physical disabilities, and compensated where there were limitations. Her outstanding characteristic was the confidence she oozed. Confidence and determination were the two pillars on which her heart stood.

Naturally, this gladdened Khulu's heart no end. It encouraged her to even greater effort, more audacious measures, prompted by the strong murmuring and urgings of her heart.

At all hours of the day, at home, in school, Mandla would play or chat, find herself absorbed within a group. Now and again, one or more of her peers would come up with hurtful remarks that tried to exclude her. They never succeeded. The girl resisted any form of bullying; her strongest weapon was her unflinching stare. It disarmed most, shamed all, confirmed her unbreakable steel.

Regular check-ups were part of Mandlakazi's life, and Khulu accompanied her even when there really was no longer any need, as the girl grew older. However, Khulu insisted, and Mandlakazi didn't mind; she enjoyed Khulu's company, with its minimal intrusion.

At Mandla's last appointment for the year, Ms Nomzi Ndonga, the social worker who handled Mandlakazi's case, was amazed at her progress; could not but compliment her. To Khulu she said, 'Ngek' utsho ukuba sisidalwa!'

Calmly the girl responded, 'Aren't we all as created by God? Asizizo sonke; sidalwe nguThixo nje?' The retort came easily; she had used it many times before.

A huge smile broke out in Khulu's heart. Her facial expression remained unchanged; but she was mightily pleased with Mandla's response, and her heart smiled.

The social worker took note. The girl's remarkable physical progress was just the half of it, she thought. This one had character! Brow furrowed, Ms Ndonga quickly ran her eye over the file; for a moment, she'd thought she might even have the wrong file. Cases like these, where there was damage in the womb, seldom showed such positive progression. This one was, if one didn't know, almost ... normal. Except for slightly impaired vision, the stutter in her limbs ... minor really, considering the usual bleak prognosis.

But not all of Mandla's appointments went so smoothly. She and Khulu returned from a visit from the local clinic with a story that was much too familiar.

At dinner that night, Khulu launched into the tale. 'Nurses – not all of them are without hearts – a few still have hearts, and I was very fortunate today; my ancestors walked alongside me today! Didn't I get into a fight with one of these educated but misbehaved and undisciplined ones? People with certificates and no manners! Nurse, she calls herself. Yhoo! I am sorry for anyone who dies and has that one caring for her.'

'Why? What did she do?' That was Themba.

'Ungaphoswa nalizulu ufel' ezandleni zentw' efana naleya ukuba krwada! Dying in the hands of such a rude one, you'd surely miss heaven!'

'Ngoba? How so?'

'Awuzukuf' uthukis' uqalekisa kaloku? Aren't you going to die swearing and cursing? You should have heard this one's mouth!'

Then Khulu acted a scene she'd witnessed umpteen times. Her facial expression, devoid of any trace of openness, to say nothing of friendliness, neck stiffly thrown back as though confined by an ill-starched shirt collar, the shoulders slightly unbalanced like those of someone carrying a heavy load, through curled lips, in a shrill voice, she screeched: 'Tshetshani! Yiza, yiza, yiza! Anizanga kufudumez' iimpundu zenu ezinukayo apha nilale! Hurry! Come, come, come! This is no place to plonk your stinking arses and go to sleep!'

No one gulped, for the scene Khulu described was far from

unusual. But to everyone's surprise, she broke into loud laughter. Then seeing the consternation in their eyes, she told the family: 'You should've seen what happened at the clinic today. I doubt the nurse who made such insults will be in a hurry to repeat the performance.'

'What happened?' several voices asked at once.

Khulu pointed to Mandla, 'Ask her.'

Mandla shook her head and strolled to the door. 'Nomabali! Story teller!' She laughed and said, 'You tell them. I have homework to do.' Still chuckling, she closed the door softly behind her and left.

Khulu then told the others how, as they were leaving, they saw a mother bringing in a sickly-looking child, sores all over: 'They were on the head, face, legs ... just about all over,' she said, her hands patting her body in description.

'Ag, tog!' Luvo said.

'Well,' said Khulu, 'you should've heard the greeting they got from the nurse, the one writing down the names of the people as they arrived.' Khulu changed her voice, mimicking this nurse: 'Hey, you! Take this thing of yours outside! Do you think we're wild dogs that eat turds? You must wash yourselves before coming here. You stink!'

Voice hushed in befuddlement, 'What is the matter with our people?' Lily asked.

'And that is a nurse?' Themba shook his head in disgust.

Apparently, the child had burst out crying at which point, Mandla rushed over to her, saying, 'Don't cry, baby!' She looked at the nurse and told her: 'You are very unkind!'

'She said tha-at?' Lily screamed. 'Good for her!'

'Mandla gave that child the apple and banana pack she had in her bag,' Khulu said. 'The poor thing did look hungry and starved.'

But that was not the end of the story. The other patients, seeing Mandla's act of kindness, were goaded into action. A rumble began: 'We stomach too much from these rude, so-called educated people!' And, 'Uyinesi, intw' ayiyo apha! She's a nurse here!' Most telling of all, 'Ufanele ukusinceda kodwa mjong' indlel' abadlakazisa ngayo abantu! She's here to serve us, but look how she mistreats the people!'

The noise rose to such a level that security called the manager. 'That lady must either have suspected or heard complaints about the nurse before,' Khulu said.

'Why do you say that?' Busi asked.

'She was told to take the rest of the day off … And I tell you, everybody there shouted, "Asimfuni! We don't want her here! Makangabuyi! Let her not return."'

'Good for them,' Themba said. 'More and more people should speak up when they see something untoward, unfair, happening.'

'Not always wise!' Luvo said. And sadly, none of those present could gainsay that at all.

Kwanele has no mountains
Not even hills or dunes does it boast.
Mind you, if it did,
Would anyone be mad enough

There to take herself before dawn?
Who knows what or who would welcome her into that space?
That is, if she ever made it that far
Did not get accosted on her way
Brutalised within sight of the house she'd just left
The house she calls home.
The tactics changed of necessity, they changed
So did the prayer spots
But the times are without variance
Pre-dawn; midday; long after supper,
When the rest of the homestead sleeps.

all through the night, she sings to me
cracks jokes with me
tickles me
whispers the secrets of her heart to me
little knowing I know all these already
little knowing I send her the words
she returns to me
believing she gifts me
bright and new
the gift she gives me is
the gift she gives my family:
Khulu is the veritable Mountain
the family of the human race entire
obedience to the law of ubuntu:
Umntu ngumntu ngabantu.

The voices were becoming more and more insistent; more frequent and louder in their exhortations, demanding to be heard.

◇◇◇

One Sunday afternoon, Lily and Luvo had visitors. Phyllis was also home. Busi and Mandla were in the backyard, mother plaiting her daughter's hair. Next thing, Busi rushed into the living room and shouted without ceremony: 'Khulu! Khulu, yiza! Come!'

The panic in her voice made everybody there jump. With Lily leading the frenzied group, they all trooped to the backyard.

And there was Mandla prone on the bare ground, half her hair in plaits, half in uncombed tufts of disarray.

'Zis' umqamelo,' Khulu said at once, 'Bring a pillow.' Her voice was calm and that staunched panic all around. However, the others stood and watched goggle-eyed.

The still figure on the ground did not stir. Eyes gently closed, face in calm repose; only deep intakes and outtakes of breath detectable by the heaving breast.

Following Khulu's lead, one by one, the others stationed themselves fittingly – men squatting while all the women righted their doeks and straightened shawls on shoulders, and sedately sat themselves down on the izicamba-covered ground, legs before them or to the side, all covered to show as little of leg as possible ... a wee bit of ankle and never any glimpse of the calf.

They all waited. And waited ... until, in a matter of a few minutes – although to the waiting people it felt like hours – the body on the ground stirred. The neck, the head moved slightly, this way and that, left to right and back again, not unlike the small movements of uphunguphungu, a beetle, in a child's hand out on the veld, showing her the way home.

Suddenly, out thundered a warning:

Lafa ilizwe, lafa! Hini na engaka indyikityha, hini na!
Zange labonwa elingaka isikizi; zange emhlabeni uphela.
Umntu akasamnakani ngani na umntu?
Indalo iyikhanyela njani na indalo iyinxalenye yayo nje?
Lafa laphela ihlabathi!

Death of the world! Woe, the magnitude, woe!
Impending doom of magnitude never seen before on earth entire.
How does humanity deny humanity?
How does nature deny nature, part and parcel of her very being?
Death of the world entire!

When the girl grew silent once again, with her breathing returning to more or less normal, Khulu instructed everyone to return inside. She waited for Mandla's return, for she knew the girl would come back a little disoriented, seeming confused. She would need rest to gain full restoration.

It was Mandla's uncle Owam who first noticed that these episodes seemed to coincide with the presence of visitors. A few days after this incidence of Mandla's being taken, he remarked on it over dinner. 'I've been thinking,' he said. 'Mandla is never stolen when she is alone or—'

'But how do you know that?' Themba asked. 'Are you with her

when she is alone?'

Everyone laughed at the banter.

'Seriously,' Owam continued when the laughter subsided, 'It is only when there are others ... visitors and not just family that it happens ...' He stopped because he realised he was not absolutely sure of what he was saying.

Lily freed him. 'Maybe what she has to say needs to be heard by more people than just her family.' Then she asked around the table, 'Have you thought of that?'

Busi was meanwhile becoming not a little alarmed about her daughter's out-of-body experiences. First, their frequency concerned her. Yes, she had not yet been stolen while at school; but who was to say it would never happen? And yes, she had mentioned something to Ms Pearl, Mandla's class teacher. But what she'd told the teacher was sufficiently vague so as not to earn her child a negative label. She'd told her Mandla suffered occasional fainting spells and sometimes 'talked' during them. She wondered what the church would say about all this: demon possession, a psychiatric symptom, ancestor worship? The last – bad in the eyes of the church – was nevertheless, in her mother's heart, the best of the lot.

CHAPTER TWENTY

Thirteen-year-old Mandlakazi was in Grade Seven, a serious gardener, and a serious scholar. During the mid-year school holidays, she had announced she wanted no new clothes for her birthday or 'other silly stuff like that,' ending: 'I'm too old for that kind of thing.'

Themba, now in a post-doctoral internship, asked, 'So what do you want?'

'Are you buying it for me?'

The whole household burst out laughing. Themba was famous for tight-fistedness. Good-hearted, he just didn't find it easy to part with anything, especially cash. Little did her family know the announcement Mandlakazi had just made was the beginning of a campaign. The girl was on the move, and life, as they had known it, was about to do a total reversal; surely, if slowly. Not just their little life as a family, but life eMzansi!

The fruit is always in the seed.

By September, excitement was tangible not only in Kwanele, but also in Bishopscourt. Since her Gracie had returned from what Mrs Bird called her self-imposed exile in what she called 'the sticks', the two had taken up the friendship where they had left off. Every other Tuesday, they either had lunch or tea or went to see a movie. Mrs B's long-ago brush with cancer had left her determined to celebrate life each day – her continuing good health also meant she could resist her daughters' pleas that she emigrate. Now, with Mandlakazi's transition into high school approaching, the mlungu woman had a new idea.

'Gracie,' she said over coffee this particular Tuesday. 'AP Couture has a sale and I want to give your favourite granddaughter a present for graduation.' Both forgot that Mandlakazi was in fact Khulu's great-granddaughter, not granddaughter. But then, who minded that little slip of memory?

Needless to say, the news was received back in Kwanele with screeches of joy. Mandlakazi, somewhat of a tomboy, was nevertheless getting into the spirit of the thing, and so was not displeased at the unexpected and generous offer. The sheer excitement all around her was catching.

This was when Khulu voiced what had been on her mind for the longest while: rites of passage for Mandlakazi.

On this matter, the entire family, except for one, stood solidly against Khulu. The exception? Strangest fact of all ... Busisiwe, Mandlakazi's mother herself, was not only on Khulu's side but adamantly in favour of the girl's ukuthomba. She knew, remembered, she'd been against it for herself; and she had always regretted not having done it. She didn't voice what she felt strongly in her heart of hearts: had she had the ceremony – thombad – not only might there have been no baby, but Mandla's life, her health, would have been very different. Of that one fact, Busi was quite, quite certain.

So, after they had argued the matter to death, a compromise

was eventually reached. Mandlakazi would thomba the following year. Enough excitement was hers this year without adding to it. Let the girl graduate and start high school, and only then think of this exercise that Khulu and Busi insisted on. Khulu wondered what would be wrong with the girl starting high school already having had the ceremony, armed with an extra ancestral blessing. However, she was happy enough there was agreement on the event – it would take place.

Although the event was nearly a year away, Khulu realised that was just about enough time to set it up. She conceded that ukuthomba of a young woman was a mammoth undertaking. It involved more than just the chief initiate and her cohorts. There was the woman who would 'nurse' or mother them through the process: inkazana. This role was not given randomly to anyone. A woman of unblemished character, a strong role model, needed to be sought and found. Then there was no guarantee that once found, she would be available and willing to undertake the duty.

The whole thing was also costly in these days where everything was for sale, including services such as these. In the olden days, the woman would have felt singularly honoured to be asked, and, in turn, the families of the initiates would gift her with a cow or horse or bags of mealies, depending on what they had; barter would be accepted as tender – good all round, good for all. No money in those days. Money came with the white man. Yes, Ntsikane's 'button without a hole' came with the white man, and as Ntsikane had foretold, it now ruled their lives. Money! Khulu thought to herself. Well, she should go ahead and prepare for this event. It was probably the last thing she would be able to do for Mandlakazi.

Nobody lived forever, and, as it was, she had almost done exactly that. Where were all her agemates? Except for MaBird, all gone. Meanwhile, this year was drawing to a close; schools would soon be on holiday. So, just as well, she conceded, to leave it for the following year.

The phone rang just as Lulama Kodwa locked her desk, bag already over her shoulder. 'Aarrgh!' she groaned, forced herself to peek at the caller ID. Yho! Better take this one. And she'd better forget she'd been busy getting annoyed a mere second before. Why, that outburst from her lungs was just a way of clearing her throat. What did she have to be annoyed about? Unlike thousands – no, millions in this country – she had a job. So that was what that sound was; and she had a right to clear her throat, didn't she? No good answering the phone with a sleepy voice that said you were already peeling back the blankets on your bed, sleep beckoning.

'Good afternoon, Sir!' She hoped she sounded cheery enough, but not excessively so. The big boss got right to the point; no banter or personal queries, she obviously wasn't what he was after. Despite the reputation that clung to him like feathers to a bird, she had always found him above board ... as far as that sort of thing was concerned. But he was one hell of a slave driver. And he forgot some of his underlings had other responsibilities besides being his grateful workers. Some, like her, were even single parents.

'This event for the disabled; the one our colleagues in Social

Development have arranged with those international funders ...' His words broke into her grumpy thoughts.

'Yes, Sir!' *What about it and why are you bringing that up now?* she screamed silently. *The blooming thing was planned nearly a year ago!* Her children-to-feed mouth asked, calm as can be: 'Are you thinking we should participate?' *Well, about time, too! After all, we are the department for people with disabilities ...*

'Are you a mind reader now?'

They both laughed politely. Theirs was not the gut-deep laughter of friends, but a half-cough, half-query neither could misread as anything but collegial exchange.

Ten full minutes later, not only had she put down her handbag, poured herself back into her seat; she had unlocked the desk and switched on the desktop computer. She'd had to call the babysitter too and make arrangements for a late knock-off time.

Lulama strode to the kitchen corner of her office, made a quick cup of tea, took that back to her desk, and started a list: prospects to invite to the celebrations. Then the list birthed another, and yet another; clients, differently-abled people ... She must ask for more details: who did her boss have in mind? Those with a specific disability, any other specific category? With the differently-abled, as with any group, one had to be careful not to exclude anyone.

And it didn't end there, oh no! On top of the list of prospective invitees, she knew she would have to include service providers of different kinds: caterers; transporters; safety officials; entertainers; motivational speakers – at least one. She made a mental note to find one eager enough to waive payment or accept a token of appreciation, some gift such as a set of pens, a mug, or a blanket

... department-branded, of course. The storeroom was absolutely clogged with the stuff.

The next morning, as soon as she'd put on the lights and hung up her jacket, Lulama Kodwa rang Ms Ndonga in Khayelitsha, one of the more enterprising and energetic social workers she knew.

Nomzi Ndonga picked up on the second ring and heard out Lulu's string of requests. All business, 'How many would you want?' she asked, adding, 'Boys or girls or both?'

Right after Lulama's call transferring some of her load, the social worker made an appointment with the matron who had run the day hospital for those with disabilities since its opening twenty years ago. Upon hearing who had made the request for participation, Matron was at first not keen to get involved: 'If they used the money they squander on themselves on providing essential services to the poor, we might have less ills besetting us.'

However, when Ms Ndonga told her the whole thing was tied to the UNMDG – the United Nations Millennium Development Goals, specifically for Peoples Living with Disabilities – she thawed somewhat. It was a whole hour and a half later that the social worker eventually left the matron's office. Matron was not only now on board, she was bubbling with enthusiasm. Sure enough, she called before the end of that day to ask for the names of candidates they would send to the affair. 'Remember,' she said when the other told her she was still working on the list, 'only those under eighteen!'

'Yes, Ma'am,' Ms Ndonga responded. Fancy that! Matron reminding her of something she had first heard from her. Time the old gizzard took her pension!

Much later, as she went through her files and made lists, she suddenly thought of that case she was handling, of the exceptional young girl. *Why not?* She called Busisiwe, the mother of the one who was so full of beans. Busi was keen on the idea, but, buying herself a bit of time, said she would get back to the social worker.

'Can you make that soon, please?'

'Will do!'

'Tomorrow?'

'Sure.'

Once Busi had thought the matter over, she shed her reservations. Then she remembered the gumboot dance that she had witnessed all those years ago. How would Mandlakazi participate in something of that nature? Would she manage? *Well, she might not be able to dance specific steps, but perhaps she could play the drums or hand rattles.*

But she wouldn't tell the child about these plans right away, not in the midst of exams. Fine once she was done with all that – not that there was any extra preparation she needed to do; from what her teachers had been telling them, she was well equipped.

The very next day, as she'd promised, Busi called the social worker back. Ms Ndonga was delighted to hear that Mandlakazi would attend camp. Then and there, the name Mandlakazi Mkhonto was added to the list.

◇◇◇

Meanwhile, as always, plans for Christmas were afoot. However, this year, what dominated were preparations for Mandlakazi's going to high school.

And as a backdrop to all this activity was the ever-present violence, prevalent as air, almost. Every news bulletin seemed to contain not one but several items of robbery, rape, murder ... heinous crimes that included those frightening cases where the victim knew the perpetrator. Mothers held their babies closer, children were not permitted to play outside the house, not even in the yards, unless supervised.

Uphill all the way. Terrible
The violence to the weak, even loved ones.
While yet another toothless campaign runs:
Sixteen Days of Activism against Gender-Based Violence
Sixteen days of pretending to care, to change.

You will be invited to take part in a special event.
Some might dissuade you from going;
Go!
Your time has come!

Yes, we know
You have not been idle all along
You have used your time well

Well done! Well done!
But not one of us would have expected less of you.

Finally, Mandlakazi was done with examinations, her last at primary school. She celebrated the event by giving away all the clothes she now considered 'little girlie stuff'. The girl now favoured solid colours – especially blues – from palest sky-blue to navy. Frilly dresses and blouses were out; she was into pants in a big way.

The next day, the last day of the school year, Mandla expected no more than the examinations report. But when she got home, she got much more than praise for her glowing report. Yes, she got the praise, her due. But with it came unexpected, startling news. Busi could hardly contain her excitement as she relayed the news of Mandla's invitation to camp.

'Rather sudden, isn't it?' Lily asked.

Busi explained that she had withheld the information, fearing it might be a distraction during the girl's final exams.

Khulu huffed, 'And you thought not to tell the rest of us?'

'Well ...' Busi stopped, stumped.

Lily wanted to know where and when the camp would be held: 'And for how long?'

Busi explained that Mandla would be part of an especially chosen group of young people to go on a two-week camp.

This led to a babble of protest. All the grown-ups were dead set against Mandla attending. How would she manage? She had never even been to a sleepover party.

'But the camp is for people my age!' Mandlakazi raised her voice enough to get everyone's attention. That achieved, she added, '... who live with one or another disability!'

Silence. Eyes out of their sockets. Busi tried to guess how Mandla could possibly know this when she had not mentioned the details to anyone.

Meanwhile Phyllis piped up, asking what the child would need to take for all that time, and who would pay for it.

'Oh,' replied Busi, 'I'm sure adequate preparations have been made.' The social worker had assured her the children would be properly equipped.

Silence again. Mandla saw the silence for what it was: a veto against her going to camp. 'Oh,' she said into the silence: 'I want to go and I am going!'

Khulu was the first to relent. This was proof positive that she had achieved her goal: making the child independent and self-assured. She had succeeded, so why was she reluctant to let go?

'Of course you are going,' Khulu said, beaming, and everyone relaxed while she told herself: *That will be a feather in my cap.* She didn't say it out loud: bragging was unbecoming, especially in an old woman. The truth was, Mandlakazi had virtually taken over her own care. She administered her own medication when it was necessary. She woke up and meditated, did her stretches. Daily, she wrote herself affirmations. She was on the ball, alert to and hands-on with her health issues. Which, thank God, were well-nigh non-existent.

The next day, Busi confirmed that as far as the camp was concerned, all was arranged. Buses would wait for the attendees at their schools on Sunday, after lunch; but each attender would be picked up by car, details of which would be sent to the child's family beforehand for verification purposes. All stuff and staff would already be at the camp site.

It was a relief to Mandlakazi's family that the instructions to those attending were to bring only their toiletries and medication, sleepwear, and a change of clothing. During the entire two weeks, they would be wearing gym gear, which the department was providing – three sets per participant! And they were particularly happy to note the precautions taken, such as transport verification; pick-up and drop-off times as well as the names and contact details of not one but two people in case of emergency. This reassured them that Mandla would be in good hands.

What they didn't and couldn't know was that the other participants would be in even better hands. Mandlakazi had been doing her own preparation; using her powers to link up those attending; for example, matching hearing-impaired with sight-impaired. Those who used wheelchairs were matched with fully mobile but differently impaired individuals. She had designed it for the benefit of each and all through co-operation and mutual assistance. Not that the organisers knew they were being directed …

Early Saturday, long before eyelids parted company
greeting the new day
I was summoned eNkundla
the last time before
I went out into the world
to do the work
for which I had regressed
once more into a flesh-being
there I saw the ones who like me
had been refashioned
by their mothers to be other

than what the Most Powerful
had planned
as I had been
by my mother
Busi-Honey
in her womb.

What have we not gone through, my mother and I?
It has been a long and winding road
we have come
here and there
straight as the bridge on your nose
at other places
hilly like a mountain range
and curved as serf's busy sickle
and it is a road that has no end.

CHAPTER TWENTY-ONE

Mandlakazi kicked off her plan on World Disabled Day. As each participant boarded their bus, they were given a package and a ticket with their seat number. Mandlazi took hers, hauled herself up into the vehicle, and stopped. She'd been smacked breathless by a stench of perfume so strong the culprit must have bathed in the stuff instead of the usual delicate dab here and there of those to the manner born. Shaking her head, she identified the source: a girl in one of the front seats of the bus reserved for wheelchair users. Pretty, if one took the trouble to look beyond the heavy mask of make-up. Mandla shook herself, walked on and found the seat allocated to her. Immediately and without emptying the bag onto the seat or floor of the bus (evidence lay strewn all about the bus), she investigated the bag's contents. The programme she pulled out looked professional, with activities galore: swimming; racing, including wheelchair racing; card games and chess; spelling bees, poetry and prose writing exercises; cooking classes; drawing and painting; sculpting small figures or making pots; photography and more. They would be spoilt for choice.

Meanwhile, great was the excitement in the bus, non-stop the chattering. From the back of the bus, a voice shouted: 'D'you all know we are going to a wine farm?' At that, a riot broke out, everyone cheering, stamping feet, whistling and clapping.

The same voice broke out in rap: 'We gonna wine; we gonna dine; we gonna do everything bad bad bad!'

Within two shakes of a lamb's tail, half the bus had joined her, each contributing to the din.

Mandlakazi surveyed her fellow passengers. If only they knew, she thought. Yes, the fruit farm and resort to which they were heading also had a winery. However, it was its campsite they were visiting, and, given their circumstances, the last thing the organisers would give them was wine.

Of course, Mandla already knew who the rapping girl was: her name was Jacquie, and she was a bit of a bully. But she had plans for Jacquie. She had already prepared each chosen soul so they would be receptive. Indeed, they would 'drive' the initiative, little knowing that the seed was already planted in them. The best way to proceed was to make each hunger for what needed to be done. However, seeing them in real time, Mandla had to admit it was fun to see kids being kids in spite of the labels with which society saw fit to burden them. So, a kid herself, she joined in, sang along, one with the rest of them. But she was troubled by that girl at the front of the bus. Boniswa was her name. Pity she reeked of vanity. Poor thing, what demons was she trying to wash away?

But then who here was perfect? Indeed, who in the whole flesh-world was perfect? Heavy, indeed, was the burden of being human. It was no walk in the park. Mandla reminded herself hers was to awaken each to the prospects they already had. None were without some gift, talent, to be put to use. And, right now, there was urgent business to which she should and must attend. Wine farm, indeed!

In a mental flash, into Boniswa's mind she went. The girl frowned, took a deep, deep breath, and let out a screech that would make a hadeda weep with envy. Hadee-dah!

The shock stole sound. In the startled silence, all eyes turned to the originator of the racket and her tiny frame. Where the hell had that ear-splitting sound emanated from, the eyes asked.

From the girl's mouth emerged the sweetest, musical tones ... but the words, oh the words, were far from sweet: 'Don't be in such a hurry to be assholes!' A steely eye swept through the bus, the girl's neck revolving as though some invisible machine controlled her.

'What the f—' a voice shouted, but was cut short by the girl who seemed to believe she was in charge.

'Assholes!' Boniswa hissed, seeming to grow taller while still seated. Something in her manner, the look she gave, radiated from every inch of her body, like vapour out a slow-cooking pot in a semi-lit room. Then she spat out: 'You already are! Don't you see that?' Her voice rose as she barked out, 'You all were born assholes.'

Now Mandla turned the tables. Enough was enough. Yes, she had had a tough life, but then none in that bus came from an elite private school or had Bill and Melinda Gates for parents. Fury sprang to life and scattered all over the bus as others put a stop to Boniswa's outburst.

'Hey, get off of yourself!'

'Who d'you think you are?'

'Go home, wherever that may be!'

'Must be a broken cardboard box from the sound of what comes out of it!'

For reasons they didn't know, didn't feel they needed to know, the passengers found this last remark very funny – as one, the bus broke into rapturous laughter. Then, like magic, the atmosphere changed. Another screech, but this one a happy one, an inviting one, turned heads.

'Yhoo! Akusekuhle apha! Wow, is it not beautiful here?' an unidentifiable voice was heard to say, and the sincerity of the remark put paid to the rancour that had been brewing. All eyes turned to the windows, and those not seated to advantage craned necks and pushed against those who were.

Someone else remarked in admiration: 'Izindlu zamaplanga!'

'Kodwa jonga indlela ezintle ngayo! But look how beautiful these ones are!'

'Kutheni ezamatyotyombe zingabi nje? Why are the mjondolo ones unlike these?'

'He-e, kakade, kutheni? Good question, really, why?'

Mandla was happy the group was now distracted. And, indeed, the beauty all around them was breathtaking. Over the wide sweep of road, tall and leafy trees on both sides with over-arching branches, their tops touching and kissing up there, their moving split marking the unmarked midway point of the road as efficiently as any formal road sign, the boring white line, trademark of tarred roads the world over. Your side: my side! This natural divider of daylight time instinctively reinforced the natural respect for one another inherent in all humanity. Indeed, inherent in all nature.

Why, the very almost but not quite touching-ness of the branches up there was proof thereof. Animals and plants in the ground observed the same law: my right to exist is a function of your right to exist. And thus was co-existence ensured.

Yes, the leafy trees spelled such splendour that the passengers on the bus were silenced as each drank it in. A little distance away from the roadsides, fruit trees boasted their own splendour. This started a guessing game, as the young people tried to identify what they could of the varying vegetation they passed. More often than not, they had no clue what it was they saw. Many had no idea of what unboxed fruit or the parent trees looked like. Their only encounters with oranges and apples had come via monetary exchange. Some would not even have been able to identify an apple tree were those not at that time heavily laden with the fruit – apple-picking season.

Softly, slightly, the sweet scent of growing things entered the bus. Without knowing that they did so, the young people deepened breath intakes, pushed out chests, and expanded lungs. Their eyes softened as the goodness of effervescent new life sank into their bodies. The long road went winding on and on and on. However, there was so much to see, not one of the young people complained that the trip was interminable. Not one voiced boredom or complained of fatigue.

At last, the buses turned off the public road and, as they did so, the speed slackened. This part of the trip gave the visitors a chance to admire what the farm offered.

Even the road leading to the farm snaked and twisted, dipped and rose, showing the visitors spectacular vistas.

Finally, they reached the farm. Right at the gate, a huge slate-grey board with bold cursive letters proclaimed: HEAVEN'S BEST!

Wine and fruit country in the Western Cape: among the best boasts of the region, and Heaven's Best was as good a representative of the ilk as any. The undulating grounds were a marvel, the lush vegetation a sight to drink in at all times of the year. At that moment, the height of summer, every fruit tree was laden and the air heavy with scent: apples, pears, grapes, quinces, pomegranates, apricots, peaches .... The heaviness of the trees was testimony to the good rains the region had enjoyed that year. Indeed, so plentiful was the crop, here and there an overburdened bough threatened to break off its parent trunk. Berry bushes, too, were festooned with bright sparks of colour – green, gold, blue, purple and red. They spotted people picking, children and toddlers too, copying their parents and older siblings.

A little way past the entrance gate, the road dipped. The farm lay in a valley through which ran a river, and the buses came to a stop midway between the gate and the main building in which the offices were housed. Farm staff members, two to a bus, welcomed the young people and gave out bags inside which were T-shirts in four colours – red, blue, green and orange; notebooks; pens; and a diary or book of gratitude.

As they scrambled down from the buses or helped off them, bottles and tumblers waited on long tables – water and an array of cool drinks, all in biodegradable containers. Smiling staff and officials were standing by, cheering the group: *Welcome! Namkelekile! Welkom!* In all three languages of the Western Cape, they bid them welcome. 'Help yourself to a drink and find a seat.'

The young people all saw and understood they had stepped into a different realm, another world, a dazzling one, stretching as far as the eye could see. Their oohs and aahs said it all.

Orientation was swift and brief. They were told to enjoy the goodies they'd find in their welcome bags. However, of special note was the book of gratitude. In that book, they were urged to write down their daily experiences at the end of each day. The last page was for them to write a summary of the whole experience and vote for the person in their group who would represent them as their speaker at the farewell dinner – their last gathering. They were to tear that page down the dotted line and hand it in the day before the final day of camp.

The item that took their breath away, however, was the list of what was on offer. Heaven's Best boasted an array of amenities and activities for campers: cycling, swimming, rafting, boating, crafting, rock-climbing, zip lining. There were horse and pony rides, the opportunity to take a train ride through the estate, a running track, and for those more inclined to walk, paths that meandered through the vales and hills of the estate, with fully provisioned rest stops along the way. There was something to appeal to everyone. It was blatantly clear the only limitations here would be one's own.

There were nevertheless guides and guards all over the place; and no activity would go on without requisite supervision.

During the Q&A session, when Boniswa seemed bent on having her own meeting, Mandlakazi noted that the girl was an egoist – pushy and apparently incapable of empathy. Then she remembered. When she'd done a quick survey of who would be at the camp with her, of all the other young people, Boniswa's situation had touched her most. Poor child! Yes, her mother worked in Parliament but, dear oh dear, what a job. Not an easy thing servicing grouches who were more often than not egocentric bullies with such low self-esteem they needed punching bags as others needed air. Boniswa's mother was one of the favoured punching bags. After Boniswa's father died in a hail of bullets, a *senji* or hijacking gone south of south, she'd gone and had herself a hysterectomy. She had realised the only job she was qualified for was using what her Mama gave her – au naturel, *indalo*! What she had not known was that abuse was a huge part of the service for which she was signing up. Boniswa suffered the spill-over.

Roll call followed, accompanied by the camp aides leading those whose names had been called to their allocated rooms, where they were to rest until just before dinner time. *Well,* Mandla thought, *who ever heard of teenagers resting before midnight?* But she made her way to her room where, she knew, she would be unlikely to get any rest.

Mandlakazi did not hurry, content to observe the others scrambling. She was near the rear of the procession up the ramp and into her dormitory building, everyone rushing, eager to see their sleeping quarters. As she neared her room, raised voices let her know there was trouble ahead. Surprise!

She knocked to announce her arrival, but didn't wait for an answer; no one could have heard the knock above the noise they were making. So she just thrust the door open and stopped there as though to survey the scene. The squabbling went on regardless.

Mandla coughed, making sure hers was a raucous, gruff cough. And that old-man cough did the trick. The last thing her room-mates expected or wanted was the appearance of an old fogey, and her cough had made them expect just such a one. Silence fell.

'Oh,' said Jacquie, the rapper from the bus: 'And who are you?'

'The name's Mandlakazi.' She turned her attention to a slight girl who stood indecisively near her bag, her hand on it as though she were of mind to drag it out and head back home. Inclining her head towards her, Mandlakazi asked, 'And you are?'

At once, the girl's demeanour changed. She thrust her chest out, straightened herself, opened her eyes a little wider. 'Glenda.' And as though she doubted Mandla had heard what she'd just said, or felt she'd been a bit abrupt, 'My name is Glenda,' she clarified, 'Glenda Booi.'

As she spoke, Mandla sensed and saw threatening tears – held back, but she knew those tears were there.

'Booi, die boere borgeltjie!' quipped Jacquie. The fourth girl sharing the room, who hadn't said a word or stirred since Mandla's arrival, closed her eyes as though she didn't wish to see what happened next; as though the confrontation she saw brewing was too much for her.

In a far from soft voice, Mandla demanded, 'Take that back! No one treats any friend of mine like that.'

Inclining her head in a show of exaggerated shock, Jacquie asked, 'Since when is *she* your friend?'

'Are you calling me a liar?'

Something about Mandla's self-assuredness alarmed Jacquie. Growing up, she had been mocked for her sideways sidle and her dragging leg, so she had responded by doling out insults. But like many bullies, she wasn't any good at an even-handed battle. If truth be told, she was a bit of a scaredy cat, even if she liked making fun of others. Now, she turned down her lips, sucked in her breath: 'I never said you were a liar.'

The fight, it turned out, was over who was to sleep where. Glenda was hesitant to climb to the top bunk, but scared to be alone at ground-floor level. What if someone came in at night? She would be Target #1!

'I'll take the other floor-level bed,' Mandla said. 'I like being grounded myself.' All laughed at the joke, even the quiet girl.

To clear the air, Mandla started the beautiful hymn: 'Lizalis' idinga lakho, Thixo Nkosi yenyaniso!' One by one, the others joined in, starting with Glenda, who had a beautiful soprano voice; Mandla sang alto. The third to join in was the quiet one. As she did so, she beckoned to Jacquie, inviting her to join the fun. With a nervous laugh, she did.

Between verses, the silent one spoke: 'By the way, my name is Nikiwe; Niki, for short.'

'Hi, Niki,' the other three said at once. It sounded as something they had rehearsed even though, to the attentive ear, Jacquie's voice sounded a little off key as that of someone who had not attended rehearsal as regularly as the others. Niki looked quite astonished at the feat she'd accomplished. She had spoken when no one had asked her; she had given her name. Could it be she wasn't a mouse after all?

When the bell summoned them back to base, the promised hour of rest had been chopped down to a few minutes, but the weather in the room had cleared magnificently. Mandla stretched out her hands, 'Shall we sing, going down?' One hand held Jacquie's, the other, Glenda's, whose other held Niki's. The four went down to the dining-room hand-in-hand, singing:

> Lizalis' idinga lakho,
> Thixo Nkosi yenyaniso
> Zonk' iintlanga, zonk' izizwe,
> Mazizuze usindiso.

Dinner was preceded by a pep talk, which was important only because of who delivered it: Dr Nomaza Vimba, the Deputy Minister of Women, Children and People with Disabilities. She welcomed them, and said she was very happy they had come to the camp, and that they would not regret it. She ran down the daily schedule of events, which each camper had already seen. Then she gave a self-conscious laugh and said, 'Happy camping! Although I wouldn't call sleeping in such a posh place camping!' She hoped they would not cause any damage to the property. 'Show the owners you are grateful for their donation to the department. Who knows, they might give it to us again.' That was it. She couldn't stay for dinner. A cancelled flight. Her child on it. She had to rush to the airport to collect him. She was very apologetic: 'But I do hope we'll be seeing one another again soon!' With a cheery wave, she was gone, leaving Ms Lulama Kodwa, who had accompanied her from the department, high and dry.

Mandlakazi wondered why the deputy minister had bothered to spin that yarn. A bad conscience? And it was not the first time, nor would it be the last that she pursued her own agenda instead of doing her job. Why had she bothered coming at all? She clearly didn't care about the issues her department supposedly existed to address.

Internally, Mandla answered her own question: *The job is a good front for what she makes via amaqithiqithi – perks – and putting spanners in the works. Each job necessitates 'calls for tenders', but the winner knows which palms to oil, or they may never win another tender again. And the tenderpreneurs 'get a cut'. But as far as this woman is concerned, she gets herself the whole body of the animal. 'Cuts' go to the smallanyana ones. She is definitely not one of those. Not bad. Not bad at all for a woman who barely scraped the few exams she sat and didn't graduate ... although that's her secret. Worth the five grand she paid for those certificates, though. She got the job, didn't she? Absolutely worth it. That's government for you!*

Dinner, as all the meals the group would share, was simple but nutritious and savoury. The best was the expedited manner of its service. The line moved swiftly. At one end, one got a number, marched on and gave that number when ordering. High on the wall behind the servers, the options were written on blackboards, the choices plain and simple: chicken curry; vegetarian curry; fish and chips; samp and lamb potjie; and for dessert, fruit salad and ice cream.

Mandla chose the veggie dish and took her seat, also bearing the same number, and within minutes, a server brought her meal. The arrangement made for ease of service and made the whole exercise run without hitches. But it was also carefully calculated to facilitate mingling among the young people; none sat with their room-mates, and, Mandla noticed, the general spread favoured de-lumping skin colour, language entities or sub-groups. It seemed that people came from a wide range of regions and cultures, and their physical and mental challenges were wide-ranging as well. Present were wheelchair users, those with crutches or braces, some visually or hearing-impaired. Some were palsied, some struggled with speech, and some had no visible physical disability, but their eyes spoke of internal limitations.

None of this seemed to affect the general buzz of young people gathered within the confines of one room, even one as large as the one where they were dining. Even the sign-language interpreters added to the busyness, their hands flying.

Mandla had already surmised that the best time to get in with this group would be either while they slept, or during the regular pow-wows – formal group meetings. The first would be easier, but the second more targeted, as it caught the subject in action; red-handed, as it were. When people shared of themselves in word or action, they were at their most receptive. The Old noticed how this was true even when people were being deceptive, or plain lying.

At the first pow-wow the next evening, the participants were asked to sit in their room groups. Next, they were given a short questionnaire that elicited their first impression of their room-mates and whether or not, within the short passage of time spent together, they had revised their initial impressions. They had to give reasons and explain their responses.

Those in Mandla's group looked distinctly apprehensive and hesitant. So when their turn came, she chose to speak first: 'I was last to arrive in my room,' she said, and saw Jacquie's head drop.

She continued: 'There was already an argument when I got there.' All eyes popped, including those of her room-mates. 'I felt right at home, and soon we were all laughing at how silly we were.'

Eyes sparkling, she turned to the other three: Niki, Jacquie and Glenda, and asked, 'Right?'

All three nodded. And – 'Yup!' said the silent one. That was a surprise: Niki had spoken, and without any prodding.

When the camp directors said each room should chose a 'prefect', Mandla dissuaded Niki from proposing her, Mandla, and convinced her to support hers instead. Jacquie therefore became the foursome's monitor. A puzzled Glenda had nodded her assent only because Mandla had gently squeezed her hand. That one knew what she was doing, surely. To her, Mandla was a hero. It would be okay.

And it was – for several days. However, one day Glenda found herself unable to keep everything in. She went and told one of the directors how she would have preferred Mandla as prefect, and then relayed the whole episode of choosing bunks on the first night of camp, and the ugly language that had been used.

Hearing about that first-night problem, the directors commended Mandlakazi for her show of leadership and compassion. 'That is what we hope this camp teaches you all,' the senior camp director said. Late that night, as staff discussed the day's happenings, again and again Mandla's name cropped up. The organisers voiced their happiness Mandlakazi was part of this cohort – their very first such undertaking.

'Let's hope these kids keep surprising us like that,' said the senior camp director.

Glenda had no idea what she had done, or what had possessed her to do it. But she had just unwittingly volunteered to be the lodestone of Mandla's project. She had not only surprised the directors, she had surprised herself. That was exactly what Mandlakazi wanted: for everyone to surprise all the others but most of all, surprise themselves. That was the spur which would invariably lead to confidence.

The staff cluster responded to the senior camp director's remark with a short outburst of laughter. 'In your dreams!' responded one cynical fellow, while another added, 'Don't forget the one who reeks of perfume!'

'Did she have to come?'

This was Boniswa, and if the staff had a choice, they would have wished her away. Because her mother worked in Parliament, the girl gave herself airs and made uncalled-for, unnecessary demands. All agreed she was a pain in the very heart of the establishment – 'and elsewhere unmentionable!' said the youngest of the crew; they all burst out in laughter.

But Boniswa was undeniably selfish and demanding, believing the world owed her because she had need of a wheelchair. Deeply self-pitying, at every moment of her waking day, she expected those around her to acknowledge her special suffering by paying her undivided attention, providing service with a smile at her first command. Better still, before she even opened her mouth to utter an order. Could they not see she needed this or that? Where was their imagination, their sympathy for those, like her, whom life had so deprived and punished?

Mandlakazi decided her aim was to help the poor girl find

peace of mind. It would be a service not only to her but to those who had occasion to encounter the 'Princess Plaintiff', as the others called her.

By the end of the first week of camp, Mandla's spirit of co-operation, her readiness to include others in whatever was happening, fun and games, discussions, meals, had been noted by many. She had a special gift for pouring oil on any and all troubled waters: an argument, misunderstanding, bullying or – as happened all too frequently for the comfort of the staff – budding love or even romances that were more than a day old and therefore ancient news, or those that existed merely in the fantasies of the afflicted one. Mandlakazi seemed able to quell any fracas, or mediate without taking sides. The organisers liked her very much, and often compared her with Princess Plaintiff, to the disadvantage of the latter.

However, Mandlakazi herself noticed how all the activities were run by able-bodied people. Simply put, the abled benefited from serving the disabled. The girl sprang into action, quietly raising awareness and forming alliances. This, of course, she had anticipated; had come with full knowledge of each participant. Had she not selected them herself? Now she got into their heads, helped them to grasp the import of the moment, of the event, and what they could do with it and get from it. Was that not her brief as one of the Old: to make the ultimate outsider an intimate insider?

Mandla noted what she of course already knew: even here,

among people who daily suffered the experience of being othered, there was othering. The sighted believed they were better than those challenged in that category; the deaf pretended to be free of any affliction; and some of those challenged in mobility cursed their Maker for punishing them even before they were born. In earnest, Mandlakazi set to work. Encounters of any kind resulted in her implanting the idea of belonging. This was followed by one-on-one conversations that looked impromptu, but were anything but.

During their free time, small groups would form voluntarily. In whatever group she found herself, Mandlakazi found a way of steering the talk toward self-appraisal, self-appreciation, motivation, and personal challenge. Her groups quickly turned to miniature pow-wows. Gradually, she built herself a following, something the staff members were quick to notice. 'OUR OWN INGROUP!' These words caught fire and soon became the camp catch-phrase.

Mandla used this mark of approval to build the larger group she envisaged out there in the real world, once they were away from the safety of camp. In everyone she spoke to, she encouraged self-revelation. Find your own strength and then find a fellow who would benefit from association with you and your particular strength; this was her motto. As her great-grandmother had always known, it is in service to others that we truly grow.

Surprisingly, to many of her peers, the idea they could be of help was a novel one. But once it sunk into their hearts and minds, it was singularly liberating. It made them happy in themselves, in who they were. They were not useless! Shy people positively sparkled. Those short of words bubbled. Those who had believed they were slow found they could, with perseverance, sponge up knowledge. For many present, it was a veritable rebirth. In return, each 'reborn' was tasked with gathering others and sharing similar lessons.

These were soon boiled down to the three Rs: Respect for self; Respect for the other, whoever and whatever they might be; Respect for the environment in its complex entirety, for, without it, we would not be here. Our breath is but a tiny part of what we get from the environment, and we should all take better care of it than we're doing at the moment.

Another of Mandla's goals was to ensure the participants grasped the importance of complementarity – teaming up with someone whose ability eased yours, and vice versa. A wheelchair-using person could be a guide to someone visually impaired; someone without mobility challenges could help manouvre a chair, as in the all-too-frequent case of finding a lift with that detested sign: 'out of order'.

Mandla was not after a following, but more of a movement.

Nevertheless, she deliberately sat out the second pow-wow. Oh, she attended; but only listened and observed, delighted to be playing 'plain fleshling'; switching off from who she really was. She also knew the truth of her great-grandfather's wisdom: that the bird who led the flock knew when to fall back, to hand over to another. But there were matters to see to, and her time, she knew perfectly well, was running out. She would soon be home in the land of forever sleep.

The third pow-wow would be their last formal one as a group.

They had been asked to bring up issues arising from the previous two, and any other matters a participant felt were important or interesting for the group.

Mandlakazi stood up and asked: 'Who am I? Why am I? What can I do about the how and what of me?'

One of the camp leaders said, 'You will have to explain those questions, I'm afraid. Also tell us why you feel they are something we should consider here.' Although the lady spoke laughingly, it was clear she was far more irritated than amused.

With astounding calmness in one so young, Mandlakazi did exactly that. 'No one, in our families, talks about us,' she started. 'No one takes responsibility for the way some of us, like me, are — toxins having assaulted our forms even in the womb. Not our mothers, nor our fathers. And not the relatives, the older people who should have guided them,' she said, then stopped. Waited for reaction; and a dam overflowed its banks.

Not all of them had been poisoned in the womb! And, well, God made them that way! 'You cannot blame your mother for your disability,' cried some voices.

But an aide took the floor. He said, 'I don't think this is about blame. But if you never ask questions about your own life, who will? And if you don't, what more important issue do you care about ... what is more important to you than you?'

After several more people had spoken, one staff member asked, in genuine puzzlement, what Mandlakazi's point was.

'A peach tree will never give you an apple,' replied Mandla.

'Wha-aat?' came from the audience.

A mischievous smile lighting up her face, Mandla put up her

hands, palms out, and the room quietened. 'If I don't know the essence of me, what makes me tick, how will I ever get anyone else to? If I don't know my strengths, my weaknesses, my fears, my hopes – how will I ever move toward my goals? Do I even have goals? What goals can I have for someone I do not know ... do not understand? And how will we ever fight for our rights if we don't know what they are ... not in the book, in the Constitution – but in our lives, our hearts, our minds? We will never safeguard what we do not understand. And we will never understand anything and anyone ... until we understand the basics of our own hearts.' Saying that last word, her hand beat against her chest. And she sat down.

Everyone applauded – camp leaders, even the cheerless one who'd laughed at Mandla's opening statement.

During the comfort break just before lunch, everybody trooped to the restrooms. There were plenty of those set aside for those who used wheelchairs. But, of course, Boniswa would not go to those ... beneath her dignity.

She'd got into one cubicle, even though it was a tight squeeze, and took out her vanity case so that she could touch up her lipstick.

However, while she was busy preening, she dropped her bag back down behind the commode. Boniswa tried this way and that way and a lot more ways in her attempt to retrieve the bag. However, even before she made the first move, she knew whatever she tried would be futile. She would not be able to reach. She tried anyway. Tried and tried and tried, growing correspondingly angrier and more upset. In the end, it was when she was beyond furious and just plain horribly tearful that Mandla found her. In seconds, the vanity case was retrieved and handed to its owner. The dejected figure tried to smile, laugh at herself ... but the attempt was no more successful than that of retrieving her bag. Finally, hiccuping, she said, 'Apologies for bothering you—' sniff-sniff. 'But thank you for your help.' Mandla bent over the wheelchair, patted Boniswa on the back, and the two embraced.

'Just goes to show, akakho umntu yedwa ... none of us is complete without the others. We all need others to complete us.'

Boniswa sighed. A clean, unpretentious smile made her pretty face a flower in bloom. They left the building laughing, holding hands.

Nothing lasts forever and, soon enough, it was the day before departure. At breakfast, the campers were reminded to hand in their feedback pages during the lunch break that day. The staff would go through them, and let whoever was the group's choice to address them all on the last day at dinner. That would give them ample time to prepare their speech.

The supervisors were not at all surprised when, upon receipt of the feedback pages, Mandlakazi's name led all the rest. She had been, throughout the camp's duration, an invigorating, hope-giving presence. She was decidedly the favourite among the campers to address the entire group. Each request included the phrase – *she's inspirational!* – or words to that effect.

Although the girl's popularity had already come to their notice, the supervisors suddenly became wary; although they would have been the first to attest that the praise heaped on the girl was well deserved, they felt compelled to ask one another, 'She's not going to charge us anything, is she?' They could not believe such popularity could come free of charge. But then the senior camp director said, 'What if she does?' Another added, 'God knows, we've paid for overpriced duds before.'

That brought a burst of laughter, for they had all encountered a few of those. The department was still bruised by an incident where someone had hired a dud to do sign-language ... on TV nogal! And the woman was not only a fraud, but the khwapheni of a top-ranking government official.

At dinner therefore, with an earnest attempt at a surreptitious manoeuvre, the chief director palmed a note to Mandla. But she was so clumsy that Mandla had to retrieve the note from under the table where it had landed instead of in her lap. The note informed her that she was the group's choice to represent them, congratulated her, and requested that she address the camp the following evening at dinner, the last one of the camp.

The next day was spent in a flurry of activity – not all last-minute, although there were a few of those encounters too ... and not all official. The campers were busy collecting contact details and taking pictures, as well as performing the inevitable and tiresome chore of packing up their belongings. Many took the opportunity to buy fresh farm veggies and fruit, as well as the butteriest butter they had ever tasted; delicious cheese, too.

At last, the final dinner began. After the first course, everyone settled themselves comfortably and the camp director began the formal proceedings. She thanked everybody, and said how she had enjoyed their camp like never before. 'Not even when I went to camp at about the same age you are now ... as a Girl Guide. It was fun, but I do not remember having this much fun. Thank you!' She made a few announcements before she turned to Mandla, and pretending the whole thing was a surprise, called her up to address her colleagues.

Mandla tried to look surprised, but her wide smile gave the game away. She stood up, nodded to the staff at the top table, looked around and said, 'I am terribly sorry to interrupt your meal. Please, go on eating. Kuphela, ndibolekeni iindlebe. Only lend me your ears.'

Naturally, giggles followed that, and a clown shouted, 'I need both mine, sorry!'

More laughter. Mandla raised a hand and the laughter died down. 'I think I speak for most here, if not all. We are outsiders, wherever we go, any day of the week. Right?'

Affirmations of various kinds followed that one.

'Well, guess what? There is a very simple solution to that. But first, so I don't upset anybody ... will those who like being outsiders, being othered, raise hands, please?'

She stopped and looked around; noticed that one of the supervisors actually stood up to take a tally.

She should not have bothered. Not one hand was raised. Mandla continued: 'Now, will those who would like to be insiders, please raise hands?'

A forest of hands sprouted.

Mandla nodded. So did the entire top table, and a volley of clapping erupted. She waited until the noise died down to complete silence as the audience waited for her to continue.

Her right arm describing a semi-circle that encompassed all those in the room, she said: 'But you have your ingroup right here. You are it! Don't you see? You already belong. You are IN. But what you MUST stop doing, something I know I do, and I have seen it here too, is this ...'

Again she stopped. Waited. And when all that could be heard was the soft, apologetic tik-tok of someone making notes on an electric device, she resumed speaking: 'Do not allow others to define you and, you yourself, do not define yourself by your disability. We must NOT do that. Everybody, repeat after me: "I am not a disability!"'

The entire group shouted, 'I am not a disability!'

'The disability does not define who I am!'

By this time, the group had sprung to its collective feet, those in wheelchairs raising arms high into the air.

In the quiet that followed as people resumed their seats, she saw the much happier faces before her, shook her head, and said: 'Since the world makes you feel unworthy, unlovable, useless ... come together and stand as a strong group, supporting one another, but, more important than that, learning how to love yourself, as an individual; and how to love others, particularly those similarly afflicted. For only when we accept who we are, do we really have the right to expect others—' and here she gave a chuckle, '—OUR OWN OUTGROUP to accept us.'

She paused for the deafening applause and whistling that came after those words. However, when she resumed, it was to affirm them. 'We can't expect others to accept what we ourselves do not.

Why would they love what we loathe, detest, avoid even naming, pretending it does not exist, is not there?'

At that point, Mandla had to wait for the table-banging to stop before finishing off with: 'Beautiful people, wake up. Together, we are strong. Let's make it happen!'

And as one, everybody rose up to their feet or waved their hands or stamped their feet, roaring their approval.

The next morning was a flurry of brief, informal miniature pow-wows during which Mandla extolled the power of the collective or mutual support; answered queries; supported the faint of heart. Thrilled at the awakening, the group decided to keep the momentum going. By the time camp disbanded, Mandlakazi's group, twenty-four young people, aged between twelve and seventeen, had agreed to continue meeting, via a closed or private WhatsApp group. They named themselves YoFoP ('Youth, fulfil our promise', borrowing from the opening words of the hymn Mandla and her friends had sung on the first night): 'So as to never forget where we are headed and what we have to offer!' Mandlakazi was unanimously elected chair of the group.

When time came for the young people to bid one another goodbye, a bone-dry face was hard to find. Last-minute cries of 'Let me get your contact details!' became the order of the moment. The bus drivers had to threaten, 'Bus going! Bus going! With or without you – going!' while noisily revving their engines.

Finally, however, bus by bus, the campers left; each heart filled with joy; with anticipation; alive to possibilities. The organisers soon followed. Each harried and harassed, remembering what loads awaited them back home. The site grew quiet.

    Bereft.

CHAPTER TWENTY-TWO

Of course, back home, everybody was curious as hell, and not just family either. The whole of Kwanele wanted to know what Mandla had done at camp; how the experience was, but, even more importantly, how she had found it – meaning, how she managed.

'Did you have a good time?' This came from Phyllis, which surprised Khulu and, even more so, Busi. Phyllis had never taken much interest in her granddaughter before. 'I had lots and lots of fun,' said Mandla.

She was careful to pay compliments to whomsoever they were due, saying: 'I couldn't have done it without your support.' She went on to name every member of the family, saying what they had done for her. Most didn't remember her words, but that didn't matter. What mattered was that no one felt excluded. However, in her heart of hearts, the girl thanked a few most fervently.

Khulu – although really you are Khokho to me
you are the one who has mothered me
Blessed Honey-girl, who gave me life
I thank you both; with all my heart, do I thank you
let me warn you, though

> *I am going to need a lot of support from everyone*
> *this is just the beginning*
> *Isende indlela ngaphambili! Long lies the road ahead!*

There was further good news, even better than Mandla's examinations report. Busi received an email, that once opened and read, led to congratulations and ululation. It was an official report from Lulama Kodwa of the Department and the social worker Ms Ndonga, who had received feedback from the camp organisers.

> SUBJECT: Mandlakazi Mkhonto: a most enterprising young woman. She has the makings of a leader.
>
> RECOMMENDATION: Offer a full bursary for her education and keep an eye on her. Might be suitable for internship position once she reaches Grade Eleven or Twelve.

This praise and piece of good news brought smiles to every face in that house, and Mandla was heartily congratulated on acquitting herself in such exemplary manner. 'May your ancestors always protect you from harm,' Khulu said.

Busi was close to tears of joy, Lily cheered and waved her arms above her head, and Phyllis broke into gospel song: 'Blessed assurance,' she belted out, and the others joined in. Khulu hemmed the singing with a brief prayer of thanksgiving.

That was also the last weekend before the madness of Christmas, followed, a week later, by New Year! Then, hot on the heels of all that excitement, the end of the school holidays arrived.

Once Mandla got back home, the holiday frenzy took over. Happily, Khulu was not mad about what she called unnecessary expenditure, and so things didn't go quite as crazy as with most of the neighbours. Among the most amusing things was how everybody, including the young gentlemen of the family, enjoyed fresh veggies from the garden – so much so they were willing, no, eager, to help out there. This development pleased Khulu to no end.

Next, the tedious chore of uniform-readying! However, Mandla found herself looking forward to the schools reopening. There would be other children to recruit, for that had been one of the mandates with which the YoFoP group had tasked itself – a membership drive. Although that came with the proviso: 'Make sure they qualify!'

So the work continued. From the word 'Go!', right after the campers returned home, the private WhatsApp group was very busy. Soon an informal register was kept that reflected not only membership, but the skills and interests linked to these names.

During all of this, Mandlakazi was busy: by stealth, she inveigled members' minds. But what she did there was far from ominous; she could only augment what was already present, perhaps undetected or undervalued. As spirit, she stole into unrealised and unsuspected dreams and woke them.

Part of the deal, however, was constant reassurance, which further camps helped to achieve. Social workers were eager to help the group, and pressed SASSA, donors and the Department of Women, Children and People with Disabilities to partner with them. The future of YoFoP was assured, especially after social workers and government officials grabbed the spotlight, showing off the budding group as their personal achievement and success story. Ms Ndonga, now their staunchest ally, always said the group was a breath of fresh air. 'You'd be surprised at the moaners we get. And here you are, disabled and all, but look at what you do for yourselves!'

Amused, Mandla saw the benefit to those who would actually run the organisation. She would not always be there; this she knew.

So it was decided to hold weekend camps every other month, with different young people with disabilities attending each time, the costs met thanks to the benevolence of donors. The excitement and anticipation this brought cannot be imagined. Having somewhere to go and something to do was a novelty for many kasi teens. To go to camp, especially when these were tied to public holidays – Easter, Youth Day, Heritage month or school holidays … what a boost to the morale of YoFoP!

Suddenly, those who had made fun or shamed members of this group now envied them. Many wondered how and why they'd been left out, and wanted to know how they could join the group.

Meanwhile, to show off his hard work, the Minister of Women, Children, and People with Disabilities had asked the social workers to bring two of their top achievers to Parliament on the day the minister would be giving the Budget Speech. Ms Ndonga immediately thought of Mandla, and the glowing reports she had received about her from the camp staff. She called her, and Mandla gladly accepted the invitation.

Even the 'boys', her uncles, were excited for her, although

they thought mostly of the food and drink that would no doubt be served at the reception afterwards. 'What are you wearing?' came from Lily, of all people – she was always going on about young people focusing on the 'exterior' instead of what really mattered, the 'interior', the real person. But to Ms Ndonga's delight, Mandla chose to go in her school uniform. Busi, in a tizz, could not shine the girl's shoes enough, although Mandlakazi kept telling her not to make a fuss about the whole thing.

'But you should be at your very best!' the proud mother said.

'Are you saying I'm usually sloppy?'

'*Mcxnfm!*' Busi sucked her teeth, rolling eyes at her. They both burst out laughing; was there anyone less sloppy in that home? Khulu, perhaps ... but that was no outright winner.

The whole family saw her off: Khulu, Busi, Lily and Luvo walked her to the gate. Neighbours came out. Why wouldn't they? Mandla was being picked up in no less a monster than a gleaming black BMW X3. The driver, in black jacket and cap, got out as Mandla approached, and opened the door for her. At the gate, Khulu took off her doek and ululated, waving the doek high up in the air.

At Parliament, they were hosted in a palatial room, with people dressed to the nines. The women were mostly in gay, colourful apparel, also sported by a few of the men. The opposite was true when it came to suits – more men than women in those.

Mandla and another student, a boy about her age, sat with Ms Ndonga and Lulama Kodwa from the department – she who had set the entire thing in motion – right in front of that packed hall. Both the English and the History teachers had asked her to prepare a report on her visit; and when the principal heard that, she said: 'But she must give a talk to the whole school!'

So Mandla made sure she listened, observed, took notes. The boy alongside her was also taking notes. Then came the turn for the address by the minister. Mandla sat up; after all, she was there at this gentleman's kind invitation.

But there were no fireworks here. 'Blah blah blah ... all protocol observed!' Followed by a whole palaver about the fantastic achievements of his department and the various ministries.

If one didn't know any better, to hear him speak, one would be convinced there wasn't a single poor person in this country. According to the fantastic job the minister and his crew were doing, along with the Ministry for Social Development, Mzansi was the land of milk and honey.

Mandla started, hearing her name called out: Mandlakazi Mkhonto and Samuel Brand were to come to the front. Ms Ndonga gave her a gentle nudge; the boy was already on his feet, blushing beetroot to his scalp, glowing through his crewcut.

The social worker walked the two young people to the podium, where the minister shook their hands, hugged them, and gestured to someone who brought packages; they handed them to the minister, who then handed one to each – Mandlakazi and the boy, in that order. All through this, he did not stop talking; telling the room, the nation, how proud everyone should be. 'Our country's future is secured. Look at the wonderful, bright and hardworking youth we have! Not all countries can boast of that ...'

Well, shaking hands with the minister was one thing. Seeing herself do that quite another. That came later, once she was home again, and everyone was watching the evening news on television.

The clamour from the neighbours was deafening. Over the wall, people were shouting: 'Mandlakazi! Mandlakazi, is that you on TV?!'

Even Mrs Bird called and congratulated her. 'Who knows?' she said. 'You might be this country's salvation – the next Mandela.'

Mandla laughed and protested: 'Oh no! Not me!'

'Somebody's got to do the job,' said the old woman, adding, 'Pity no one's asked Thuli Madonsela. She'd make a good, clean, honest president.'

But the most surprising and gratifying call came from Boniswa, who video-called Mandla via WhatsApp, beaming, eyes batting rapidly – she was that excited to talk to Mandla – who was on TeeVee! 'They don't believe me here,' she shouted. 'I'm telling them I know you!'

Mandla raised her voice too, shouted back: 'Tell them we are friends!'

Gleefully Boniswa shouted, 'Niyeva ke? Hear that? She's my friend!' Coming back to Mandla, she said, 'Tell them, friend of mine. Tell them who you are.'

Word of mouth is like a veld fire during a drought. To Mandla's surprise, all of Kwanele seemed to know of the event; and were thrilled that one of them, a girl from kasi, was mentioned by name during the Budget Speech. They had heard that with their own ears, seen it with their eyes right there on TV!

In no time, Mandlakazi's name was on every lip in every home where a differently abled person lived. Family, friends and government employees entrusted with the improvement of the lives of People with Disabilities got to know her name. For her purposes, Mandlakazi was extremely pleased that this meant more similarly afflicted people coming into her orbit. It soon became apparent that there was a growing number of such cases; people who fell under the umbrella of YoFoP. Here, for once, they felt at home; felt they belonged, that what they said mattered.

Soon the YoFoP group had so many members, it could split into smaller groups, with each one choosing a name that best represented its mission. Mandla's group was called 'Potatoes' – for food growers, 'Potatoes' was as good as any other veggie name. They held earnest discussions about the meaning of gardening, its import not only to self-preservation but to independence and human dignity, and many became instant gardening enthusiasts. Although they met for mini-camps, the essentials were covered via electronic and digital means. Mandlakazi deliberately kept a low profile in the group, keen not to be seen as the leader. If truth be known, however, her heart was with her Potatoes. They worked hard: planting and weeding and reaping and distributing the food they grew ... and all the time, learning what worked best where and how.

But they also made sure they had fun. And always but always, they reminded one another why they were there, what brought them together: 'Always outsiders, here we are INSIDERS!'

As did all YoFoP subgroups, the Potatoes recited their motto at the beginning and end of meetings:

1. We are role models for future generations, our descendants
2. We define who we are by what we do
3. We firmly believe we can do anything we set our minds to
4. We are a community, committed to self-development
5. We are helping one another get there; make it; enjoy life
6. We love who we are unconditionally
7. We accept limitations, but refuse to let them define who we are.

And to affirm the credo, at every meeting, some time was given to song and dance. It didn't matter whether one was in a wheelchair, visually or hearing impaired ... dance dance dance! came the call. And everyone, as best they knew how, as best they could, danced. And again, according to the credo to which they subscribed, they danced together, helping one another to dance dance dance!

A ritual developed: in the throes of the music and the movement, a whistle would suddenly shrill, and everyone would stop in whatever pose they had struck. The leader would sweep eyes over the gathering and demand: 'ARE we HAPPY or not?'

'HAPPY! HAPPY! HAPPY!' without fail, each time, would resound. Mandlakazi, always there, even when physically absent, would nod, heart smiling.

It was not all a bed of roses, though. Some had never before realised the role their mothers had played in creating the children's disabilities, consciously or unconsciously, with or without intent. Others knew but only vaguely so; it was as if their mothers had accidentally made the wrong moves, wrong choices. But now, with the awakening of self-awareness and growing confidence, issues of speculation and discussion arose among the young members. There was a lot of weeping, a lot of anger, and bags and bags of bewilderment. No one was happy to cast their mother in the role of the evil stepmother or the Wicked Witch of Crocodile-Ville. But the crude facts of their bodies would not be denied; stared them straight in the eye of the soul.

So discussions were far from frivolous; people had real issues confronting them, and the group offered a platform many had not realised they had needed. Now that it was available, wondered how they could have lived without it. They knew that now that they'd stumbled on it, this pool of mercy, they would not be able to do without it.

> *You learn, dear ones*
> *you learn:*
> *in wheelchair, wearing stocky-heeled shoe*
> *eyes that barely make out shapes—*
> *happiness tastes the same in every heart*
> *touch it! Smell it! Taste it!*
> *Let it soak into the marrow in your bones!*

At one particular meeting, the last of the year, Mandlakazi was challenged to do something different with which to present her family.

'Something visible,' said Glenda.

'Sure!' Mandlakazi replied. 'But what?'

'I know,' offered Boniswa, now an integral part of the group. 'Dye your hair!' And proceeded to offer to do it, 'free of charge!'

As the whole ethic of YoFoP was based really on the disruption of commonly held beliefs about disability, and she was always urging the others to 'jump in and take risks', how could she refuse? But she made as though to demur.

'No risk, no gain!' came the cry, a phrase she used to urge others to action.

So Mandla agreed, but she drove a hard bargain. They could dye her hair any colour they chose if they all promised to start growing their own food. All agreed, and it was not surprising that the colour her friends picked was green!

They dye my hair
I dye their minds, their hearts and their souls
get in there and
plant understanding deep, deep, deep.

Well, if Khulu didn't freak out. Mandla almost laughed at her great-grandmother's reaction. *You'd think I had done something like Busi did all those years ago, getting herself pregnant with me. Look, here I am preparing for Grade Nine – am almost out of high school – well, almost at the midpoint, anyway. Time to show a little rebellion!*

'Green hair?' Khulu shrieked before Mandla had even put both feet over the threshold, umgubasi! 'That's the trend!' Themba announced through a mouth full of the sandwich he was gormandising. *Someone should teach him not to talk with food in his mouth,* thought Mandla: *no wonder he has no girlfriend.* But Sazi does! Met her at an AA meeting, but she's turned out to be his mainstay. With her by his side, he's doing really well.

'What trend? What does it mean?' Khulu fired one question after the other without waiting for an answer. She obviously didn't expect one. These were not questions, but statements of bewilderment and disapproval. More the latter than the former, in fact. *The hair is not a healthy green, either; I don't know what those girls did to me, but now it's a green that makes poor Khulu think of vomit ...*

Surprisingly, Aunt Lily was the one to bail Mandla out.

'She is grown; makes her own choices,' she said.

'What kind of choice is green hair? What does it say about her? About us?' This was the day of questions in a string, Mandla noticed, without letting on that she was the least bit interested. Nonchalance was the word.

Lily continued her defence: 'That she is who she is.'

'Who is ...?'

'Mandlakazi, a high-school student?' Her family still used such archaic terms. They fairly made the girl blush. *Student*, indeed!

'And this is what sets her apart? Isn't "colour-this, colour-that" the so-called trend with the young these days? How then does it set her apart? It announces to all and sundry she has joined the crowd – has become a follower!' Khulu spat the last two words.

Next she resorted to tradition. 'Siphi ke esakhe ngqo isimbo – exhentsa ngezabanye nje? Where then is her own dance step or trademark – since she is dancing the dance step of others?'

For once, to everyone's surprise, Phyllis opened her mouth to gainsay her mother, even if quietly.

'Maybe, Mama,' Phyllis said and all eyes popped. But as though she did not see that, as though she had no idea of the consternation she was causing, she went on, said, '… maybe the child just wants to belong.'

'She belongs here!' Khulu huffed.

'I mean,' Phyllis coughed before she raised her voice just a little and said, 'Mandlakazi probably wants to be accepted by oontanga bakhe, her peers.'

Khulu sucked her teeth, shrugged, and went to her room. But the thought had been planted. Like all teenagers, Mandlakazi desired to be accepted by other teens … especially those, as in her camp group, with whom she shared so much more than even Khulu could really know. It was time, the old woman thought. It was time, all right.

CHAPTER TWENTY-THREE

Not long after the 'green hair' lawaai, Khulu plonked a big, pail-shaped grass basket on the table – one of those open ones with no handles women carry on their heads loaded with groceries from the shop or veggies from the garden. She put it right down in the centre after dinner. That stopped what little conversation had been going on, as everyone was thinking of bed. She must have had the basket beside her on the floor during the evening meal. When she saw that she had caught everyone's attention, she said: 'This is the best time to catch all of you. The basket you see before you is for each of the grown-ups to fill.'

'With?' Lily asked.

'Your contribution toward ukuthomba kukaMandlakazi, Mandlakazi's initiation into womanhood.'

Luvo looked a little taken aback. 'Then you don't want me around.' He made as though to get up from where he sat.

'What makes you think we don't?'

'Ukuthomba is an affair of women.'

'Not the preparations,' Khulu said. Once she saw him nod, she continued: 'I think it is time to prepare for the traditional rites of passage. Why delay?' She added, 'Before she surprises us with yellow or red hair ...'

'Mama,' Lily said, 'what are you talking about?'

'Nifuna ndiphinde laa nto sayigqiba ngoNoquku? You all want me to repeat what we decided ages ago?' She looked at each person present long enough for their eyes to meet, as if taking in votes of agreement and making sure of their attention. Although only Lily had asked the question, Khulu suspected a collective opposition. Had they reneged on their agreement? So she included each one of them. If they were not in opposition to the plan, why were they not supporting her?

'We agreed, remember?' Without waiting for her daughters' responses, Khulu continued, 'Lo uza kuthomba – nithanda ningathandi! This one is going to thomba – like it or not!'

Khulu went on to spell out once more what ukuthomba meant, and its relevance to modern life: 'Time does not change living; what it changes is the manner in which that living is done. The rules remain the same; it is the how of it that changes.'

'I don't understand,' Phyllis said.

Khulu turned the tables on her, asking: 'Bekuthonjiswa ukuze? What was the significance of ukuthomba?'

'Kwaziwe yilali yonke ukuba intombi ikhulile. That the whole village gets to know the girl has grown; that she has matured.'

'Yena? What about her?'

'Yena ntoni, Mama? What do you mean, what about her, Mama?'

'Yena uza kuyazi loo nyaniso? Will she also know that truth?'

'Ewe nje. Ingani nguye lo uthonjiswayo! Of course. Isn't she the one undergoing the rites?'

'So, you agree with me, ukuthombisa was a signal to the girl and her world that she was no longer a little girl but had transitioned into womanhood. Yes, young womanhood, but womanhood nonetheless.'

Surprised at the simplicity of this, Lily and Phyllis said at the same time: 'That's true!'

Khulu followed with a question. 'How has that changed? Don't girls grow up and become women today?'

'They do!' Lily agreed.

'And they know that?'

'Yes,' said Phyllis.

'And all around them know that?'

'Yes, but ...' Phyllis stumbled, adding, '... eh ...'

'Go on! But what?'

Lily helped her sister out. 'But we don't make a song and dance about it.'

At that, Khulu rose to her feet, leaving the others seated. Her voice noticeably higher, just below shouting pitch, she said: 'That's not true – well, not completely true. You do indeed, and I will tell you what song and dance you make and how that works ... but only to some extent ... in the same way as the old. Your young do not go through rites of passage as of old. True. But they undergo certain rites which mark the passage of time, and also show all that they are a step further than they were earlier.'

Phyllis asked, 'What do you mean?'

'What did you do when Mandlakazi here passed ... what do you call Standard Six these days again? When she gradyu – wagreda.'

Busi, who had been listening quietly until then, corrected her: 'Graduation.'

'Of course! Oo heke!' from both Phyllis and Lily.

'That tells you, you who are doing that gradyu thing, that you are marching along in the path of life,' Khulu said and stopped to glare at her daughters. 'These signs that mark the path we travel are important. They remind us of the very purpose of life, our life. Each person is born to a purpose. However, life is so full of things that pull us this way and that, we forget our purpose. And these rites of passage serve as reminders – to us and those with whom we live, that we must take responsibility for our lives.'

The old woman sat back down again, but held her posture upright. 'Gradyu— is for that, today. However, it doesn't seem to quite have the same or full impact on the young as the rites of old did. And I blame the secrecy or exclusionary manner in which today's rites are performed. Rites are the finishing steps to the process of growing. From birth, the child learns to be as the people around her. At ukuthomba, for girls, and ukwaluka, for boys, the training is perfected. AmaJuda, like the Birds and their friends, do this for their children when they turn thirteen. Now, *there* are people who have stuck to their traditions. Thina, we just turn our noses up at ours. That is why our young are filling the jails, why they have all these first-borns.'

Phyllis asked, 'Mama, what will ukuthombisa do for this one? She is already a sensible girl, doing well at school. Everyone says she is wise for her years.'

'Wait and see. While in seclusion, she will be taught the ways of womanhood. What it means to be a grown woman. What behaviours are expected, which frowned upon, and which out and out forbidden.'

Frowning, 'Such as?' Phyllis asked.

'What do you mean, *such as?*'

'Which behaviours are forbidden women?'

At once, Khulu's face took on another look, one of weariness, as she asked herself how far to go; what exactly to voice. She sighed and said: 'The same as for men. Most are in the Bible. Many more are in the tales of our forbears, the stories we were told growing up. And all are about the promotion of peaceful co-existence: how to live a life that contributes to the life of the village; a life that destroys nothing and no one; a life that brings joy, help, and grows or encourages all things good in life. That is the essence of being human.'

'I suppose it can't do any harm,' Phyllis said reluctantly. Never mind, Khulu told herself. Half the battle won. She smiled, an inner glow warming her.

Lily interjected, 'Phofu iyafana nje nale yeenwel' ezimabalabala; yindlela entsha yokufikisa, I suppose. It's the same as this thing of multi-coloured hair. It's the new way of ukufikisa – ripening.'

The family once more in agreement, Khulu smiled broadly and said, 'Here's something that will make you see I also march with the times, nam ndihamba namaxesha!'

A little sarcastically, Lily said, 'Surprise us, Mama.' She didn't believe Khulu would say anything she hadn't said before, at least a hundred times.

Khulu took a deep breath. 'Remember how I'm always going on and on about how we should not be wasteful?'

Phyllis groaned; Lily sighed. 'Is this new or wha-at?'

'Well now,' Khulu went on. 'I suggest we stop the insane extravagance that has become the norm in all our affairs: weddings, funerals, circumcision, whatever ...' She paused and gave all present a steely look. There was not even a hint of a smile in her demeanour. 'When tradition started, and until recently, within living memory, the scale of all these affairs was very different – miniscule compared to today's ridiculous numbers.'

Again she stopped, waited for questions or comments. When none came, she continued: 'But we have not adapted our manner of doing things to fit our changed circumstances.'

Luvo jumped in. 'For example, Mama?'

'Thank you, Nyana,' Khulu said, straightening in her seat. 'I'm glad you asked that question. Let us take umngcwabo, a funeral. Long ago, we buried the body the same day, if death happened very early morning. In any event, burial took place within two days after death, before the body spoiled. There was no time or means for hundreds of people, all needing refreshment, to travel to the family. Now, with modern technology, it can be weeks, even months before a person is laid to rest. Not so?'

Khulu gave a few more examples, all illustrating the imbalance between intent and method. She then suggested that the process in the matter before them – ukuthomba kwentombi, the girl's rites of passage – be adapted to suit the present while still honouring tradition. 'We must observe the spirit of the custom and the teachings imparted to the initiate. Not the trappings! That is paramount,' said the old woman.

So time, space, and fare were all refigured. The girl would remain in isolation, in her room, for one week, instead of a month.

A chicken at the start and another at the end of the ceremony would serve as offering instead of an ox and a goat and two or three or more sheep, depending on the numbers that descended on the family, honouring them as they honoured their ancestors. Respectively, Khulu and Busi would serve as inkazana and ikhankatha, nurse and aide looking after intonjane, the initiate, while she was in seclusion. Busi, a social worker, had the knowledge of today while Khulu had that of yesterday. Intonjane would get the full benefit of both; she would be in good hands. Phyllis was charged with bringing the light: candles, matches and white ochre. These would signify her entry into the spirit world.

Relief was palpable. Each had feared, if silently, the debt this would call for. But Khulu was not quite done and also, seeing the glee in their eyes, thought to burst their bubble a little, just for the fun of it. She went on: 'Njengoba nani nisazi, as you also know,' laughing out loud, she said, 'Akukho mcimbi kungekho tywala – there is no ceremony without utywala – liquor!'

The ensuing debate was short but bittersweet. Not everybody was thrilled at the idea of shrinking drinking. But none had the courage to say this openly. Khulu was firm: only umqombothi – traditional home-brewed beer – would be served and that in limited quantity: ifatyi for the first ceremony, and another for the coming-out ceremony. Ifatyi, a vat or three four-gallon tins of it. Absolutely no bottled liquor: 'We lie when we make objects we cannot make ourselves the centre of our observances. Siyaxoka xa sisenza isiko ngezinto esingakwazi nokuzenza.'

CAMAGU!

Do we hunger or thirst?
Homage to us should not be bondage
To our beloved earthlings.

CHAPTER TWENTY-FOUR

D-DAY!

That week of the initiation of Mandlakazi into womanhood, the house was a beehive in early spring. As had been agreed, however, this was no extravaganza, but all the basics were present in modest quantities.

For a while now, Mandlakazi had been both prepared and preparing for this event.

The night before the actual day of umngeno, a Thursday night, the procedure began: alone, she left the house she called home. Away, she walked, bare-footed, a lone figure completely covered in an old blanket beneath which she had on only boxer shorts. From the house, in measured steps, she walked to the gate. Exited!

This marked her exit from her earlier being, whom she had been until then. Now she would not be called Mandlakazi, but Intonjane – Initiate – and perhaps given a name for the duration of her ukuthonjiswa, initiation. This also marked her withdrawal from society; she would not partake of any social activity, including staying at her girlhood home; her 'father's' house, the house she had until then called 'home' was now out of bounds to her. Her language too, was circumscribed; there were words she was forbidden to say, and she had to substitute others by way of ukuhlonipha – great respect. All her childhood was in her past now; play and frivolity were no longer hers to have; the serious, deliberate acts of adulthood, grown womanhood beckoned, and that was the business of her seclusion: instruction into that onerous role.

Once she cleared the perimeters of her home and walked a little way from it, without turning, her back to the main house. Intonjane knelt on the ground. On the bare, bare ground, just outside the gate to her home, the girl knelt; and bowed low, as though in prayer. A forlorn figure, out from one world, the world of girlhood, a world she would never again return to, she knelt; leaving it behind her, irreversibly.

The pupa was knocking. Knocking at the door to the other world, the world of her ancestors, so that they would intercede on her behalf, so that she would be given entry and guidance and blessings into the new world she sought – womanhood: a blessed and fruitful womanhood.

A little while later, inkazana emerged from the main house. With slow, measured steps, Khulu walked towards that figure of total obeisance; took her by her left hand, helped her to her feet, and led her around the main house to the back room, where the soothing scent of impepho enveloped her as she entered. Everything was as clean as new. For the next week, her bed was isicamba, her speech in hlonipha language, voice barely above a whisper. Immediately, inkazana directed the pupa to shower: 'Only cold water, remember!'

Intonjane returned, minutes later, and her idindala gently anointed her body with white ochre. From head to the sole of her feet, intonjane was covered with the stuff. And then she got robed so that under the blanket, she was hooded in a black doek tied under the chin, clad only in inkciyo and boxer shorts. The white clay that covered her body from head to toe indicated her nearness to the ancestors and thus her withdrawal from society.

Throughout that week of withdrawal from society, small groups of girls the same age as intonjane visited in the evenings and sat in on the instructions given. These were no secret and, indeed, increased in value as they were shared, became common knowledge.

One such evening, intonjane was stolen, the one and only time during ukuthomba. But unlike her visitors, who were much surprised, inkazana and ikhankatha kept calm. They kept calm for they knew what was taking place, but by so doing, they helped calm the girls who had come to pay homage to their agemate as she transitioned into full womanhood. And so, much as the girls were surprised, to give them credit, they kept their collective heads, knowing the two women in charge, inkazana and ikhankatha would take care of things ... and of them too.

All was calm. Eyes strained towards the figure prone on the floor.

Her voice just above a whisper, she first spoke to her inkazana; sang her clan praises, including some the woman herself barely knew, had forgotten, or now heard for the first time ... for the initiate went deep ... deeper than even inkazana knew, much to her surprise and even a little chagrin.

Then she greeted each girl there, said something pertinent that would leave the addressee wondering how on earth she'd come to know of it. When she had spoken to all, revealing each to herself, she grew quiet. For a brief moment, she lay there, silent, seemingly not even breathing.

And then again she stirred, returned in the earlier form, spoke with the voice heard seconds earlier. Now, she repeated something she had said years before; but those with her at this very moment had no knowledge that this was a repeat performance. To them it was a new and frightening revelation. Those who'd heard it or heard of it in long-ago Sidwadweni had all but forgotten it.

Rising noticeably, and now speaking as with multiple voices, the words came:

> *In great jubilation, we played*
> *and the world played with us.*
> *Who has forgotten that time?*

The voice, or voices, then called the names of the winning teams, mentioning something pertinent about each: the captain or a brilliant player, one who'd scored the deciding goal in a heart-and-gut-wrenching battle. Three of the young women present were familiar with what she was saying. One was herself a player; two had brothers interested in football, and were au fait with the game because of that.

A brief silence fell. Like mist over a hill, awe slowly filled the room, creeping up all inside them and filling each girl with dread as they heard the initiate's breathing change. Progressively, it sounded heavier, more and more laboured. It was as though she were straining to breathe, as though the air had turned thick or wet or odour-laden, making inhalation a complex and hazardous process.

At that point, one of the girls, the soccer player, made as if to rise and assist the labouring initiate. But inkazana, the house mother, put out one arm, stayed her as if a gate.

Communal breath held as though by celestial order, in silence, all waited. Watched and waited. Waited, each second a full year.

Suddenly, from the breath-strapped form came a startlingly loud, harsh in-drawn breath that sounded as though there were teeth in the initiate's nostrils or further down the respiratory tract, in her throat or windpipe. The air seemed to rake and scratch over some substance or blockage ... no one could picture or guess ... but all did wonder. Then, once more, the multiple voices came. But now they were distinctly and ominously different, clad in heavy sorrow, wailing as if at a wake:

Now – the world will not play
– the world will die!

Like a world-renowned and celebrated music score, a Bach or Mozart composition, practised and well remembered – what followed was an exact replica of the Sidwadweni announcement the girl had made more than a decade before. The pitch of the voices was even the same; authoritatively, they decreed:

So few years.
Oh, so very few! Another event,
bigger ...

> *Not for playing, but for burying*
> *— Oh, so-o soon,*
> *Ngomso lo, like tomorrow!*
> *No cups or trophies, but caskets instead*
> *The ground will not be able to swallow all the dead!*
> *O-oh! The multitudinous dead!*
> *There will be none left to bury the dead.*
> *Earth will no longer be able to swallow more.*
> *Calamity of calamities!*

As can be expected, that prediction alarmed the company of girls, but inkazana was not chosen for the role lightly. Her stately demeanour, her eyes, and the occasional nod toward one or another of the girls went a long way toward maintaining calm. The bewildering phrases they heard would haunt them for years to come, though; haunt them well into their old age.

But right then, the imminence of a colossal disaster singed itself into the hearts and minds of those present. Even the grown women minding them felt their bowels loosen, ants crawl in their armpits, their bloomers mist. A fear was at once etched in every heart and mind of those whose ears the dread prophecy had penetrated.

Then voices spoke softer, more slowly, but their message remained no less frightening.

> *This may seem a long, long way from home;*
> *but it is not so.*
> *China is like Woodstock to Cape Town,*

It is like Kwanele to Hermanus,
For all humanity breathes the same air.
Therefore, be not complacent China burns
If it burns, you burn.
Iyatsh' iTshayina! China is burning!
They are human beings. We too are human beings.
We burn with China therefore.
We burn.
All humanity burns!

When intonjane finally fell into the aftermath of sleep, inkazana put up a curtain around her, and shifted the others accordingly. She followed that with instruction regarding what they had witnessed; emphasised their responsibility and respect for the experience. As part of their culture and also their growing up, the mysteries of the Old had been revealed to them. 'Each one of you knows you are doubly blessed,' she ended. Inkazana spoke more truth than she knew.

Khulu, as usual, spoke more truth than any knew
this time I was not alone
izihlwele, the multitude of the Old was in and with me
we were all there, as always
but this time they voiced their presence
My time is coming
and what we sowed is seed the wind will blow about
sow in the minds of many whose lives cross these children's
the Old have spoken!

◇◇◇

But this instance was a singular one. For the most part, the days that followed were spent in learning what it meant to be a grown-up, a woman, wife, mother, active member of the community. Sex education was certainly part of the training the girls received. Other duties were connected to keeping a home: cooking, cleaning, gardening, animal husbandry; prevention and cure of common ailments such as running tummies, coughs, headaches ... using roots and herbs. There were lessons in beadwork; plaiting hair; doek-tying and building body strength so as to be able to carry a decent-sized inyanda on one's head, a baby on one's back, even while ploughing and reaping fields.

Khulu was at her best in this role. To intonjane and her peers, she said: 'You are grown, no longer a child, a girl, but a woman. The sacred blood shows you can have children. With womanhood comes responsibility – responsibilities to yourself; family; society, then and now. Do not throw away custom without first examining the meaning of it. Only when you have done that and found its worth no longer applies, should you consider throwing it into the sea of yesterday. Most of what our esteemed forebears did, you will find worth preserving, if adapted to today's ways of doing things.

'Let me start with sexuality, one of the most misunderstood concepts of our tradition. First, sex is your natural right; enjoy it. But, like all freedoms, it comes with responsibility. Sex can and usually results in procreation. Children come into the world totally dependent on the adults who beget them. Today, young people look at the practices of their grandparents and disrespectfully throw them into the toilet. But they miss the wisdom of those practices. Today, men and women have contraceptives. They have the responsibility to monitor the begetting of their children. If, with the methods you all find crude, the old managed this matter as well as they did, then there is NO excuse for fatherless children, a plague in our country right now. This is a crime against children ... a crime, if not a sin.'

Another day, inkazana explained: 'Any unfinished childhood business must be complete by the time of your re-entry to society. You leave childhood here, at this time. Serious work now takes the place of play. You are now your own supervisor. It is up to you to keep your body healthy and strong, for the duties of a woman are strenuous, even in these days of appliances and help. Exercise and diet should be your form of prayers to your body. Pay attention to nutrition; gluttony and poor diet lead to lifestyle diseases such as diabetes, high-blood pressure, kidney problems and asthma, among others. Your health is your life, and your life is in your hands.'

On the very last day, inkazana repeated teachings she had been presenting all week: 'Check your attitude: humility is not stupidity. Loyalty to self and loved ones is essential. Kindness and empathy – an open mind, willingness to be of worth to the world; this is how we build ourselves, our communities, our society.

'But is the will there? Is the sense of responsibility there? Lukhona na uhloni? Is there respect for self, for the other, for the environment, the mother-house of all that lives?

'Never forget, you are never alone! Hence this ceremony, this celebration.'

On that final day, what Kwanele would remember foremost was the dignity of the ceremony, and also the family present to the initiate: a bank account!

Busi surprised all present, including herself. As uSosuthu, the mother of the solo celebrant, as well as ikhankatha, Busisiwe qualified for the right of first appearance. Strangely, she ceded this, choosing to go last.

When her turn to speak eventually came, she surprised even herself with all the tears that came flooding down her face, before all those people, some complete strangers. But once they started, there was no stopping the tears.

In a clear and sincere voice, she said: 'Mandlakazi, my child, forgive me. It is a hard thing I ask of you, but if you can find it in your heart, forgive me. I will be part of the work you do, bear witness. All women of child-bearing years need to hear my story, which is your story; how you got to be what you are: a child maimed, deliberately maimed, by your mother, me—' Here, Busisiwe stopped and repeatedly beat a hard fist against her chest, tears pouring down her face. 'Young women must be reminded that when they carry their young in their bodies, whatever they ingest and drink, the baby also ingests and drinks. Therefore, they should take great care that whatever they eat or drink will do no harm to the precious being they carry. You can count on me to help. I offer my assistance whenever it is needed. It is the least I can do … that is, if you will allow me to be part of the work you plan.'

For answer, the emerging woman went and knelt before her

mother, put her head on Busisiwe's lap. The two hugged tight as tight can be. Then the new woman straightened and leaned towards her mother's ear. She said: 'Mama, I forgive you, but will that bring you true healing? True healing can only come from self-forgiveness, and that comes from forgiving those who have wronged you. Only when you have achieved your own forgiving do you even have the right to ask for it of others. Only when you are grudge-free, are you able to take responsibility for errors in choices or deeds you committed, not blaming others.'

Even as Busi heard those words from her daughter's lips, faces from her past marched swiftly, relentlessly, before her eyes. It was as though she were watching a film or TV: Papa, Mama, Brian, Aunt Lily, Thandi ... and as each face flashed past, the ugly that person had done her flashed through her mind. But, reaching deep into her heart, she found she no longer had any hate or anger stored there. She turned to her daughter, a sad smile on her face, her eyes glowing with unshed tears of relief and joy.

Busi nodded several times. With each nod, her smile grew bolder and brighter.

Again, the two hugged.

Busi turned to the gathering, still holding her daughter's hand. She shouted above the din that had arisen, shouted until quiet returned: 'All mothers who have harmed – abenzakalise – their children now know, cannot but know what it is they did. What is more, society knows what it has allowed to happen to millions of its children; allowed and even encouraged. To be the leading country in the world in foetal alcohol syndrome should make each and every South African ashamed. Ashamed of what we permit while of sane mind. I know I am! With universities, institutions of religion, legal institutions and more, how do we choose to lay waste human potential?'

Khulu burst into tears. Even had she tried, she couldn't hold the tears back; she was deeply gratified to see the rent between mother and child mend, and mend so beautifully, so authentically. With purpose and determination to do the work so sorely needed in Mzansi.

Busisiwe,
Blessed Honey-girl
you are grown; healed; whole
for as you forgive others
so you may
forgive yourself.

CHAPTER TWENTY-FIVE

In the wake of this much-talked-about initiation, new clubs sprang and grew from the association with Mandla and YoFoP. These showed the interests of the group: needlework, gardening, cooking, animal husbandry, and building. Although Mandla encouraged the diversity, her heart of hearts was with the gardening group. This thrived, as members researched which food and medicinal plants did well in the local soil, and what they could do to enhance the soil's fertility.

But the work didn't stop there. Mandla urged the members to 'Spread the word! Infect friend, relative and neighbour with the gardening bug!' For, as she reasoned with her camp sisters and their recruits: what is good for one is good for all. Moreover, she joked, 'Let us make gardening fashionable, the in-thing!' She was leaving her footprints; planting thoughts and burying beliefs in people's minds. And it was not just young people with disabilities; able-bodied boys and girls, young men and women, flocked to join these groups.

Street by street, gardens grew healthy and strong. And there was more in store for the young gardeners. Mandla led them on expeditions of discovery: finding soil on slopes, in caves, gullies and along old, dried-up swales where water once sang.

These fertile grounds became the group's 'Fields of Hope', as they came to be known. Here they planted staples: vegetables and practical crops such as maize, beans, potatoes, sweet potatoes, pumpkin, butternut, flax, marogo, madumbi. Some members expressed fears that people would help themselves to their produce, but Mandla responded: 'Sibiye ngegunya lezinyanya! Our fence is our ancestors!' She dared any thief to 'trespass' although she quickly added, 'Wrong word! For no one owns God's land.' However, she said, 'What we plant, none may plunder!'

Miraculously, the Fields of Hope were not raided – not even once; as in the days of old, when thievery was unknown, and respect ruled supreme. Respect for self; for others; for the environment, by the kindness of which all life, particularly frail human life, survived, dependent, and without whose beneficent bounty nothing would live.

A few of the more adventurous or curious members wanted to prove Mandla wrong; test the efficacy of the ancestral protection. But the Old fenced the Fields of Hope with rings of will that no fleshling could break. So each time different young women by themselves or accompanied by friends, ventured to the fields by stealth, they never could find them. Not even once. And when one mischievous one told Mandla of her failed attempt, saying she'd happened to be in the vicinity and wanted to show a couple of friends what she was involved in, Mandla told her, 'You are lucky. Go home and make an offering of thanks to your ancestors. They protected you.'

Those who heard that shivered, for their imagination most probably far outstripped reality. Who really understood

Mandlakazi and the air of mystery she wore? Oh, she didn't flaunt it, but it was there ... indefinable but tangible.

By day and by night
From the land of forever-sleep
We come to safeguard the seed
From it, ubuntu's rebirth shall come.
Time is almost nigh. Time is almost nigh.

The Fields of Hope thrived bounteously; the harvests the gardeners reaped were unbelievably rich and plentiful. That, coupled with the harvests from their gardens at home, gave them such good nutrition that their health was all but ensured.

As the gardeners shared their food with others, selling at very low prices, when they did sell, they enjoyed the grateful thanks of their neighbours and customers. Not a few began small businesses, taking advantage of being right at the customer's doorstep and providing super-fresh produce; not to mention their very reasonable prices!

'Fields of Hope' soon became a catch-phrase, and business boomed. So did friendships, old and new. The Fields of Hope were featured in community newspapers and on radio talk shows. Soon thereafter, they made their way into local magazines and daily newspapers. Before long, they were among those projects receiving high praise from government and international organisations. The stellar not-for-profit organisation, Gift of the Givers, which provided disaster relief all around the globe, offered their support, advice and any guidance they might need. 'Just ask!'

WHEN THE VILLAGE SLEEPS

◇◇◇

It was not just crops that were ripening. The initiation ceremony had brought about a rapprochement between Mandla and Busisiwe. Although their relationship before had never seemed distant or lacking in affection, the new closeness had an almost sisterly quality about it – more intimate. Among the new ventures on which the two embarked was hiking. Mandla, always an outdoorsy person, introduced her mother to the joys of beach, veld and mountain. She wasn't able to climb rocks or steep inclines, but as long as there was a distinct path, she could manage. Meanwhile the bug bit Busi to such an extent she became the prime mover in their regular forays.

This is my mother, Busisiwe,
honey-sweet
as the time draws nearer and nearer
for Khulu to go to forever sleep
she, it is, who will take over, carry on
therefore, I do with her as I have done with Khulu
Isina idedelana – the old yields to the new
but I, Mandlakazi,
soon, I will be gone
gone before Khulu
to welcome her home
It is a small kindness I can do for Khulu
Who has done so much for me in flesh-life.

One fine Saturday, the sky the colour of a calm summer sea at noon, mother and daughter were out on magnificent Boyes Drive. That morning, they had taken the south-bound bus from Claremont to Simonstown so as to make their way back on foot, a pleasant walk along the sea on one side, the mountains towering on the other. Boyes Drive would take them as far as Muizenberg – at least, that was the plan. However, high above Kalk Bay, Mandla tripped and fell, bumping her head on a boulder. Fortunately, although dazed, she remained conscious, but found she couldn't move. She had cracked her left shin.

'Don't panic,' she told Busi, who was beside herself with anxiety, but managed to summon help. A party of hikers helped carry Mandla down to the main road, where they could get her to hospital.

When Busi returned with the news, Kwanele was riled. Didn't she know mountains were dangerous? They were lucky they had not been assaulted or raped or murdered. But when Mandla rang from hospital and said she would be coming home the very next day, tempers cooled and laughter returned.

And, indeed, the next day, Mandla was back. Yes, she walked with the aid of crutches and the leg was in plaster but she was cheerful. She could go to school but, of course, no more hikes for her – not even walks could she manage. This was irritating enough. But it was being hindered from gardening that brought her to tears of frustration almost every day. Her garden itself did not suffer; her friends rallied and the work continued as before … perhaps with a little more earnestness for none wanted to disappoint Mandla or make her think they had slacked off in her absence. Even Boniswa sat in her wheelchair setting seeds in planting trays.

Thanks to Mandla's robust health, it wasn't long before she was fully mended, the bone knit. It was at this point, when many would have expected Mandlakazi Mkhonto to shine in the limelight that she receded. Little by little, she pushed Busi and the more outstanding performers in the group forward. This core became the board of directors of Fields of Hope, with Busi recognised as the CEO. Popular now not just throughout Kwanele, but the entire nation, Fields of Hope registered as a not-for-profit organisation.

Hlombe's words resonated. Behold a flock of birds in flight. For a moment, a season in the benevolent aerial currents of waves, one will lead while behind that one, the others follow in orderly fashion. No sooner than she falters, feeling the burden of leadership begin to weary her, overcome her strength, her judgement, than another thrusts himself forward. Not envious or grumbling or boastful. But in humble obligation, relieving the courageous leader. And assuming that when time comes for him to relinquish the lead, another worthy will just as willingly take over the obligation he now takes.

True glory dwells not in the self, but in service rendered to others for the greater good. There is no nobler pursuit than contribution to the common good – never forgetting that ISINA IDEDELANA!

My job here nearly done;
my Agemates call me back;
now we must plant the seed.

◇◇◇

Then began the year of the deadly and infectious Covid pandemic, throwing the entire globe into disarray. On 23 March 2020, President Cyril Ramaphosa announced the country would be on lockdown for four weeks, beginning in three days' time.

Three days of grace, for some. Three days of a frantic scramble to stave off death by starvation for many.

That very same day the president announced the imminent national lockdown, visible panic spilled out of houses and shacks, and spread everywhere. With only three days to gather stocks, putting together enough food and other necessary supplies, including sanitary items of every kind, including disinfectant, became a major undertaking. Those who could, people with money in their purses or bank accounts, went shopping as though Christmas and all the other public holidays put together were upon them, all rolled into one. But those who lived from hand to mouth or, worse still, waded through each day in a sea of miserable penury, saw death beckoning. How would they survive with no means of begging, with everybody shut inside their cozy homes?

Lockdown, a clear death sentence to the destitute, meant that lines longer than those depicted in celebratory pictures of the 1994 election formed wherever rumour had it that food might be given away. Lines formed in scorching sun and harsh winds. Social distancing went out the window. Those escaping death through empty stomachs had little thought of death via infected lungs. To their way of seeing things, the former, an enemy well known, witnessed perhaps more than once when friend, relative, or colleague fell at its stroke, was more real, more dangerous; the other, more theoretical, perhaps less visible.

Disabled people were in those lines, waiting for food parcels.

The elderly, the infirm, were there too, even if they were barely able to walk, stand. They had no other means to stave off that belligerent hunger.

Government promised food parcels and other measures to alleviate the suffering of those who had absolutely nothing. Large amounts were reportedly spent on procuring food parcels, blankets, medical supplies, and other items the desperately poor needed.

But soon strident voices were raised regarding the chicanery of government employees. Cadre deployment made daily headlines as money went into the pockets of corrupt officials. The hungry starved as food rotted in warehouses while bureaucrats squabbled, or food parcels were used as bribes for votes, or were simply stolen. Tenderpeneurs splurged on luxury cars while nurses fought for masks and patients fought for oxygen in hospitals laid waste by a terrible pandemic.

Meanwhile, government spokespeople advised: stay indoors; wear masks when venturing out; observe social distancing! However, from day one, the banality of evil, the rottenness of graft, the failure of poverty alleviation: these were laid bare for all with eyes to see.

Mandla's visitors at her initiation remembered the prediction she had made. In the remembering, they gleaned for clearer meaning; afraid to scare themselves more than necessary. But the informal mbizos only affirmed and reinforced their fears.

They asked and answered the question themselves, surprised by the clarity of vision that was theirs in this hour of desperate need … a growing need. Had they not pledged not to live for themselves, but for the good of others too – the good of the community?

In hundreds of thousands, the poor poured onto the streets, seeking anything they could feed their children. 'Social distancing' and 'wearing masks', steps so carefully articulated by the president meant nothing to the majority of the citizens of Mzansi. Their needs were basic: food to satisfy howling stomachs – theirs, their children's, and the elderly.

> *See what you grow!*
> *Lines of beggars*
> *Lines of dispirited, hungry,*
> *Downtrodden by and with your help*
> *What help is that which nails one to poverty?*
> *Disaster after disaster*
> *– GRAFT –*
> *The poor robbed blind*
> *Robbed by civil servants they trust …*

But this was no time for courage to fail. YoFoP and its satellite groups and clubs stepped in, roping in any mothers willing to work with them. Grandmothers too! And Fields of Hope came into their own, providing the hungry with food, staple vegetables and more.

What was more, they did not offer food parcels only. With each food parcel, the person was given advice and the option of taking seeds and pamphlets on how to grow their own food. And very few refused the offer.

In ever more frequent interviews, Mandlakazi and Busi spoke out: 'See what you grow? Poverty! All those people the government purports to help are out on the streets, poor as poor can be!

What has happened to all the helping they've been getting? Has it improved their lot, even a jot? No, what government help does for the poor is cement them in poverty. Ask yourself, "Why?"

'The answer is staring you in the eye: as long as people stay poor, they will not bite the hand that feeds them. Government largesse ensures votes – and the poor are nothing but voter fodder!'

The work done by Fields of Hope and YoFoP gained recognition from those grateful for the help the group provided. But their popularity was rapidly turning into notoriety from certain quarters, especially when pointed questions were asked about *why* the work was still there to be done. With strong leadership and an uncorrupted state, there would have been no need for anyone else to 'step in' and help those starving and desperate. But the rumbling criticisms and plain animosity did not deter the gardeners. The people they served, thrilled at the sight of them, hailed: 'Na!' uncedo lokwenene! Here comes help that is real!'

One cold and wet morning, Mandla, Khulu, Busi and members of YoFoP were ladling soup into various food containers, even plastic bottles and tins, held out by those in the long lines of desperately hungry people. Cries of frustration filled the air. A man rushed forward and snatched some sandwiches. A collective groan broke from the crowd, and people began pushing towards the tables.

Mandla shouted to restore order when she spotted police running towards them. Khulu, unaware of this new development, was berating some of the men breaking the queue. Yelling at the top of her voice, Mandla stormed towards Khulu, waving her hands, her face distorted with deep foreknowledge.

A shot rang out. Mandla jerked and fell forward.

Khulu dropped to her knees and pulled the girl's body onto her lap – the body she knew so well, the body she had nourished and nurtured. It was clear from the amount of blood that Mandlakazi had left for the light that sent her.

Khulu lifted her face and uttered a primordial roar. Of absolute loss. Of stark grief. Of blind despair. She flailed like a wounded lion over the girl. The Old had abandoned her.

> *The poor policeman who shot me*
> *was but an instrument of my will*
> *I had done what I had come to do*
> *the time had come to return to the source*
> *my fleshless colleagues were calling my name.*

There was a national, a global outcry at this, yet another case of police brutality, and one sure to go unpunished like most of the others. Mandlakazi's name went around the world.

Khulu thought she would die from heartache, while Busi was inconsolable. But the spirit that bound them, the child they mourned, brought them even closer together. Comforting each other, they found comfort. In the end, they established a trust: AMANDLA: a programme aiming to establish self-sufficiency by teaching people to grow their own food. And in the few years she had remaining in flesh-life, Khulu would see and hear both Hlombe and Mandla in her dreams.

The police officer responsible for the shooting was suspended. To this day, no conviction has been made.

ACKNOWLEDGEMENTS

My special thanks go to:

- ◊ the National Institute for the Humanities and Social Sciences (NIHSS) for their financial support, without which the dream would have died in utero;
- ◊ Dr Meg Vandermerwe, my supervisor, for considering me worthy of the journey;
- ◊ Prof Chris Stroud for suffering me in his great unit, the Centre for Multilingualism and Diversities Research (CMDR) at the University of the Western Cape (UWC);
- ◊ Mrs Avril Grovers for all the help when the computer would be spiteful;
- ◊ Albert Omulo who so kindly and patiently coached me through the intricacies of proposal writing;
- ◊ Thokozile Fezeka Sayedwa: more than a daughter; my first reader and severest critic;
- ◊ Phumeza Magona for her unstinting research support;
- ◊ Helen Moffett: editor peerless; and
- ◊ Andrea Nattrass: alias IP. In my book, her other name is Infinite Patience.

Last but not least: my parents, Lilian and Penrose Magona, who brought me up with a profound respect and reverence for our ancestors and all living things.

◇◇◇

The following sources have been used and adapted:

Jordan, A.C. 2004 [1968]. *Tales from Southern Africa* (translated and retold). Johannesburg: Ad Donker Publishers.

Mqhayi, S.E.K. 1914. *Ityala Lamawele*. The Lovedale Press, Alice.

———. 1929. *Udonjadu*. The Lovedale Press, Alice.

———. 1973. *UAdonisi waseNtlango*. The Lovedale Press, Alice.

ABOUT THE AUTHOR

DR SINDIWE MAGONA writes in both English and isiXhosa and translates for various media, including film. She has authored over 120 children's books; four stage plays; two books of short stories; works of autobiography and biography; novels; radio plays; and a screenplay. Dr Magona is a graduate of Columbia University and has been awarded three honorary doctorates. Before relocating back to Cape Town, she spent 25 years living in New York, working for the United Nations in the Anti-Apartheid Radio Programmes, until June 1994; and in the UN Film Archives until her retirement from the organisation at the end of 2003.

Dr Magona's published works for adults include two autobiographical books, *To My Children's Children* and *Forced to Grow*; two collections of short stories, *Living, Loving, and Lying Awake at Night* and *Push-Push and Other Stories*; three novels, *Mother to Mother*, *Beauty's Gift* and, in 2015, *Chasing the Tails of My Father's Cattle*. Her most recently published work is *Theatre Road*, a collaborative biography of Thembi Mtshali-Jones.

She is the founder of the Gugulethu Writers' Group, which she runs on a voluntary basis, to encourage women who might not otherwise write their stories. Dr Magona is currently a writer-in-residence at the University of the Western Cape in Cape Town, South Africa, and a PhD candidate.

AWARDS

2020 – Honorary Doctorate from Nelson Mandela University

2020 – Ellen Kuzwayo Award from the University of Johannesburg

2018 – Honorary Doctorate from Rhodes University

2016 – The English Academy Gold Medal for distinguished service to English over a lifetime

2014 – Flora Nwapa Literary Award

2012 – Imbokodo Award

2011 – Awarded the Order of iKhamanga by the President of the Republic of South Africa

2008 – White Ribbon Award for *Beauty's Gift* from Women Demand Dignity

2007 – Lifetime Achievement Award for contribution to South African literature

2007 – The Molteno Gold Medal for promoting isiXhosa culture and language

2007 – The Grinzane Award for writing that addresses social concerns

2006 – Award in acknowledgement of contribution to South African literature from the Department of Education

2005 – Greenaccord Award for literary work that addresses issues of the environment

2003 – Proclamation (NY State Senate Democratic Leader, David A. Patterson, on World Aids Day 2003) in recognition of artistic work on the issue of HIV/AIDS

2000 – Bronx Recognizes its Own (BRIO) Award: Fiction

1999 – South African–American Organization (SAAO): Women Who Changed Lives Award

1997 – UNdimande – Grand Prize Winner, Bhala Writers Short Story Contest and Xa ndisiy' emsebenzini, ndihamba naye; First Prize in the same contest

1997 – Xhosa Heroes Award from the Xhosa Forum of the Western Cape

1997 – New York Foundation for the Arts Fellowship: non-fiction category

1993 – Honorary Doctorate in Humane Letters from Hartwick College, Oneonta, New York

1982 – ITT International Fellowship, for study in the United States of America, awarded by the Institute of International Education in recognition of outstanding scholastic achievement.